# A LESSON IN SEX AND MURDER

## DAVID UNGER, PHD

Artwork by Damonza

ISBN-978-0-9967613-8-3

DavidUngerPhd.com

### Author Note

One of the challenges I faced writing about the 80s is that many of the things we now hold as fundamental values were not in place at the time. I have endeavored to have my characters hold respect for others in the forefront of their interactions, but wanted to stay true to the tenor of the times. Their actions and words might not always be as sensitive as they could be, but historic wrongs can only be righted if we acknowledge them. Where they appear here, they are a deliberately mindful reminder of how far we've come ... and how far we still have to go.

# PROLOGUE

"THE BEST I ever had? Whew. That's a tough question. Not that I have all that many to choose from."

"Sure. Sure. Come on, fess up."

"I suppose the best was years ago. I was a hairdresser and one of my co-workers brought in his sweet seventeen-year-old cousin who was visiting. He came in the salon every day for a week and just hung around. I'd catch him looking longingly at me, but he was so shy he'd fumble every time I talked to him. He was so cute and innocent I just wanted to make him feel better."

"So?"

"So my co-worker told me his cousin was about to have his eighteenth birthday and I decided he was old enough to get a grown-up present."

"You didn't."

"I did. I asked my friend if I could have a key to his apartment, and before sunrise on his birthday I slipped under the covers."

"Just like that? What happened?"

"You could say he was pleasantly surprised and rose to the occasion. He wasn't quite sure what to do but he was a quick study. We spent a glorious morning together and by the time I'd left he'd learned everything he needed to know to get a head start with his sex life."

"I wish I'd gotten a birthday present like that. Even now!"

"Me too."

They laughed in unison.

"So he learned enough to give him a head start. What about you?"

"I also learned a thing or two. Things like good deeds reward the giver. And, of course, as if we needed a reminder, young men are more energetic and grateful. Plus, they don't fall asleep after they climax."

"I hear you."

*Me too.*

"That's my story. What's yours? What's the best sex you ever had?"

I wanted to hear that myself. I felt a bit awkward standing in the hotel check-in line behind these two middle-aged women as they reminisced about their sex lives. I don't really consider myself overly voyeuristic, but this was hard to pass up.

"There's one thing that comes to mind. If that's the right organ."

They giggled and continued, oblivious to my posed indifference.

"The best, and most romantic and sexy time, was this incredible fantasy that happened to me at a Club Med. You'll never believe it because I don't even believe it myself, but I swear it's true."

"I believe. Now tell me."

"In order to believe this, you have to understand being at that place put you in a state of perpetual arousal. It's not like it is now. This was in the days when Club Med meant sex, sex, sex."

This was one of the only times I was glad a line was moving slowly. However, I wanted her to hurry up before they got to the front. Fortunately, a lot of people were checking into the hotel for the conference so hearing the end of her story looked promising.

"I remember. So tell me already," said her friend.

"One evening after a long day of tanning and drinking, I went for a walk by myself on the beach to watch the sunset. It was a lovely evening and a fog was starting to roll in. I was strolling along, trying to commune with nature. Remember how we used to do that?"

"I remember."

So do I, but that's not why I'm eavesdropping.

"I was ambling along the water's edge and this man came strolling toward me. He sorta came out of the fog. I didn't think much of it, but as we got closer it began to feel like one of those TV commercials. The nearer we got, the sexier I felt. As we approached each other, everything seemed to move in slow motion. He seemed so statuesque and assured."

"And," her friend prompted as she paused to embrace her memory.

"And when we were at arm's length, we stood still and just looked into each other's eyes. It seemed like forever. And then, very slowly, we started to kiss. I couldn't believe it was happening. It was so picturesque and perfect and weird and sexy all at the same time."

"You didn't say anything? Not even hello?"

"We never said a word to each other. We just kissed, embraced, and then lay right down on the sand and made love. It was like that scene in *From Here to Eternity*. It was all too glorious..."

We each stood there quietly and pictured the empty beach and the lovers at sunset.

"I looked up as the stars were coming out and said to myself, 'Now this is a vacation.'"

"I'll say."

*Me too.*

"And the strangest part was, after we'd finished, we slowly got dressed, kissed, and walked off without saying a word."

"What? Come on, you didn't even get his name or room number?"

"What for? The whole thing was complete as it was. To say anything would have spoiled it."

I agreed though I didn't say so. Although if it had been me, I'd have kicked myself later on for not getting her phone number.

# CHAPTER ONE

# FOREPLAY

**August 22, 1977**

**Monday morning**

I WAS SITTING at a small table by the window in my hotel room, enjoying the ocean view and my over-priced fifteen-dollar continental breakfast, thankful the school was picking up the tab. That was more than I wanted to pay—if I'd been paying. Free of that burden, I read over the workshop catalog and debated which morning presentation to attend. Would it be "Introduction to Talking About Sex," "How to Enjoy Sex When You're Afraid of Disease," or "Sex Games to Revitalize Your Relationship"?

There was a knock on the door. Britt was standing there looking like she'd been up most of the night.

"I have to speak with you," she said as she strode into the room.

"Come on in."

"I don't know what to do," she said hesitantly. "I'm afraid and I'm not even sure I should be here talking with you."

"What's the matter?"

She turned to leave, then blurted out, "Can I trust you?"

"I don't know. I hope so."

"That's not very reassuring."

She sat down at the table. "You're the only person here who I know doesn't know anything."

"Thanks," I replied, trying to show I didn't have a glass jaw. "Just what is it I don't know anything about?"

"You don't know anything about sex."

"Excuse me? That's hitting a bit below the belt Besides, you don't know me that well. Maybe after we've known each other for a while you could say that. But— "

"You don't understand. It's not that you don't know anything about sex. You just don't know about human sexuality."

If that had been meant to make me feel better, it wasn't working. I started to feel uncomfortable and unsure; that's not uncommon for me but rarely first thing in the morning.

"What do you mean I don't know anything about human sexuality?"

"I can tell you haven't formally studied it."

"Only in a fumbling way," I said, trying to invoke some humor into the situation. Which I often do when I'm uncomfortable and unsure. In the therapy business, we'd call that a defense mechanism.

"Why does it matter that I haven't formally studied sex?"

"Well… it means you don't know Dr. Goodst."

"I've seen him on TV a few times and was looking forward to seeing him last night."

She started to cry.

"I can see how upset you are. Why don't you tell me what's going on."

Her tears soon subsided and she stood up, went to the window, watched the sail boats breezing by without seeing them, then reached into her pocket.

"Here," she said, handing me an envelope. "Read this."

It was a plain white envelope with Britt Pearson printed on the front. I opened it, took out a standard piece of paper, and read:

Dr. Goodst is being held hostage. If you ever want to see him again, you will leave $5,000 in small bills at the Goodst Institute by Thursday noon. The sooner you pay the better. If you inform the police, Dr. Goodst will die.

I looked it over twice and handed it back to her, then realized my fingerprints were now neatly placed on the note. Putting my concerns in the background, I said, "This is serious stuff. No wonder you're so upset."

"What do you think I should do?"

I have to stop here and point out something all therapists are taught. You might not be interested in this insider information but, since I'm a therapist and a professor, I'm gonna share some therapeutic approaches and theories along the way. You can grade me later.

What therapists are taught is, of all the things we can say or do, the least useful is to give advice. Of course, that doesn't stop me.

It might be hard at first to discern why giving advice would be the least useful. After all, we've all been the recipient of some excellent advice that's improved our lives. And we've all been the recipients of a lot of advice that's gone in one ear and out the other. But that's not why it's unhelpful.

When someone gives you advice, they're basically saying they know better than you. That's fine when you're trying to do something you know little about. But when it comes to relationships and how to respond to what life presents you, it's usually best to remember what therapists are taught—"What advice would you give yourself?"

I must admit, when Britt asked me what I thought she should do, my initial reaction was to say, *Forget about Dr. Goodst and spend some time with me.* But I knew better than to blurt that out.

Britt was right. I didn't have any formal knowledge of human sexuality. I could joke about having obtained my full share of informal experience, but I'd never studied human sexuality in graduate school or anywhere else. My lack of knowledge was, in fact, my reason for attending the 1977 Annual Meeting of the National Association of Sex Therapists and Surrogates—a week-long event devoted to learning the latest research, innovations, techniques, theories, and practices.

The sixties had birthed the sexual revolution and now, almost a decade later, sexuality had gone out of the bedroom and into the classroom, the workplace, and everywhere else. All kinds of therapists, educators, researchers, journalists, and surrogates were gathering to find out the newest methods to help the needful public with their sexual concerns.

It was also a good excuse to spend a week in San Diego and learn a few things that could help me out professionally and, I hoped, personally.

The dean had informed me that the school's resident human sexuality teacher was taking an emergency leave, and she wanted me to teach the course. I needed to fill three hours once a week for ten weeks. Surely I could do that, she'd opined. Wanting to stay on her good side and glad she trusted me, I'd assured her I'd be able to fill in.

Earlier in the year, the dean had sent me to the First West Coast Computer Faire where two twenty-one-year-olds named Steve Jobs and Steve Wozniak had informed the audience there were between twenty and thirty thousand computers in the country and one day everyone would have one. I'd told the dean the conference was useless as computers were destined to join the dodo but sex was here to stay. I was glad that after wasting the school's money on the computer faire, she'd been willing to invest in my attending another conference.

My first reaction had been it would be fun and challenging. Not to mention a little provocative. I'd recently read Erica Jong's *Fear of Flying* and knew she'd created a second wave of feminism that had opened up the sexual dialogue. Surely I could keep the conversation going.

As soon as I got hold of a couple of textbooks and started reading, I knew I was in trouble. I'd thought Vas Deferens was a Spanish explorer and vulval orgasm the title of a porn movie that takes place in a foreign car. If I was going to be teaching this stuff, I'd need to learn it.

I'd talked it over with the dean and she'd told me the school would pick up my expenses. So here I was, on a mission to spend the week learning as much as I could about human sexuality and how to teach it. All in all, not a bad homework assignment and certainly open to a range of interpretations.

Whatever I'd learn, I needed to do it fast because the following Monday afternoon I was scheduled to teach my inaugural human sexuality class to fifteen graduate students who would soon be therapists.

## CHAPTER TWO

# GOT A GOOD FOUR MINUTES?

*August 21, 1977*
*Sunday evening*

THERE WERE A few pre-conference workshops scheduled before the welcoming session. Eager to learn as much as I could, I sat uncomfortably in a room with about fifty intent-looking adults while a speaker in a floral dress pointed to various charts and explained how to build a better orgasm. Now here's a subject that would interest most of us, but the speaker managed to make it sound similar to repairing a flat tire.

According to the research and the various charts and diagrams, most people lie about their sex lives—to their partners, their friends, their doctor, their therapist, and anyone else who happens along. They also lie to themselves. With all that lying, it was difficult to get a clear picture of what people were actually doing. Researchers found it much easier to put people in a laboratory and observe them. I don't know about you, but I'm not sure I could do my best work under those conditions.

It turns out if I could just slow down, breathe more, be in the moment, take a few short breaks, and think about the Dodgers now and then, it would help. As far as I could tell, that's basically what I was already doing with limited success.

While the speaker droned on about exercises we could do, I took a closer look around the room. I don't know what you do when you first get settled in a room, but being a single guy, I tend to give the place a good going over to see if there's anyone that might make my heart take flight. Or at least pique my interest.

I'd scanned the room on arrival. Now, with boredom coming into play, I took a closer look at the fair-skinned redhead in her late twenties sitting on the aisle. Initially, she'd looked like a contender. She still did.

She seemed focused on the material, which I took as a good sign. She also looked like the kind of woman who knew more about sexuality than you can learn from charts and diagrams.

I've spent enough time on earth to know looks can be deceiving, and what you see across the room doesn't always manifest itself when you get up close and personal. Nevertheless, I was interested in getting a closer look.

I got lost in my thoughts and the next thing I knew, she was gazing back at me with enough of a look to imply possibility. Before the glance became awkward, she turned away. I noticed that, along with the red hair, she had a pair of blue eyes that came with a bit of a sparkle.

The speaker was trying to get the audience involved in her presentation, asking what we did to make our sex lives better. I toyed with saying first you needed to have one, but opted for discretion.

When she announced a break, I went to find the redhead. Opening lines are not my forte. I usually come up with a few good ones on the way home. Supposedly it doesn't really matter how you initiate a conversation—it's sustaining it that counts. You don't even have to do it for long; people usually decide if they're interested in knowing more about you within four minutes. Personally, one or two seems more like it.

I was hoping I had a few good minutes in me. When I found her, she was talking with a group of women. It's never easy for me to approach a new woman, let alone a group of them.

I once asked my students if they'd want to go to a party where they knew no one. Most said no but some said yes. The appeal for the want-to-gos was the excitement of meeting new people. The rest said having to make small talk with strangers was too anxiety-provoking. We realized one group was curious about others while the other was self-conscious.

My takeaway from that discussion was:

- keep my focus on other people and find out whatever I can about them;
- don't pay so much attention to my own fumbling ways.

Easier said than done.

I ambled over to the group and stood on the perimeter. One of the women was wearing a button stating *If You Think You Feel Good, Feel Me.* I was trying to come up with something witty to say when thankfully she noticed me and said, "Why don't you join us? We were just discussing what Dr. Michaels was saying, and it would be good to get a man's opinion."

"I'm happy to give you my opinion and a feel to go with it," I said, quickly gesturing at her button lest there be any misunderstanding.

She smiled awkwardly.

"What exactly are you talking about?"

"We were discussing her contention that you can prolong arousal states by focusing on the moment and not rushing ahead. Most of us already do that, and, in our opinion, it's the men who are rushing. What do you think?"

"Well, I've been accused of rushing, so that does sound familiar. We rush because we're so excited to actually be having sex that on those occasions when it happens, we want to jump on it before it goes away."

Most of the women avoided eye contact and left me hanging. Finally a short dark-haired woman asked, "But can't you stop yourself from rushing?"

I was relieved she'd at least responded, but somewhat reticent because her question seemed more accusatory than inquisitive. "Sometimes. It depends on how caught up in the action I get. I like to savor the moment, but I also know how quickly those moments of appreciation can be overcome by a wave of lust. I have to remember to slow down and think about the Dodgers. If I can do that, I can hold my own for a few minutes."

"What happens when you don't think about the Dodgers?" the woman asked.

"I end up taking my seventh-inning stretch in the third," I replied to a less than enthused audience.

I wasn't sure how this would count with those four minutes but felt a ray of hope when the redhead said, "Would you be able to sustain yourself longer if you focused more on the other?"

"Depends who I was with," I replied suggestively. Then, in an attempt to be more inclusive, I added, "But to tell you the truth, I wasn't sure what Dr. Michaels was talking about. If I had to think too much about being in the moment, it would take away some of the spontaneity."

"You don't have to think about it that much when you're engaged, but you can consider it now," said the dark-haired woman.

I nodded. She was right but that didn't mean she wasn't starting to annoy me.

The redhead bailed me out. "One needs to be considerate of their partner as well as themselves, and love-making ought to be about communicating and sharing one's needs and desires."

We all agreed.

It isn't easy for me to talk openly about sex. Especially with women. I worry about offending them and saying the wrong thing.

Being politically correct was the talk of the land, and at the progressive college where I work it was expected of us to walk the walk. While I agree with that, old ways of talking and thinking take time to be replaced. Remembering to call people mail carriers and police officers requires a certain diligence with language. Probably the same diligence it takes to focus on the moment and not jump ahead.

Mercifully, people started heading back into the room. I excused myself and headed for my seat. I tried to concentrate and take notes so when I got back to school I could teach prospective therapists how to interact with their future clients. One thing I'd already learned was that to teach future therapists how to talk about sex, I needed to get out of my own safety zone and be willing to talk about things I usually didn't.

CHAPTER THREE

# IN LIEU OF

**Sunday night**

Dr. Wilhelm Goodst was due to give the opening speech: "Sexuality: Today and Tomorrow." His name was on every brochure and he was widely regarded as one of the foremost experts on human sexuality. He'd taken up where Masters and Johnson had left off, bringing their theories and plenty of his own into many households in the land.

*Dr. Goodst's Good-Time Sex Hour* was a long-running weekly TV show broadcast from his institute an hour and a half east of San Diego. He was suave and smart, someone you'd like to invite into your living room, providing your partner wasn't there. He had a reputation as quite a lady's man… and man's man. It was rumored much of his knowledge of sexuality was the result of varied personal experiences.

I went into the hotel's ballroom-turned-auditorium, found an empty seat, sat down, and waited for the program to begin at 8:00 pm. There was a table with two chairs on the stage. While I waited, I watched the crowd fill the place.

I admit it—I like to people-watch. Yes, I like to watch women but also men and children, not to mention animals and pretty much anything else.

I was also entertaining myself. People were dressed in a variety of styles. There were tie-dyed T-shirts, velvet dresses, guys in flowered shirts and bell-bottoms, and women in jersey wrap dresses. Mustaches and miniskirts abounded. There were easily a few thousand people in the room. I couldn't spot the redhead.

At eight fifteen, the crowd was becoming restless. Many in the audience were therapists used to running their lives by the clock.

At eight twenty, a man came on stage and announced Dr. Goodst had been delayed. There was a slight groan but the anticipation continued to build.

At eight thirty the same man reported they were trying to determine just when Dr. Goodst would arrive.

At eight forty-five, he told us they were unable to locate Dr. Goodst. The evening's program would be rescheduled for later in the week. He apologized and hurried off the stage.

People slowly began to leave. I didn't feel much like going back up to my room and decided to look for the redhead. I hurried out of the ballroom and took up a semi-casual position where I could spot her if she hadn't left already.

I waited a good fifteen, twenty minutes and figured I'd missed her, but good fortune was mine—except she was engaged in conversation with another group of women including Feel Me, the short dark-haired woman, and a tall well-dressed blonde with a Scandinavian look about her.

I wished for something profound to come out of my mouth. I ran over a few options in my head but they all sounded contrived. I took the leap and went over. When there was a slight break in the conversation I blurted out, "It's too bad about Dr. Goodst. I was looking forward to seeing him." Maybe it wasn't profound, but at least it was truthful.

"Yes," said Feel Me. "I wonder what could have happened."

"He's probably off doing some research," I said, hoping to add some inappropriate humor to their concerns.

"It wouldn't be the first time," said the redhead, nodding at me. Given her slight encouragement I rushed ahead. "So, what are you all planning on doing tonight? I was hoping someone would have a good idea and invite me along."

There was an awkward pause. It seemed I'd failed to be in the moment.

"I'm going to my room and catch up on some reading," said the dark-haired woman snidely. She seemed irritated I'd interrupted, adding, "When we finish our discussion."

That garnered its own awkward silence. No one seemed to want to continue the discussion or offer any other options until Feel Me said, "Anyone want to take a walk on the beach?"

I immediately thought of the woman in the check-in line. It wasn't sunset and Feel Me wasn't the woman in the line so the fantasy died there.

"That sounds like a great idea," the dark-haired woman replied. "Maybe tomorrow night for me. I guess I'll just go catch up on my reading. I'm finally reading Indira Gandhi's *What Educated Women Can Do* and can hardly put it down."

There were some nods of approval though I couldn't tell if anyone else had read the book. It hadn't made its way to my bedside table.

It was time to take care of basics. "Before we decide if there's anything we want to do, I'd like to introduce myself. My name's David," I said, extending my hand to the redhead.

"I'm Britt," she replied with a firm handshake that lasted a moment too long, though that could have been wishful thinking. "It's good to meet you."

"It's good to meet you too," I replied.

"And I'm Marie," said Feel Me as she shook my hand.

I'm not great with remembering names, and as soon as Marie

said hers I knew I'd most likely remember her as Feel Me. Not the best of nicknames but one I was unlikely to forget.

"I'm Rhonda," said the dark-haired woman, reluctantly offering her hand. "And I'm going back to my room. See you all later," she said, making eye contact with everyone but me.

With that there were some good-nights and see-you-tomorrows, and the group was reduced to Britt, the tall blonde, and Feel Me.

The blonde thrust her hand out and gave me a very firm handshake. "I'm Astrid."

"Good to meet you as well."

I looked at the women and said, "What'll it be?"

"How about we walk around town?" Britt suggested.

"I'm not up for that," Astrid replied.

"What about that walk on the beach?" said Feel Me.

We brainstormed some ideas and hung out for a while before we agreed to call it a night. I wasn't pleased with not being able to spend more time with them—well, Britt—but the introductions had been made and I was eager to see what the week would bring. Plus, it was inching up on my bedtime and I was ready to call it a night.

I asked if I could accompany them to their rooms and received some questioning looks. Feel Me's seemed to imply she thought I was a perpetrator and she quickly said good night and headed off.

"How about it?" I asked Britt and Astrid. "I'm happy to escort you to your rooms. I know male chivalry is a form of chauvinism but I've learned the importance of everyone being safe at home. Ever since I became a therapist and started working with parents with teenagers, I realized having everyone home safe at night provides a better night's sleep for all."

"That's very considerate," Britt said.

"Thanks, but no thanks," said Astrid at the same time.

"Okay. How about I walk with you back to your room, Britt, and we say good night to Astrid?"

I've learned to ask for what I want. I don't always ask and I certainly don't always get, but I like me more when I ask.

They looked at each other, then Britt said, "Actually we're sharing a room. We're both freelance journalists covering the convention and thought we'd save some money and get to spend some extra time together."

"Oh."

We headed toward the elevator and when they got in, I followed. Britt pushed 3 and I smiled at them. "Same floor." I shrugged.

We walked down the hall and they stopped at 315. "Hey, I'm right down the hall in 327. What a coincidence."

Astrid opened the door and stepped in. Britt was about to follow her when we all noticed the envelopes on the floor just inside the room. Each envelope had one of their names typed on the cover. I stood outside the doorway while they opened the letters. I couldn't read what was written, but it was easy enough to read their response.

"Oh my God," said Britt.

Astrid slammed the door in my face.

# CHAPTER FOUR

# NEW WAYS TO USE A SLIDING SCALE

### Monday morning revisited

BRITT CAME TO my room. She wasn't sure if she could trust me. After all, we'd met just briefly the evening before. But she'd decided to show me the ransom note.

"Why would anyone kidnap him? It just doesn't make sense," she said.

One thing I've learned is when someone asks you a question, there's usually a statement behind it and you're better off knowing more about the statement before you answer the question. Why are they asking? What do they want? What are the circumstances that prompt the question? The answers provide context, enabling you to offer a more responsive reply.

Of course, what I've learned and what I practice are not always perfectly aligned.

"Sounds like they want money. Although, these days, five thousand dollars isn't a whole lot to ask for in a kidnapping."

"They wanted fifteen thousand from Astrid." She started to pace.

"They wanted more from her? Why's that?"

"I don't know. Maybe it's because she makes about three times more than I do."

"These kidnappers are working on a sliding scale? I've never heard of that."

"I don't know what it means. Astrid and I have been talking about for it most of the night. I still don't know what to do."

"If you're reluctant to go to the police, you could always pay the money."

"Astrid says she's not going to pay. She says he isn't worth anything to her, and while she doesn't want him harmed, she doesn't really care. She thinks the whole thing's a publicity stunt."

"Why does she think that?"

"You know these show-biz types. Anything for a rating."

"Do you believe that? That sounds pretty cynical."

"I don't know what to believe. It could all be a hoax or some sort of experiment he's conducting—using us as guinea pigs."

"I know he's a researcher," I replied, trying to sound knowledgeable. "This would be a pretty explosive exposé if he was studying how his kidnapping affected sexual behavior. While that doesn't sound likely, it's not impossible."

Britt stared out the window. "People have made death threats against him. He's a very controversial person. There could be people out to hurt him, profit off him, or get him to renounce his work."

"That certainly thickens the plot. He could've staged the whole thing. Or someone had it out for him. Or some other reason entirely."

Time spent speculating on the whys and wherefores, while a popular pastime, is mostly a waste of energy. But I do it.

I decided to move things along. "I guess for the moment it comes down to whether you call the police or pay the ransom."

"Or both. That's the hard part. Astrid isn't going to do either. Right now, I'm inclined not to call the police, but maybe I'll pay the ransom. But that's a lot of money to me and not something I just have hanging around."

"Yeah," I said. "It's not an easy decision."

"What do you think I should do? Don't worry—I won't hold you responsible. I'd just like to hear another point of view."

"What do you want to do?"

"Don't give me that therapist crap. If you want to be helpful tell me what you think."

So much for those therapist insider tips I'd planned to pass along.

"If I were in your shoes, I'd call the police and pay the money, but I'm not in your shoes. I don't know how well you know Goodst and how important he is to you. Certainly everyone is important to us all. It's just that some are more so."

She turned from the window and stared at me. "That sounds reasonable. But, then, this isn't a reasonable situation."

"There you have it. There's no right or wrong. While one action might be better or worse than another, you have no way of knowing. You have to do whatever you think is best. Regardless of how it turns out, that's the intention you could use to guide your process. What do you think is the best thing to do right now? I'd go with that."

"That sounds very therapy-esque. It's also somewhat reassuring. But we both know if what I do harms him, I'm going to feel pretty bad about it."

"Yeah. Of course. But, still. Whether you do nothing or something it will beget the next step and you'll go from there. I know that sounds like therapy pablum, but I believe it. I imagine there'll be some back and forth with the kidnappers, and whatever you do now will evoke a response."

She looked away from me and gazed out the window. After a couple of minutes she turned back and asked, "Any thoughts about what to say to Astrid?"

"I'd tell her your truth. You're thinking of calling the police and paying the ransom and she's not inclined toward either of those actions. So be it. You each do your own thing. Knowing me, I'd try to convince her to see things my way."

"Would you speak to her with me?"

"I don't think she likes me."

"She doesn't take to a lot of people. But give her some time. Maybe you can win her over."

"Not sure about that. I'm happy to help you explain your point of view and request she reconsider her own, but regardless of what she does, your choice needs to be your own."

"I know that. I'd just feel better if we were both on the same page. If she can convince me to follow her path I'd be just as happy with that."

"If you say so."

"I do. Now come on back to my room with me. We can talk with her together. Then I have to take a shower so I can get downstairs for the morning presentation."

When we got to their room, Astrid was dressing in the bathroom and I could partially overhear Britt asking her to talk with us.

Astrid came out and gave me the kind of disgusted, hopeless look that my high-school chemistry teacher had been fond of sharing. However, she did look great. She was wearing a full beige skirt with western boots and a black silk blouse and vest. Her hair had that shiny look I've never been able to attain, though her face looked pretty worn out. She'd probably had as rough a night as Britt, but she'd certainly nailed the trendy western motif.

"Good morning. You look great."

"Thanks," she replied, though her tone implied anything but gratitude. "I feel like shit." She headed toward a chest of drawers, and came up with some turquoise earrings, which brightened up her face if not her countenance.

"Britt seems pretty upset about the kidnapping and ransom. How are you doing?"

"That really is none of your business."

"Well, you're right. I didn't mean to trespass into your personal space. I was curious what you think about paying the ransom and notifying the police. It seems you and Britt have differing opinions and I'd welcome hearing your thoughts."

That was about as nice as I could muster.

"What's the use of talking about it with you? Goodst is gone and they want money to give him back. Personally, that's not how I want to spend my money. Britt may want to. That's her business. I just think the world would be better off if they just killed him and did us all a favor."

"Not your favorite person?"

"You got that right."

"Why do you think someone kidnapped him and asked you two for money, especially given your opinion of him?"

"You're awfully nosy, aren't you?"

"I miss my clients."

As I've mentioned, I turn to humor when I get uncomfortable or just want to lighten things up. I was uneasy because it seemed Astrid really didn't like me. While I can be an acquired taste, usually people don't start off not liking me.

"Truthfully, I'm just curious. It's not every day someone I was due to hear speak is kidnapped. I was hoping to hear what he had to say and I'm certainly curious about what's happened to him. Plus, I can see the kidnapping has distressed Britt if not you."

"I'm plenty distressed," Astrid said quickly. "I'm distressed Britt brought a stranger in to talk with us. I'm distressed my friend is so upset she's acting in questionable ways. And I, too, am not used to kidnapping and ransom notes."

Britt took a shot at the peace process. "We're all distressed. We need to support one another. Now, I have to shower. You two can talk this out while I'm gone."

And with that she left. Astrid and I tried not to look at each other. Finally, she said, "Why don't you make yourself useful and call room service. Get us some coffee."

"I'm happy to do that, but by the time it arrives the morning's presentation will have started. You're better off going downstairs."

"Thank you for the advice. Now will you call and then leave, or just leave?"

"Sure. I'll call and then I'll go. I just don't understand why you're on my case so much."

"Listen, guy, you don't understand. I'm tired. Britt is tired. We're stressed out, and you come along and try to be the cavalry. Frankly, I don't need or want the cavalry. If I ever do, I'll give you a call."

"Okay. I didn't know I was being the cavalry, but obviously I seem that way to you. I'll just call room service and take my leave."

I made the call while she went into the bathroom. By the time I was almost finished, Astrid came out and said to cancel it because Britt was just about ready.

I did as she asked and was about to leave when Britt called out, "Don't go yet. You can come downstairs with us. I'll just be a minute."

Astrid glared at me. I tried not to smirk back. We waited in silence.

## CHAPTER FIVE

# IN THE LOBBY

THE LOBBY WAS full of commotion—close to a hundred people clustered in groups, talking in raised voices with a lot of hand-waving. Many were brandishing envelopes that looked like the ones Britt and Astrid had received.

Britt and Astrid made a beeline toward a group of women. I followed them but hung back. I recognized the dark-haired one but couldn't remember her name. The other women were all new to me. Well, everyone was.

I stood on the periphery and listened. It seemed all the notes said the same thing except for the ransom figures, which ranged from a hundred thousand dollars down to two thousand. Why wasn't entirely clear. I couldn't hear what the person with the hundred-thousand-dollar note was saying, but given her fashionable attire and the overgrown diamond on her hand, her net worth might have earned her the higher asking price. Then again, perhaps the numbers were based on who wanted him back more, although Astrid's note didn't exactly support that conclusion.

It seemed everyone was either a past or present client, or had attended one of Goodst's workshops at the Institute. Everyone was busy sharing their notes, theories, worries, and listening to hear if anyone had anything new to add to the mix.

A wave of information from a "reliable source" swept through the room. The morning presentation would be postponed; instead, in an hour there'd be a meeting in another conference room for everyone who'd received a note.

I was on the outside looking in. I usually don't mind that position. In fact, many a therapist has noted voyeurism as part of their career choice. You get to be privy to someone's inner life and hear about their escapades without ever leaving your chair. As comfortable as I am being an observer, I also get a good degree of pleasure from being a participant.

I didn't want to be on the outside for this meeting. I'd joked earlier about missing my clients, whose lives I could probe in the name of therapy. But that wasn't the whole truth.

Therapy is all about being true to yourself. And to be truthful, I'm nosy by nature. Or maybe it's nurture. Either way, like Popeye, I am what I am.

I knew if I were going to be true to myself, I'd have to put my curiosity into action and take a chance.

Goodbye, safe observer. Hello, dicey participant.

## CHAPTER SIX

# THE MEETING

I WENT TO the reception desk and asked where I could find the nearest stationery store. I fast-footed it a few blocks and realized how nice it was to be in a city where you didn't have to drive everywhere. When I got to the store, I stopped at the rack of postcards and bought a few as well as some plain paper and envelopes that resembled the ransom notes as best as I could recall.

I hurried back to the hotel and asked the receptionist if I could use one of their typewriters for five minutes. They politely said no, but would be happy to send one up to my room for $10 a day. I had to stop and have a brief conversation with myself.

*David, I know you like mysteries, but are you sure you want to continue? You haven't done anything over the line yet. Is it so important you try to sneak into the meeting?*

I had the typewriter sent up immediately and set about re-writing the ransom note as best as I could recollect. I set the requested amount at fifteen thousand dollars (hmm) and typed my name on the envelope. I'd toyed with twenty thousand—to one-up Astrid—but decided I didn't have to be childish about everything.

I figured Britt wouldn't mind my sneaking into the meeting, but wasn't so sure about Astrid. If she outed me, at least my note would be equal to hers for whatever meaningless reason that mattered to me. I decided to wait until the last minute then slip into the meeting and find an inconspicuous place in the back.

Turned out I didn't need to worry that much. While the place wasn't as vast as the ballroom, it comfortably sat the hundred-plus people in attendance. No one was checking for ransom notes at the door so I promptly spotted a seat next to a good-looking thirtysomething woman with copper skin and dark curls dressed like Cher and an equally attractive Roy Rogers-looking man wearing snakeskin boots and a bolo tie.

"Good morning," I said as I squeezed by and smiled. As soon as I sat down, the man put out his hand. "I'm Chet Walker and this here is Layla Diamond."

They each gave me a hearty handshake.

"I'm David. It's good to meet you both."

"You from these parts?" Chet asked.

"Sort of—I'm from LA."

"Never been there, but I hear if you can deal with the phonies and the traffic the rest is pretty fine."

"I'm sure the place has more than its share of phonies and traffic, but for the most part if you're going to live in a city it has a lot going for it," I said in the way that most LA residents find themselves defending the city. "Of course, that doesn't keep us from complaining. That is, unless we're talking to someone from out of town, in which case we sound like the Chamber of Commerce."

"That's true about every place," said Layla. "We're from Denver and we complain a lot to each other about everything, but once an out-of-towner shows up, we're all about the bragging rights."

"She's right," replied Chet. "We don't bow down to anybody. Of course, when we lived in Texas we said the same thing."

"Well, you have the dress code down right," I observed. "If

I were doing a better job of representing, I'd be in a T-shirt and flip-flops."

"Yeah, you LA people like to flaunt your weather," Chet said. "I remember one New Year's Day when I was nursing a decent reminder of the night before and I caught some of the Rose Bowl and lots of guys were shirtless."

"I've seen the same thing at some of your football games when the snow's falling."

"That's a macho drunk thing you put behind you once you're out of college," Layla said, giving a little wink and a shiver that accentuated her curves.

The audience quickly hushed as the man that had been due to introduce Dr. Goodst the night before came out to speak. He took out a piece of paper and read a statement about this being an outrage. He was sorry this had put a pall over the conference but he was sure Dr. Goodst would want us to carry on. For the time being, anyone who wanted to speak was welcome to talk so we could support each other during this trying time.

At least that's what I think he said. I'd been a little distracted by that wink and the shiver that had accompanied it. I wasn't sure what it meant, but it had divided my attention.

Once the man stopped speaking, chaos reigned. Many people got up to speak. Some shouted; others patiently waited their turn. Some wanted to call the police; others were afraid to and were upset with those who wanted to. Evidently, most people had woken up to find the envelope by their door and had hurried down to the lobby. The rest had been up most of the night, worrying about what to do or waiting for their bank to open.

I didn't speak up, but I did wonder why anyone would be willing to pay. Would you pay thirty thousand dollars for your therapist? More importantly, would my clients pay it for me?

Was there some special reason why no one was asking, "Why

me?" Instead, everyone seemed to know. They might not pay, but no one was questioning being asked. Or if they were, they weren't speaking up. Instead, the bulk of the bickering was about calling the police. The whole thing was fast becoming a shambles when a strikingly beautiful woman stepped up to the podium and the place quieted down.

"As most of you know, I am Dr. Goodst's executive assistant, Gabriela Barbosa. Like you, I'm terribly upset and unsure about the best course of action to take. We each need to search our soul for our own solution. As of this moment, it doesn't seem anyone has called the police." She looked out to see if that were true. If someone had called the police, they weren't saying so. "Personally, I prefer to pay the ransom and hope Wilhelm isn't hurt. I know some of you feel the necessity to call the police, and if that's your choice, so be it. I'd hope instead of arguing with each other we can find ways to support one another and collectively send out our wishes and prayers for a safe resolution."

That quieted things down. The man who'd started the meeting said the conference would continue as scheduled, and gradually the meeting broke up without any formal decision about how to proceed. I took another look at Gabriela Barbosa. She had the kind of striking good looks that quieted rooms when she entered. She was statuesque, like a model, and certainly had a runway strut. Her hip-length jet-black hair and tan skin made her look like she'd grown up on the beaches of Ipanema and now was an unobtainable goddess.

I heard Layla ask me if I'd like to join her and Chet in the bar before the evening session. I quickly said yes and headed out the door. I wanted to make sure I got out of there before Britt and Astrid spotted me... although I did take a look over my shoulder for one more glance at Gabriela Barbosa.

# CHAPTER SEVEN

# THE ENVELOPE PLEASE

**Monday afternoon**

I WAS HAVING a snack in the hotel's Sunset View Café, enjoying the Mediterranean décor and ocean vista. A middle-aged man with a ponytail came rushing in and hovered over a nearby table of four. I overheard him saying the police had arrived and we were all supposed to come back to the meeting room. The group quickly finished their meal and headed out. I took my time so Britt and Astrid would already be there and I could fade into the background.

My timing seemed to have worked as the room was mostly full when I arrived. I sat down while an experienced-looking police officer tried to reassure everyone, but I could sense a lot of fear and resentment in the room along with some hope. He was advising people not to pay the ransom, but if they insisted on doing so to please let him know so the bills could be marked. He and the rest of the officers would be setting up individual interviews and everyone should leave their envelopes at the door. There would be sheets on a table outside the room on which we could indicate the workshops we'd be attending for the rest of the day, where we were staying, and how we could be located.

I started to feel uneasy. I wondered if I could get out of there without handing in my envelope. I looked at the door. Two officers stood ready to collect them. Comeuppance might be heading my way.

In the meantime, I wasn't feeling particularly reassured by the police presence. Especially as it pertained to me.

I smiled warmly at the officer as I handed over my envelope. *Now, you've done it, David*, I heard a voice say. I went to one of the tables and figured out how to spend the rest of the day before I had to do some explaining.

I spotted Britt and, despite some familiar faces nearby, approached her directly. "Hi. How you doing?"

"I'm okay."

"Really?"

"Really. At first I was pissed off someone had called the cops but Astrid told me it wasn't her and, to be truthful, it's comforting to have them here."

"I'm glad you're feeling more comfortable," I replied in a kind of a therapist-rote way. I could have lingered in that moment, but I jumped ahead. "I was hoping before the evening's workshop you'd like to have dinner."

"That's very kind of you. A group of us were planning on having an early dinner in town before coming back to see *The Harrad Experiment*. I'm sure it would be fine if you came along."

I put on a brave smile. It wasn't a rejection, just a reminder to take things a step at a time. To use a baseball analogy, I tend to want to get on base before I come to bat.

I needed to touch base with Chet and Layla. We'd agreed to meet before the evening session and, while that was still a ways off, by the time I got back from dinner it might be too late.

Chet's last name had slipped my mind but I remembered Layla's. Diamond. And she was a diamond. Plus, she'd winked at me. I figured Diamond wasn't her real name, but maybe the wink had been genuine.

I asked the receptionist whether Layla Diamond had a room at the hotel. I didn't know if she and Chet were sharing one but left a note addressed to both saying I was sorry to have to miss our drink and hoped we could catch up another time. Maybe after the evening's presentation.

"Maybe" because maybe something would happen with Britt that would keep me away. There's nothing wrong with wishful thinking. There's also nothing wrong with giving yourself some wiggle room just in case. And who knew? There might be some follow-up on that wink.

I'm nothing if not hopeful.

# CHAPTER EIGHT

# HISTORY AND PERSPECTIVE

FIVE OF US sat in a soft-colored health-food restaurant with whitewash-pickled wood interior. I learned Marie, otherwise known as Feel Me, was a sex therapist in Marin County who specialized in working with erectile-challenged men and pre-orgasmic women. To balance things out she also did sex-ed workshops in schools and spent a lot of time in her garden. In addition to Britt and Astrid, there was another woman who was very quiet but spoke briefly but memorably about attending the first love-ins in 1966. All she could remember was Timothy Leary saying, "Turn on, tune in, drop out."

I guess there wasn't much to say after that. It was one of those factoids everyone remembered about her and would say, "Oh yeah, you know who I mean. I can't remember her name but she was at those early love-ins." It made me wonder what reference points people would use to remember me—"Oh yeah, you remember him. He's the one who didn't know anything about sex."

As we were eating our organic sprout-laden salads, I threw out this question: "How do you all know Dr. Goodst?"

After finishing her mouthful, Marie answered. "Dr. Goodst, Wilhelm, was my first supervisor. When I was doing my hours for my psychologist license, I interned in a hospital and became friends with the social worker. She told me vasectomies were becoming increasingly popular, but a lot of men were having psychological and physiological complications. I knew nothing about how to help them with this problem so I went to one of Wilhelm's workshops to learn more and then followed up with some individual supervision."

"That's somewhat how I know him," said the love-in woman.

I looked over at Astrid, who looked back at me. Finally, she said, "I first heard of him a few years ago when I'd just started freelancing. I was doing an article on how women are portrayed in modern literature and thought it might be helpful to interview someone about sexuality. I was referred to him and interviewed him. I thought he was a sexist pig and viewed women as objects." She paused, then added, "To his credit, he gave me some good quotes for the article."

I wanted to ask her more about the article and the focus of her writings but I also wanted to hear what Britt had to say. So did everyone else and all eyes headed her way. She was quiet. Hesitant. Soon some words came out in a quiet monotone.

"I was a client of his. When I was growing up my stepfather sexually abused me. When I started dating, I didn't feel comfortable being sexual. I decided to see a therapist and Dr. Goodst was recommended to me. I had the freedom to live anywhere so I moved out here for a couple of years and saw him pretty regularly."

"I'm so sorry to hear this," Marie said, and the other women and I nodded.

"It was a long time ago."

There was an uncomfortable silence. It seemed like Britt's abuse wasn't news to Astrid. I wanted to reach out, find some words to relate to her pain, show some compassion. Instead I blurted out, "When did you see Dr. Goodst?"

I got some "You're-an-insensitive-lout" looks, but Britt didn't seem to mind my obtuseness as we skipped past the emotion of the moment.

"I transferred to UC San Diego in my junior year of college and stayed until I graduated. Then I moved to Seattle."

"I'm glad at least you were able to see Dr. Goodst," I said in an attempt to show some degree of sensitivity. "I hope he was helpful to you."

I got another round of disapproving looks. If they'd been able to inflict physical harm, Astrid's would have knocked me down.

"Yeah. Sure," Britt mumbled.

It made me wonder if the good doctor hadn't been good to her.

I decided to skip *The Harrad Experiment*. I'd read the book in the early sixties and, as titillating as the movie might be, I didn't want to see the Hollywood version. The book had made quite the splash when it came out as it described a college where students participated in a New Age experiment where free love and experimentation were the norm. It had been part of the groundswell for the sexual revolution and had helped expand my own parameters. I preferred to retain my own images and fantasies than see them transferred to the big screen.

I decided to take a stroll on the beach. Perhaps I'd been recalling the conversation from the check-in line—I'd be remiss if I left that out—but mostly I just wanted to take advantage of being near the sea.

I don't know if it's the endless ocean, the clean air, or the sand underfoot, but ambling along the ocean's edge calms me. I was able to spend some time appreciating the moment. I tend to be the guy who foregoes foreplay so I can just get to it, whatever it is, already. I rush through a lot of things, but right now I was just enjoying the moment.

# CHAPTER NINE

# LAYLA AND CHET

I WENT BACK to the hotel bar in hopes of running into Layla and Chet. There were some people I recognized from the conference but no one I'd met. I found a seat at the end of the bar with a good view of the televised Padres game.

As I watched, I thought how baseball used to be the national pastime and now people were saying it wasn't exciting enough. It was much slower than basketball or football, and when things heated up the game slowed down. Baseball stretches its moments out. Maybe watching the game would help me in that capacity.

I didn't get to absorb much before Layla and Chet appeared.

"Hey, partner," Chet said, resting his hand on my shoulder. "We missed you before but glad to catch up. Looks like the Padres have another lousy team."

"Looks that way. Although I wasn't giving it much attention. Do you think baseball is too slow?"

"Not for me," Layla said, putting out her hand for a rather long handshake. "I like it slow. Gives me time to languish in it."

I'm not sure whether Chet was languishing in that moment—I couldn't tell—but I kind of was.

"What brought you to the conference?" Layla asked.

"Among other things I'm a teacher. The university where I work asked me to teach a human sexuality course and what better place to learn about it than at a sex-therapists and surrogates conference."

"You've come to the right place," Chet said. "You're going to learn everything you need. Heck, Layla could teach you all you need to know."

I looked at her. She was dressed in tight bell-bottoms and a crochet top. Her curly hair resting on her shoulders highlighted her hazel eyes, which were very inviting.

"Chet," Layla said, teasing him. "Don't embarrass me. Not that you can. And don't be modest—you could teach him as well, and maybe even some things he didn't know he needed to know."

I was enjoying their interaction—kind of provocative, playful, sexy, and earnest.

"How come you both know so much about sex? Are you teachers?"

"Of a sort," Layla said, turning to Chet for some acknowledgment.

"We're the best kind of teachers," Chet said. "We're hands-on. We've both been surrogates for years. You stay in this business long enough and you get to thinking you've seen it all. Of course, that ain't true, but Layla and I can teach you what you really need to know."

"Oh, yeah? What exactly is it I need to know?" I asked. Since I'd been accused of knowing nothing, maybe I could at least learn something.

"You need to know," Layla said, "how to make love. How to be loved. All the research, proper names of body parts, psychological/physiological/sociological pontificating is really just head stuff. Human sexuality's in the body and soul. It's about loving your body, sharing your body, and being in union. A union of mind, body, and spirit. The rest is bullshit."

"You tell him, babe," Chet said, cheering her on. "In one way most of this conference is bullshit. There's a lot of this theory and that theory and this and that laboratory research, but what does it all mean? What's it for? It's to sell products, get tenure, make a buck. You want to spend your bucks, spend some time with a surrogate—your toes will curl, your body will shriek, and you'll know what human sexuality is all about."

"Where do I sign up?"

Chet took out a card and gave it to me. "Just in case you're ever in Denver. In the meantime, Layla and I will see what we can do to help you out."

"That would be great. To tell you the truth, I really do believe what you're saying. I want to help people express themselves fully and honestly. I also know I need to also expose them to various theories and practices in the field. After all, I don't work at Harrad; I'm at a real college."

"Now that would be a good gig," said Chet.

"You got that right," Layla said. "No typical academic bullshit at Harrad. But since you don't work there, you'll have to play the game. In the meantime, let me and Chet show you what it's really all about."

"Hard to argue with that."

"There you go," Chet said.

"Help me understand. If the conference is really not that helpful to you, why do you come?"

"Two things," said Chet. "Number one, referrals. You're not the first person I handed out my card to. There are a lot of therapists here who would welcome having good surrogates to refer to. And Layla and I are good. We're very good."

"I believe you. You've got me convinced I can learn something valuable from you."

"Not *from* us," said Layla. "With us."

I could tell why she was good. "What's the second reason?"

"The soirées," they said in unison.

"What soirées?"

"The ones at the Institute," Layla said. "Business-wise, they're also a great referral source. But they're more than that, way more."

"I don't know if you're going to get a chance to experience one," Chet said, sounding disappointed. "Every Friday at the Institute, Goodst sells a hundred or so tickets to a select group for an evening of many things."

"What kind of many things?" I asked.

"He always has a great buffet of healthy food and a well-stocked bar. And the smell of marijuana blends in with the night-blooming jasmine. He usually has a Q&A session for about an hour, then people drift off and do their own thing."

"What's so special about people going off and doing their own thing? It sounds like every party."

"Yes, in some ways it is," Layla told me. "There's a big pool and spa area. People swim and sunbathe. It feels like the tropics. There are some nice garden paths to take and romantic spots to visit. Lots of short strolls and long interludes."

I couldn't tell if the smile on her face held promise for me or a pleasant memory.

Chet interrupted my wishful thinking.

"Yeah, that's true," said Chet. "Usually at most parties, if there's fucking it's a quickie in the bathroom or on the coat pile. It's not in one of the guest bedrooms with circular beds, mirrors on the ceiling, and all sorts of paraphernalia on the bedside tables. At the Institute, people are fucking in groups or by themselves. Some are dancing naked or in lingerie, and the whole place reeks of sex."

"Okay. That's different. I get that it's erotic and not your, or at least not my, everyday fare. But why is this orgy-type scene so extraordinary? The way I hear it, it's happening more and more these days."

"Let me begin by saying every orgy scene is extraordinary, even if it's happening in suburbia on a Saturday night. But this is not your ordinary swinger's party. People come to the soirées to take things to a different level. They dress up; they dress down. It's visually overwhelming. Some things you see are beautiful, others grotesque—you don't want to look but you do. Sometimes you want to join in; sometimes you don't. Sometimes they want you; other times they don't, although they usually do. It's just a whole different reality."

"And," Layla added, "not only are you in a stimulated state the whole time, but you actually see, hear, smell, and taste new things, and learn new things about yourself and others. And, of course, teacher, you get to learn a whole lot about human sexuality. It's field training at its finest."

She raised an eyebrow invitingly. I was intrigued. "Okay. Another reason to root for Dr. Goodst to be rescued."

"Or maybe the show goes on without him," Chet added. "They make some good money those nights. Those tickets ain't cheap."

"Not sure I can get the school to pay for that. How do I get one?"

"We'll see if we can get one for you," said Layla.

"Great. Thanks." I wasn't sure about being a participant but I knew I'd like to be an observer. "You certainly are painting a different picture of Goodst than the TV show. I've only seen parts of it and, to be honest, I didn't think much of him. Just sort of re-hashed platitudes. But now I'm getting a fuller picture."

"Yeah, don't cut the cat short," Chet said. "He didn't build his empire by shooting blanks."

"I'm sure," I replied. Then, as is my wont, I moved on. "So, what do you think about this whole kidnapping thing?"

"Chet thinks it's a publicity stunt, but I'm guessing someone figured he'd be easy to kidnap and people would pay the ransom. They must have known about the conference and that many of his supporters would be here."

"How much do they want from you both?"

"Five thousand," they said in unison.

"How come that amount?" I asked.

"I spoke with a few other people who I know from the soirées," Layla said, "and they all got asked for the same amount."

"It sounds like a lot to pay just to attend one of his soirées. I want to ask you something—and if you don't want to answer I'll understand—but why would you pay that kind of money? Is it really just to get him back to hosting his parties so you get referrals and do some serious partying, or is there more?"

"Listen, Dave," Chet said, putting his hand on my shoulder. "You'd pay it too."

He tried to sound convincing but I wasn't buying it.

Layla didn't say anything, which made Chet uncomfortable, and he quickly added, "I don't know about the rest of the folks here, but I'm happy to pay it. You'll see, he'll get"—he put his fingers up, made quotation marks and smiled broadly—"released. Then he'll have a hostage-release party and you'll know why everyone paid up."

Back in my room, I had a lot on my mind. First and foremost, I wanted to go to one of those soirées. I'd heard from friends about Sandstone Ranch in Topanga Canyon, where clothing was optional and swingers had their fantasies come true. No one I knew had gone there, and while I'd had some interest, fear of contracting an STD had outweighed the allure.

Going to one of Dr. Goodst's functions with a group of sex therapists and surrogates sounded appealing. But, really, five thousand dollars apiece? There had to be more to it… or I really needed to go to one of those soirées.

That got me thinking about just what kind of person wants to be a sex surrogate. Let me ask you, would that be a career path you'd want to follow? I didn't even know there was such a thing as a sex surrogate until I got to graduate school.

I liked Chet and Layla. They were comfortable in their skins, which is a good thing to be in their business. I guess if you feel good about your sexuality and want to help others with theirs, why not?

Heck, wouldn't we all want greater happiness in our sex life? And if someone helped us get that, well, wouldn't we be grateful?

The sexual revolution had ushered in an open-minded view of

sex and, perhaps, if you wanted to be a pioneer in a new frontier you might give it a go. I just couldn't fully understand the psychological disposition and process by which you arrived at that decision.

Being a therapist, I'm always interested in how our pasts affect our present. I wondered what had happened in Chet and Layla's developmental years that had laid the foundation for their wanting to be surrogates. Lots of questions ran through my head. Unfortunately, the answers weren't keeping up.

I lay in bed trying to sleep but my mind wasn't ready to cash in its chips. Finally, I told myself it was time to let it go. I did what I do most every night. I thought back over the day to find the moments that stood out in a positive way. I thought about Layla's wink, the stroll on the beach, and Britt bravely telling us at dinner about having been abused. Recalling them gently rolled me into sleep.

CHAPTER TEN

# ABERRATIONS

**August 23, 1977**

**Tuesday morning**

I WAS FOCUSED on the "ABCs of Aberrations." I hadn't realized how many people were discovering creative ways to use everyday objects. According to the workshop presenter, some sexual aberrations are:

a. fun;
b. dangerous;
c. okay with me if they're okay with you;
d. a possible indicator of a history of sexual abuse; or
e. all of the above.

The presenter made it pretty clear all sex is good sex just as long as all parties are in agreement. If one person says no, their word needs to be honored. If they say maybe, it's acceptable to proceed but you need to continually check in with your partner to make sure they're okay with what's happening. If the person says yes, everything's fair game just as long as the yeses keep coming.

I could understand the bottom line of mutual agreement. If someone wants to smoke, overeat, do drugs, or have an intimate encounter with an inanimate object, who are we to stop them? We might think it's not in their best interest to do what they're doing and might voice our thoughts, but it's their life to live just as long as they're not directly hurting anyone else.

I was curious what Layla and Chet would say about aberration. Is it one of those things that once you try it, going back to more standard practices loses appeal? Do you become jaded and need to keep pushing the limits to be satisfied? Plenty of substance abusers had taken it to the limit, crashed, and been able to give up their addictions and build meaningful and fulfilling lives. Would that hold true for people who strayed so far outside the sexual norm?

I tried to frame what I was learning to share with my students. Learning how to become a therapist means learning how to engage in all manner of conversations.

Talking about sex doesn't come easy to most of us, so the more I could get students talking about various sexual topics, the easier it would be for them to talk to clients. You're not going to be doing therapy long before someone talks about their love life, sex life, and mother. Ideally, you're at ease talking about them all; realistically, sex talks always come with an extra emotional charge and level of discomfort. That, too, I'd need to share with my students.

I was wrapped up in my thoughts when the session ended. I had no idea how long I'd tuned out. Everybody who's ever sat in a class knows you can spend a certain amount of it lost in your own thoughts. I hoped I hadn't missed anything too critical, but I'd gotten what I wanted—a class on sexual aberrations. Only had another nine to put together.

I wasn't sure where in the rotation a class on aberrations would go but I knew it wasn't going to be at the beginning, although the bottom line about mutual consent would be an ongoing theme. I must have been overly absorbed in my thoughts because I didn't notice Britt until I heard her clear her throat next to me.

"Hey. How you doing?" she said, greeting me with a warm smile.

"Actually, I'm in a bit of a fog. I've just been listening to someone talk about aberrations and my understanding of normal just moved a couple of steps toward the weird. Do you know how many people have to go to the emergency room to get all sorts of things removed from places they weren't intended to go?"

"Yes, I do. And good morning. I was in that workshop and I don't get it. You have to have a pretty warped sense of things to want to experiment in that way."

"Yeah. Sorry. Good morning to you. It's good to see you too."

"I suppose it's okay if all parties agree," she said, "but who actually thinks about this stuff?"

"I don't know. It's one thing to take a cucumber and see what you can do with it, but some of those things were just beyond the pale."

"It's disgusting. I don't know about you, but if I had a cucumber lodged somewhere where I couldn't remove it, I'd have a hard time telling the nurse."

"We therapists call that embarrassing moment a natural consequence. You play with fire, you get burned. I imagine the ER people get a lot of laughs out of those emergencies."

I could see her wave of repulsion settling down, but it was clear the presentation had disturbed her. It wasn't the best moment to ask her if she wanted to spend some time together, but, as you know, I tend to push forward.

"So how about we go have lunch together and talk about other things?"

"Not now. I've something serious I want to ask you."

"Okay, but my lunch invitation was serious."

"Thank you, but let's hold off."

I frowned a little to let her know I was disappointed but also pleased she wanted to ask me something.

"I've been thinking about what to do about the ransom. If you're willing, I'd like you to go with me to the bank and police station. Then we can drive over to the Institute and drop it off."

"I don't know," I said, teasing her. "I was thinking about the 'STDs and You' workshop this afternoon. But, truthfully, while that holds some potential interest to me, it really doesn't compare to my wanting to accompany you."

"Thanks," she said with some measured relief. "I don't really want to walk around with five thousand dollars in my pocket. Astrid is busy so she can't go with me."

"Happy to help out, even if I'm second choice."

"Hey, not long ago you were no choice. You're moving up. Besides, maybe we can have a late lunch when we get back."

"That sounds great," I said, because it did. "And maybe I can brainstorm with you some ideas I have about how to teach human sexuality to would-be therapists."

"I'd like that. Anything to get my mind off this ransom business."

"Sorry to hear it's troubling you so much. I'll do my best to get you thinking about other sexual matters."

I knew it as soon as it was out of my mouth—I'd moved too fast. I didn't need to see the displeasure on her face; I could hear it in her words.

"Don't get any fancy ideas. We're going for a drive, dropping off the money, talking about your class, and then, maybe, having lunch."

# CHAPTER ELEVEN
# THE INSTITUTE

As we headed to the Institute, I asked her to tell me more about what had brought her to the conference. She told me how she was on assignment to cover the convention. As a new reporter she had aspired to write for *The New Yorker* and *Atlantic*, but right now she was writing for "*Mother Jones* for my soul and *Cosmo* for my supper." Since I'd never read anything in *Mother Jones* about sex, I guessed she was working for her supper.

She asked me to tell her more about my work so I filled her in on how I'd been teaching graduate students for a few years but had been pulled in to teach the human sexuality course at the last minute.

I asked her for suggestions of topics I could cover. Instead she asked me what I was thinking of covering. That's when I realized she was an investigative reporter.

Once we got out of San Diego proper, the road was close to deserted. The highway weaved its way across rolling hills and mostly modest homes. The Institute was spread over ten thousand acres just outside Julian, a small gold mine/horse ranch town about sixty miles east of San Diego.

We drove past a long wooden fence and came to a big archway with a bronze sign proclaiming our arrival at the Goodst Institute.

We proceeded down a winding driveway lined with eucalyptus trees. There were several parking areas off to the side with a few cars in them, but Britt chose to drive up to the drop-off area in front. Two cars were parked there: a gray convertible Mercedes 450SL and a spotless black jeep.

The Institute comprised a rambling ranch house and some outlying buildings surrounded by olive trees, palm trees, and yucca. Pathways headed out in all directions to small gardens with sculptures. Probably some of those short strolls and long intervals Layla had mentioned. A few miles away lay a range of hills covered with oak trees. A gentle breeze rustled the olive branches. Goodst had picked a pretty idyllic spot.

Britt grabbed her large purse full of bills and headed into the building. I got out and stretched my legs and waited. I could smell the freshness in the air and wondered why I lived in a place where the stench of exhaust fumes dominated. My thoughts didn't go very far as Britt came running out from the far side of the Institute.

"Quick!" she said, hurrying into the driver's seat. "Get in the car."

I jumped back into my seat as she started up the engine and made a getaway that would have held its own at the Indy 500. Gravel went flying as we took off.

"What's going on?" I said as we passed the blurring eucalyptus.

She glanced at me then back at the road, seemingly deliberating about how to respond. "I saw someone in there stealing files. I want to follow him."

We got to the end of the driveway and she glanced left and right, then made a sharp left onto the road. I could see a car a few hundred yards in front of us heading back toward San Diego.

"That must be it," she said.

"I didn't see any cars leave the place."

"Most likely he was parked in one of the side lots you couldn't see from where you were. But there's no one else around so that has to be him. He was just a minute in front of me."

"How do you know he was stealing records?"

"The receptionist left to go into one of the offices. There was a room with office supplies and filing cabinets and the door was ajar. I could just see in. After a few moments, I saw a man sneak into the room from another entrance. I didn't see him the whole time, but I did see him hurriedly open a drawer, pull out a file, and rush back out the side door. I wanted to tell the receptionist but she was gone and I didn't have time to wait so I just bolted out. I want to see what he's up to."

"How do you know he doesn't work there?"

"I could tell. He was sneaky. And I'm sure that's him in front of us." She slowed down and settled in three hundred yards behind him.

"Do you think this is connected to the kidnapping?"

"How would I know? I just know I want to find out the story."

"Okay," I said as I buckled up. "But I have to tell you, just because I enjoy the mild adrenaline rush of reading a good mystery doesn't mean I'm fully enjoying this."

She gave me an exasperated look.

# CHAPTER TWELVE

# FOLLOWING UP

Britt kept her distance behind a dark-blue Camaro. As we got nearer to the coast, the traffic became heavier and she needed to move closer. He turned off the freeway and headed into La Jolla, the lovely spot just north of San Diego that most of us can afford to visit but not live. He slowed down to accommodate the surroundings as he weaved alongside the ocean, down Calle de la Costa.

He parked by an oversized hedge that hid what looked like a pretty decent estate on the bluff. As Britt drove past, he got out of the car. He was about forty-five, wearing an overcoat, and carrying a duffel bag that looked mostly empty. He entered a walkway cut into the hedge.

Britt parked the car down the block and we hustled back to the hedge. She slowed down as she approached the archway and peeked. "Come on," she whispered as she started to enter. "Let's sneak up to the house."

"No way," I replied. "Let's go to a neighbor's house and call the police."

"No," she said adamantly. Then she opened a latched gate and headed down the flagstone walkway.

"Wait," I said, and rushed over to the mailbox and opened it. It was stuffed. I took out some of the letters and looked at the name: Dr. Wilhelm Goodst.

"This is Dr. Goodst's house," I whispered loudly. "We definitely have to call the police."

She gave me a look that shut me up. "Are you coming or not?"

"I'm not," I said as I inched up to the gate.

She was a good ten yards in front of me and it was another thirty to the house. Surrounded by expansive evergreens, the house was a two-story colonial and looked as expensive as it probably was. The guy was nowhere to be seen. I scanned furtively, worried he might jump out of the bushes.

I felt like a whiny, scared kid. I didn't know if I was more afraid I'd find him or he'd find me. I just knew I wasn't cut out for this kind of moment. I'm a teacher and a therapist. I talk to people for a living. I don't follow them in cars, trespass on kidnapped people's property, or search out unnecessary trouble.

"Why don't you go back to the car?" Britt suggested as she took off toward the house.

Not moving either way, I stated the obvious. "I don't know what to do."

"Go back and wait for me." She threw me the keys. "If he comes out and I don't, honk the horn. I'll come back then. If I don't come out, then you can call the police."

"But…"

She didn't hear the rest as she closed in on the house. I felt pretty chickenshit. Well, a lot chickenshit. But, truthfully, also relieved.

I crossed to the opposite side of the street so I might not be so obvious. I took my time getting back to the car, keeping the archway in view. What were we doing at Dr. Goodst's house? And where were the police? Shouldn't they be here? You'd have thought a police car would be in the driveway. Wait, maybe there was. Where was the driveway?

I saw it at the other end of the house and started to head toward it when the guy came rushing out of the archway. The duffel bag was flung over his shoulder and was much fuller than it had been.

Where was Britt? He started up the car. If she didn't get out here quickly, we could lose him. If she didn't get out here... well, I didn't want to think about that. That extra weight in the duffel bag hadn't looked like a body, but I had no idea what a body in a duffel bag looked like.

He started to drive away.

Britt stuck her head out of the bushes. I exhaled. I hadn't really thought she was in the bag, had I? Nah, I was just nervous.

As soon as the guy was a good way down the block she bolted for the car. I rushed back with her.

"What happened?" I shouted.

"It's strange. Very strange," she replied as we got to the car. She floored it, made a squealing U-turn, and we were back at it. A couple of blocks later, we saw him up ahead. She took up her position a few hundred yards behind.

"I snuck around to the back of the house," she said. "I could see where he'd broken a window in a French door to get in. I wasn't sure whether to go in after him or not."

I could relate to that. "What did you do?"

"I went in."

*Of course*, I said to myself. "What happened?" I said to her.

"I heard some noise on the second floor so I slowly made my way toward the staircase. I was about to go up when I heard him in the hallway upstairs. It sounded like he was headed toward the stairs so I ducked back and hid. He hurried across the room and back out the doors. When he was out, I quickly ran upstairs and down the hallway. There was one room where some videos were thrown all over. He must have taken a bunch. Did you see how big his duffle bag was?"

"Yeah. It looked like it could be heavy enough to hold anything. It likely was a bunch of videos. Any idea why?"

"You know as much as I do."

# CHAPTER THIRTEEN

# JOHNNY'S

THE CAMARO GOT off the freeway on Hancock Street and headed into a mixed-use neighborhood. We followed, headed downtown, and saw a fair number of sailors in uniforms, bars, and X-rated movie theaters.

He parked on Sixth Street between an adult entertainment store—fetchingly called Johnny Trombone's House of Sex, offering twenty-five-cent movies—and the less creatively named Oriental Massage Parlor. Britt drove past and found a parking space. We watched him take the duffel bag out of the trunk and head down an alley. We got out of the car and ran to the alley, only to see him disappear into a doorway at the back of the store.

"Come on," Britt said to me as she headed toward the door.

I gave her a pained look. We went in the back of the shop and found ourselves in a hallway with a less-than-enticing bathroom and some doors with stenciled signs that read "Private Screening Room." At the end of the hallway was the store. The man was nowhere to be seen.

"Let's go," said Britt as she started toward the store.

"I suppose it's cheating to call the police and tell them he's here."

She didn't bother to answer. I followed her into the store. Inside were a couple of men—long-time-between-dates types—and a similar-looking guy behind the cash register, all leafing through magazines. Nobody made eye contact. I couldn't help but make eye contact with some of the covers. I wondered if any would make their way into some of the conference presentations.

There was an open doorway that led to some stairs. By the time I reached the bottom, Britt was close to the top. When I got to the top, I could see a warehouse-like space directly above the store and another hallway with rooms off it that modeled the layout downstairs. Most of the doors were closed but I could see Britt inching over to an open one at the end of the hallway.

I approached slowly. A few more steps and I'd be next to her, just outside the threshold. I crept forward, anxious to see what was happening.

Britt looked in, spun around, quickly moved past me toward the stairs, and gestured for me to leave. My knee-jerk reaction was to follow her but I'd swallowed my fear this far so, surprising myself, I moved to the threshold. The man was watching TV. There was no sound but I could clearly see two people fucking. One of them was Dr. Goodst.

I turned and took off after Britt back out to the car. Evidently, she'd found what she wanted because she started the car up and drove off. I started to ask, but she cut me off.

"Please. Be quiet. I need to think."

She smiled weakly and focused on the road. She drove as if distance was imperative. It confused me. First, she'd wanted to follow him; now she wanted to get away. Britt's journalistic impulses and her own personal interests had pushed her to follow the story. But why catch the guy and then leave? What had she learned so she now knew all she needed to know?

And what was she going to do with that knowledge? Wasn't it our responsibility to tell the police? Even if she wasn't going to tell them, that didn't mean I couldn't.

CHAPTER FOURTEEN

# BRITT'S REQUEST

**Tuesday lunchtime**

BRITT DROVE US back to the hotel. When I asked why she was so
quiet, she told me she needed time to think. I mentioned some
people find it advantageous to think out loud.

I can only bite my tongue so long. By the time she'd parked the
car, my head was full of tangential questions and elusive answers.
As we approached the lobby, I was on the verge of interrupting the
silence when she said, "We have to talk. But I don't want Astrid to
find out."

I was about to point out we'd just had a pretty good opportunity
to do just that, but knew better. Instead I said, "You want to come
to my room?"

She must have detected the various layers of interest in the question as she stopped and looked closely into my eyes. I didn't know
whether all my motives were showing but I hoped some sincerity
was coming through.

"Let's get a late lunch," she replied as she headed for the Sunset
View Café.

We were seated in a booth where I could view the sky above the ocean. Since the sunset was hours off, it was easy not to be too distracted, although gazing at Britt took care of that. Her fair skin and red hair made her blue eyes sparkle.

We looked over our menus until a well-worn waitress with a name tag that read Cindy came over, and poising her pen on her pad said, "Who wants what?"

"I'll have a Caesar salad and an iced tea," Britt said.

Cindy turned her pad toward me. "I'll have a turkey sandwich—hold the mayo; Dijon—and a Corona."

By my watch it was close to mid-afternoon, which almost put it in the socially acceptable time for a beer. In the therapy business we call that a rationalization. Most people just call it bullshitting yourself. Whatever. I could deal with the name-calling as I felt I'd already logged in enough of a day to warrant some alcoholic soothing.

As soon as Cindy had left, Britt leaned toward me. "You're the only person here I can trust, except for Astrid, and she's fed up with me."

"Glad you trust me. Sorry to hear about Astrid. I'm nowhere near fed up. Why is she?"

"She thinks the whole Goodst business is him trying to strum up headlines and I'm crazy for paying the money. She got pretty upset with me the last time we spoke about it. If I told her what we did today, she'd think I'd gone over the edge."

"Well, that was pretty edgy. I've never done anything like that before and really don't want to again. I can understand being a reporter and following a story, but that was truly scary."

"I was scared as well, but it's important for me to find out what's happening."

"Why's it so important?"

"You don't seem to understand. I'm a reporter."

"What does that mean?" I asked, my tone mildly confrontational.

"It means," she replied with some irritation, "it's my job to find the connection between Dr. Goodst and the guy we followed."

"And you don't have any misgivings about not telling the police?"

"Do you?"

"Yeah. A few."

"Does that mean you're going to call them?"

"No. But it does mean I want to call them, and I'm uncomfortable not calling them. If things get more involved, I might have to. But I'm not going to call them now."

"Thanks." She smiled at me, removing any misgivings I might have had.

"You're welcome. I'm happy to try and help you, but, I have to tell you, I'm not sure how much more of this I can take."

"I'm sorry to hear that, because there's one more thing I want to do and I could use your help."

"Do I want to hear this?"

She looked out at what we could see of the horizon.

"We have to go back to the Institute and then back to Goodst's house."

"We do?"

"Actually," she said, "you do. I know you hardly know me, but I wouldn't ask this of you if I didn't think it was extremely important."

I had one of those I'm-not-sure-what-to-feel/think moments. Whatever I was feeling/thinking, it wasn't good.

"What exactly is it you're asking?"

"I'm asking if you want something else. We're out of Corona," Cindy said.

Normally I don't like it when people interrupt conversations, but this time I was thankful.

"Whaddaya got?" I asked.

"Bud, Bud Light, Michelob, Heineken, and Dos Equis. Sorry about the Corona."

"That's okay. Let's stick with the Mexican and go with Dos Equis."

As soon as she left, Britt continued. "I'd like you to go back to the Institute, find my file and videos, and take them. Then, if the videos aren't there, go with me to his house and find my videos if that guy didn't steal them already."

I leaned over and whispered, "You want me to steal your file and videos?"

"I want you to retrieve them. They're mine. That's all. Just like the guy we followed did. He got his and I want you to help me get mine."

"I know you told me you used to be a client of his, but if I'm not being too pushy or invasive, what's the problem with Goodst having your file and session videos? He probably has hundreds, even thousands. And how do you know he has videos of you?"

"It's a long and very personal story I'd rather not get into. Maybe another time."

"I respect your privacy and know I ought to just let it go... but what you're asking me to do could have serious consequences. I could go to jail. Lose my license. Job. Life as I know it. You want me to trust that your reasons for having me do this outweigh the potential cost to me. That's a big leap for me."

"I get it," she said with a mostly compassionate look. "I know I'm asking a lot of you. We don't even really know each other and you have no way of knowing if my concerns have any real merit. And, yes, you could get into some trouble. But I don't think you will. It will be pretty easy to get them both and I'll help you all the way. I just can't show my face at the Institute again."

"That's comforting. You can drive the getaway car while the police arrest me."

"Stop it. I'll help you as best I can and be there for you. I'll tell you some of why this is important but I'm disappointed you won't just trust me."

"I do trust you. That's why we've come this far. I just need some context so I can tell the part of me that wants to run away we're doing this for the greater good. Whatever that may be."

"That's very sweet," she said with a look in her eyes that drew me in. "It's just telling you this that embarrasses me. I feel very stupid and exposed. I don't want you to judge me harshly because of it."

"Hey, I know a lot about stupid. While I could judge you harshly, it really isn't my thing. I might judge you because I do that all the time. We all evaluate the people we meet. It's a survival-of-the-fittest thing."

"Okay, Teach, that's enough of that. I've only shared this one other time and that was a long time ago."

"In that case, I'm honored you want to tell me."

"Tell me," said Cindy. "Will you settle for a Bud? These sex therapists sure drink a lot of Mexican beer. What is it with that?"

"Sure. Make it a Bud. Maybe those sex therapists know something I don't."

"Yeah, like it goes well with Acapulco Gold."

Britt told me her story.

# CHAPTER FIFTEEN

# BRITT COMES CLEAN

BRITT'S FATHER HAD died when she was very young and she'd missed his presence in her life. Her mother remarried when she was eight and she'd been happy to have her stepfather's attention. However, that attention had soon become physical. He told her if she said anything, he'd leave her mother and they'd be broke and living on the streets.

Britt had relented and for two years he'd forced himself upon her. She couldn't tell anyone... had to pretend everything was wonderful. She'd been a prisoner in her own home. She'd protected her mother but hated her at the same time for not being able to see the truth.

And she'd hated herself.

She couldn't forgive herself for giving in to him for so long and keeping silent about it. Intellectually, she knew she'd been just a frightened child and many people had done, and would do, what she'd done. But emotionally she a hard time forgiving herself.

Even though she'd been able to stop him from molesting her when she was eleven, she'd kept it a secret and tried to be the "good girl." In high school and then college she'd been afraid to go out on dates or to parties. She'd lived a pretty sheltered life. Then one day in college, her roommate called her on it. The roommate suggested a therapist she'd heard about in her psychology class and that's how Britt found out about Goodst. After corresponding with him, she decided to transfer to the University of California in San Diego.

Cindy brought the food, this time without comment, perhaps sensing she was intruding.

"At the start, just like with my stepfather, Dr. Goodst was like a good dad to me. He talked gently and never rushed me to speak about anything until I was ready. One day, after I'd been seeing him for a couple of months, he asked me if he could hug me. It freaked me out but I hugged him. I was scared and unsure, but believed him when he told me if I was ever going to be physical with someone, I should start with someone I trusted.

"Soon, at the end of every session, he'd hug me. I sensed it was wrong but it also felt right. He was soothing, comforting, and he was the therapist. I didn't trust my own judgment. It was all very confusing.

"One moment he'd ask me to trust him and the next he'd say or do something that didn't feel safe to me. Then one day he told me he could tell from my behavior I wanted to have sex with him but was unsure whether it would be best for me. He'd thought about it and 'agreed with me' it would be the best thing for my healing to have a truly loving, caring sexual relationship where there were no expectations of anything more than the intimacy and healing of sex."

I didn't like where this was headed. I'd heard there were therapists in the sixties and early seventies who'd instigated nude encounters and conducted group-therapy sessions in the hot tub. But as far as I knew, having sex with a client was always considered a no-no. That said, it's thought Freud had sex with at least one of his.

Licensing boards have reined in this behavior, yet sex between therapists and clients is still the number-one thing—in addition to insurance fraud—for which therapists get in trouble.

Dr. Goodst had framed his own sexual desires and hung them

on her in the name of her recovery, and in the process caused her more damage. He was the-rapist, not the therapist.

"I told him I was too scared to have sex with anyone. He told me I didn't want to live an asexual life and now was the time to do something about it. I trusted him. He told me he wouldn't rush me, when I was ready he'd be there for me. Thinking about it now, I can see how manipulative it was, but then I felt he was caring for me.

"Eventually I told him I'd do it, even though I was frightened and wasn't sure it was right. He said what could be more right than a doctor healing his patient and assisting her in building a healthy, robust sex life?

"I remember it clearly," she said haltingly. "He turned on the video camera to document our time for his research. He came over to me and gave me a big hug and told me how proud of me he was for having the courage to face my fears. I did feel empowered about tackling my fear and was proud of myself, but that was the only thing I felt good about. He took me to his personal 'file room' next door; it had a giant circular bed with a mirror over it. He had some of his favorite research videos beside it and told me maybe mine would be there as well. He lit candles while I stood there. He asked me to undress myself and then to undress him. Then he told me to lie down on the bed and he slowly began to kiss my feet. Then he massaged them. He continued to do that until he'd kissed and caressed every part of my body. Initially I was very tense and at times I thought I'd scream, but I stayed and slowly I surrendered to it."

She paused, overcome by her emotions. I knew better than to say anything. We stayed quiet for a few minutes, then she continued.

"He entered me and stayed inside me until he was finished. Then he slowly got up, dressed, and told me to rest; I could leave when I was ready and he'd see me at my next session. He said this stage of therapy was critical to my healing and for it to be successful

I needed to keep it secret. That didn't feel right to me but I had no one to tell, so it became yet another secret." She looked disgusted as she spoke and looked away toward the ocean. "I hate telling you this but you need to know I went back. Just like I did with my stepfather. I was dutiful. I took it and kept my mouth shut. It went on like this for months. Always the same. He hardly talked to me anymore. If I wanted to talk, he told me I was resisting the therapy."

"Wow. That's quite the manipulation."

I could see her anger rising. "The whole fucking thing was a manipulation so he could get his rocks off. He videoed our 'sessions' so he could use them for his research. I was naïve and afraid to speak up. When I finally got the nerve to speak up and tell him I wasn't sure I wanted to continue, he got mad and told me I was frigid and would be an old spinster if I didn't do the therapy."

"That's so not okay. He sounds like a complete asshole. I'm sorry you had to endure that. What happened?"

"Finally, I just stopped going. But he called me and told me I was undermining the therapy and this would only make things worse for me. I told him I no longer believed him and didn't want him bothering me anymore. He kept calling and every time I'd hang up on him."

"I'm sorry to hear this. It's a horrible thing that he did to you."

She wasn't listening to me. She was struggling with her composure. I could tell she didn't want to cry but the tears were there and wanted to come out. Usually when I wear my therapist hat, I shut up at this point and let the client settle the struggle. But we were in a restaurant and I didn't want to be her therapist.

"So how come you came to the conference? Have you seen him since then?"

"Only once," she replied, moving a little away from her tears. "A few years later I went to a woman therapist, and when I told her what had happened, she encouraged me to confront him in person."

"You made an appointment and told him?"

"I had it all planned out. Yes, I made an appointment. I wanted to be composed and strong, but seeing him I instantly got upset and started screaming at him. He must have pushed some hidden buzzer because a couple of his assistants came running in and dragged me out of there."

"Did you and your therapist report him to the licensing board?"

"No."

"How come? Your therapist ought to have done that even if you didn't want her to."

"At first I was afraid I might have to testify, that he'd deny everything and it would be a he-said, she-said thing... and it would damage my reputation."

"You mean damage his reputation."

"No. I was worried about the backlash against me. But the more I thought about it, the madder I got until I decided to report him."

"Good for you."

"Not that good. Turns out he has no license. He lost it years ago. He doesn't need it to do what he does. There was no place to go with it. I wasn't a minor. I'd consented. There were already stories about him and his escapades and I'd be just one more voice in the wind."

"That must be hard to live with. At least you got to confront him and let him know how upset you were with him."

"That did help a little but it really felt incomplete."

"Yeah, that's rough. I wish there was something I could do."

"There is."

Oh no. I hadn't really meant it that way. Sort of like when you see someone and say, "How are you?" You don't really want to know. I didn't really want to do anything other than listen to her and try to comfort her, but it was too late now.

"I want you to go to the Institute and get my file and videos if they're there. And, if necessary, go to his house."

"I forgot you wanted me to do that."

"Will you do it?"

"Maybe. But I still don't know why I have to steal them. I know he fucked you over and you have every reason to be upset with him, but why do you want to have your file and tapes?"

"Because if the police read the file or see the tapes, they might connect me to the kidnapping. Especially since I got thrown out of there because I was so angry."

"No way. There must be lots of files of people with motives. Many celebrities get hate mail and threats I'm sure are worse than your screaming. That doesn't prove anything. And if you didn't kidnap him, you don't really have anything to worry about."

"I'd just prefer there's no record of my involvement with him. If I can get my file and videos it will help me get on with my life. I can put all this behind me."

I could hear the resolve in her voice and understood that having the file and videos might help give her some closure.

"But why me? You just went over there. Why not go back and do it yourself? I can go with you." As soon the words were out of my mouth, I felt a wave of shame. She was asking me for help and I was putting it back on her. A very therapist thing to do but better kept in the office.

"I can't go back there."

I could understand about not wanting to go back to where she'd been abused, but she'd already overcome that hurdle. "Why not? Nothing happened when you dropped off the money. They didn't give you any trouble."

"Jordana was at the reception desk and didn't recognize me at first. She was just happy to see I'd brought my portion of the ransom. When I gave her the money and then my name, I sensed her tensing up immediately. She acted like everything was normal but she quickly excused herself, told me to wait, and went to one of the back rooms. That's when I saw the guy from Johnny Trombone's and I raced after him."

"But you could go back. You're not sure Jordana was going to do anything. Maybe she just went to the bathroom."

"Even if that were true, and I'm pretty sure it isn't, they'll get suspicious if I return after having left so abruptly. Even if I made up some excuse, I just don't feel comfortable. Please will you go? It would mean a lot."

I didn't feel like I had to go. I preferred to think I wanted to. I knew this was what I'd dreamed about when as a boy I'd read *King Arthur and the Round Table*. I realized it was a sexist, dated concept, but I wanted to be the one to rescue the damsel in distress, to be the hero.

But I could just as easily be the fool. It's a thin line.

"Okay. I'll help out. I know you're distressed about this. I still don't totally get why, but if I can snag them for you without getting caught and it'll give you some peace of mind, well, that's a good thing."

"It's not just peace of mind. It's insurance. I came to the conference intent on writing an exposé about him. I wanted to find other people who he's fucked over so we can destroy him. And I want to make sure he isn't able to destroy me in return."

That made more sense to me. But I still had a couple of questions.

"Whose files and videos do you think the Johnny Trombone guy stole? I don't think they were all his."

"I have no idea. I hope he didn't take mine. That's what I want you to find out."

"Okay. One more question. After all that's happened between you and Goodst, why would you want to pay money to get him back?"

"Because I don't want them to kill him. I want my story to do that."

# CHAPTER SIXTEEN

# WHAT SHOULD I DO?

**Tuesday, early evening**

AFTER BRITT CONVINCED me of the heroic role I could play in the destruction of the evil Dr. Goodst, I needed a break. I don't know if you've ever been lured off course by a pretty face and a compelling story, but I needed a consultation with my conscience, which seemed to have taken a vacation.

Is stealing in the name of helping someone because you're attracted to them explainable in court? What if you're exposing sexual abuse? I wasn't sure two wrongs made a right.

Ethical questions make me squirmy. I kinda knew what I should do, but doing what I should isn't always a route I like to travel. There are lots of things we ought to do. Things we've been taught are correct and proper. My mother taught me about writing thank-you notes and being polite to strangers. I knew the proper thing here was to tell the police. That's what I should do. But sometimes shoulds evoke a rebellious part of me.

Britt had shown courage in sharing her history with me. I wanted to honor what she'd told me and try to help her. And, I'll admit, I was curious about where she was in her journey. To my eye, it had been about a decade since she'd seen Goodst. How had those years affected her? Had she had partners? How able was she to build an enjoyable and meaningful sex life for herself? And, of course, did she see any possibility of having a meaningful and exciting sex life with me?

I wasn't sure what I wanted to do. Not an altogether unfamiliar position, but usually it doesn't involve the police.

# CHAPTER SEVENTEEN

# THREE STEPS TO A SEXIER SEX LIFE

I saw Chet in the lobby. He seemed both happy and relieved to see me, and more than a little upset. He asked if I'd take a walk around the neighborhood and I said sure. As we headed through the lobby, I saw a poster for the next workshop, titled *Building an Even Better Orgasm*. I hoped it wouldn't be a long walk.

"Did you hear the news?" he said.

I was about to give a wiseass reply but could tell he was rattled. "No. What happened?"

"Elvis died."

"What? No. Really?"

"Yeah, it's all over the news. He had a heart attack."

"That's horrible. He wasn't that old. How are you doing? You look pretty shook up."

"Yeah. I'm all shook up." He tried to smile.

"I'm sorry. I didn't realize I was throwing out a song title. This is really sad. He was a transitional figure. I know a lot of people think he was over the hill but he popularized rock and roll. In his prime he was the King."

"Still is to me. I'm really bummed out."

"I can see that. Anything I can do to help out?"

"Yeah, you can go get an ice cream with me and help me forget."

"Happy to do that. Not sure I can help you forget about it but, if you want, we can talk about other things, although, as a therapist, I can tell you it's better just to stay with your sadness until it organically lifts."

"Let's get the ice cream," he said, pointing down the block to a Farrell's Ice Cream Parlour. "You know, for a country that's supposed to be health-conscious, we sure do consume a lot of ice cream and cookies. Will you explain that to me, Doc?"

Since he'd decided to change the subject, I joined him. "It's a good question. Do you think life is hard and we all need some things to sweeten things up?"

"I don't know about that, but when I leave the house and pass a Farrell's, I feel driven to go in."

He opened the door.

"I hear you. Public consumption of ice cream and cookies is now a respectful act. You no longer have to sit at home alone on your couch and consume a pint while watching *The Rockford Files*."

"Now," Chet said, stepping up to the counter, "you can come to a swanky place like this, get a cone, and take it out on the street with no shame."

"Something I gather Elvis did quite a bit of, although he liked his ice cream fried."

"Along with those peanut butter and banana sandwiches."

He took his butter pecan, I my mint chip, and off we went. The town was succumbing to tourists. Local services had been pushed to the side streets. The pharmacy, shoe repair, and post office had given way to mass-produced art stores and cheap souvenirs. Fortunately, a few original galleries and a bookstore were holding on. When we'd finished our cones, we went in.

Chet and I headed off in different directions. I went to the magazine rack and pulled out copies of *Mother Jones* and *Cosmopolitan*.

Britt had said she was writing for *Cosmopolitan* for her supper and *Mother Jones* for her soul. I scanned the tables of contents to see if there was anything by her. No such luck, but there was an article by Goodst in *Cosmo* entitled "Three Steps Toward a Sexier Sex Life." I kept the *Cosmo* and bought an *Esquire* to balance things out.

Chet opted for *The Shining*, Stephen King's just-released book, and pointed to it when he saw me. I gave him a thumbs-up but he seemed hesitant to return the gesture for the *Cosmo*.

As we left the store I asked him, "What do you think are the three steps toward a sexier sex life?"

He gave me a strange look.

"Oh!" I said, relieved to be able to show him why I'd bought the *Cosmo*. I pointed to the side of the seductively posed model where the article by Goodst was listed. "I thought I'd read what the good doctor thinks, but since you're in the business I'd value your thoughts as well."

"Three steps to a sexier sex life. Aw, that's easy," he said with a big smile. "Goodst has been preaching those for the past couple of years. Number one is opportunity. You have to set aside time for sex to happen. You have to decide how much of a priority it is and then you have to devote time to it on a regular, consistent basis. Number two is honesty. You have to tell the person what you want and what you like. You have to tell them what they do that you like and what you want them to do. Don't tell them what you don't like. Just focus on making sure they know, with a capital *K*, what you like that they do and what you'd like them to do. Keep the focus on the positive."

"Making it a priority sounds right to me. Of course, I've found while sex is a priority for me it isn't always so for others."

"Exactly. That's why you need to see Dr. Goodst, so he can teach you how to get on the same page. Believe me, he knows all the angles."

"So I gather," I said, but he didn't catch my tone. "Telling your partner what you like and avoiding the negative seems wise. If you like what they're doing, it really is in your best interest to moan and groan and otherwise let them know how much you like it. What's the third thing?"

"Number three is connected to number one. You have to really want to have a sexier sex life. If you want it, you have to walk it not just talk it. If you can't walk it, it means you really don't want it so quit complaining about not having a better sex life. If you want a sexier sex life invest the time, energy, and money into making it so. Otherwise it isn't really a priority. Which is fine. We all have different priorities. But the true test of a priority is in the pudding. You're either in the pudding or you ain't."

"That makes sense too. Sort of like money. A lot of people say they want more, but the people who have a lot of money are people who really, really want it. They make the pursuit of it a major priority in their life. They work for their pudding. Or, at least, most of them do."

"The rest inherit it or marry it," Chet pointed out.

"Yeah. I suppose if having a sexier sex life is a priority, you'll look for someone who also has that priority, and together you make it happen."

"And, if your partner doesn't want exactly what you want, you'll either find it elsewhere or sublimate it in some way."

"Hey, that's therapist talk. Where did you learn that?"

"Just because I have sex for a living doesn't mean I don't read." I couldn't tell if he was teasing me or a little upset. "The Stephen King is my summer reading. In the winter I break out the self-help books."

"Okay. That's good to know. Glad it's summer. Some of those self-help books can get you down."

"You're right, there. I just remembered another thing Goodst has to say about the sexier sex life. He thinks most people want more and better sex but are afraid to really go for it. So they end up living repressed, regretful lives because of it."

"That's horrible."

"That it is. But it pays his and my bills. Yours too."

Back at the hotel, Chet and I bade each other an awkward good-bye. Did we shake, hug, backslap, or offer a see-you-around nod? There was an uncomfortable pause and then Chet gave me a hearty bear hug.

Male bonding, or female bonding, was what they were calling it in the self-help books—a non-sexual relationship with members of your own sex. Most people call it friendship. Whatever the terminology, I felt a kinship with Chet. He was what my mother would call a character. A modern cowboy sex surrogate who liked Elvis and didn't mind traveling halfway across the country to party. Or so it seemed.

## CHAPTER EIGHTEEN
# ONTO THE INSTITUTE

**August 24, 1977**

**Wednesday morning**

I LAY IN bed, reluctant to step out and face the world. Often when I wake up I want to linger. However, it wasn't a peaceful, easy feeling that was keeping me; it was the dreams I'd tossed and turned through. The night had been full of images of me on the front page of the newspaper with my hands covering my face as the police led me off to the big house.

While I'd been able to rationalize away my ethical discomfort, my unconscious wasn't letting me off the hook quite so easily. There'd been no sanctuary in sleep and I wasn't so sure there'd be any in the day ahead. I didn't want to get out of bed and have my nightmares become reality.

I was about to put my life in jeopardy to help out a damsel who may or may not have been in that much distress. I've certainly done my share of stupid and embarrassing things in the pursuit of romance, but this was number one with a bullet.

I don't like to think of myself as soft-headed or an easy touch even though I might be those things. But I couldn't deny that because of my attraction to Britt I was putting myself at risk in pursuit of her good favor. What happened to flowers and remembering her birthday? I guess we'd missed that stage.

One thing I know about life is the ante keeps going up. And not always in easy increments. I could follow a person in a car, go into a porn shop, and stand outside a house while Britt snuck in. But having done that, I'd now be leaping to committing felonies.

I rationalized that as long as Goodst was missing, it ought not to be too hard to sneak into the Institute. After all, the Johnny Trombone guy had just done that. Why couldn't I? All I had to do was go to the front desk, ask some questions, inquire if there was a bathroom, go down the hall, slip into the office, find her file and tapes, and get out of there without anyone seeing me.

Yeah, sure, that's all I had to do. No big deal.

She drove up in her rented car looking worth the risk. She wore a denim skirt that accentuated her legs, a white blouse that outlined her torso, and a beckoning smile.

On the drive we debated the merits of sneaking in versus walking in and offering my volunteer services to help out in their time of need. The volunteering option felt iffy and might get me roped in to another thing I wasn't sure about. So sneaking in it would be.

The plan was I'd go in and hope no one was at the reception desk. I'd quickly head down the hall. The fourth or fifth doorway down the hall was Goodst's office, and connected to that was his personal file room with his private papers, video equipment, circular bed, and perfunctory ceiling mirror,

If I encountered someone, I'd say I'd heard about the place and I wondered if I could have a brochure and schedule of events. Once I had those, I'd ask to use the bathroom, which was across the hall from Goodst's office. From there I could sneak in, search for her file and tapes. If I had no luck, I could open the door to the adjoining file room and search there. If that didn't pan out, I'd have to go down the hall and into the real file room, but the videos were least likely to be there. If I got caught in any of the rooms, I'd say I was searching for the bathroom. It wasn't much of an excuse but it was better than having to think on the spot.

Or so I thought.

The parking lots were just as empty as the last time. The black jeep was still in front and a few other cars were in the outer lots. When we got to the entrance, I loitered in the car. I really didn't want to go in but knew it was too late to back down. Britt gave me an encouraging smile and gently pushed me out of the car.

"Go on, Mr. Bond," she said, holding her hands together with a finger pointed up and shooting me a piercing look. "Everything will be all right."

I smiled weakly in a very un-James Bond way as I slowly made my way to the entrance. The lobby had a high ceiling, beige walls, contemporary Scandinavian furniture, and a curving reception desk made of birch and framed in aluminum. There were plants and pictures of what looked like the gardens surrounding the Institute. Behind the desk sat a very Southern California-looking middle-aged woman with a beach tan, brown shoulder-length hair that looked sun-bleached but might not have been, and a name tag that said Jordana Handler, Director of Operations.

"Good morning, Jordana," I said.

"Hello." She offered a strained smile.

"This is a beautiful place," I said, figuring a compliment was usually a good way to kick things off. "I'm visiting the area and heard about the Institute. I thought I'd drop by and see what I could find out."

"I'm afraid we're closed now."

"Oh, that's too bad. I was hoping I could attend a workshop, get a massage, or do whatever it is people do when they come here."

"All those things are available, just not right now. If you want, we could put you on a mailing list and send you information about upcoming events."

"That's a great idea," I said, gushing. "Do you also have a brochure or schedule?"

"Sure thing." She leaned over and pulled out a glossy pamphlet with a picture of Goodst standing outside the entrance. She handed me the pamphlet and a clipboard with a mailing list.

I hadn't been in the robbery business long enough to have given myself a witty moniker. Instead, I wrote the first thing that popped into my head, Travis McGee, 77 Sunset Blvd, Los Angeles, CA 90028. I smiled as I handed her the clipboard, which she put down without a look.

"How come it's so quiet? I thought the place would be busier."

"Yeah. It's pretty quiet now. Perhaps you haven't heard. Dr. Goodst has been kidnapped."

"Yes, I have heard. It's horrible news and I'm so sorry for you all. I just thought even with his being missing the place would be carrying on. But obviously that's not the case."

"We've canceled everything until he returns. Some people have dropped off ransom payments, but that's about it. The quiet makes up for when the police and press were storming all over the place. Things were crazy enough and then we had the robbery. Yeah, today is, thankfully, a quieter day. Well, so far. But that's what I thought yesterday morning at this time. You never know."

"I'm sure the calm is appreciated. I didn't hear anything about a robbery."

"Well, we didn't find out until it was too late to make the papers. But we're getting the word out so things might get busy any minute. Yesterday, some asshole came in here and stole all the ransom money."

"That's terrible. What did you do?"

"Earlier we called everyone who'd paid and requested, if possible, they pay again. We just called the people at the conference. It'll be on the news tonight."

Britt hadn't told me about a call, but they'd probably called her home phone and she wouldn't get the message till she checked her answering machine.

"Hopefully you'll be able to gather enough to get him released."

"We hope so. We're keeping positive thoughts and prioritizing his safe return."

"Yes, let's hope for good things," I said with a supportive look. "I know there are no activities happening today, but would it be okay for me to roam in the gardens? They look so lovely and it would be a nice way to relax before I drive back into town."

"That would be fine. It's a lovely garden."

Not one to leave well enough alone, I added, "Oh, yeah. One more thing. When they announced at the convention Dr. Goodst was missing, his executive assistant shared some information."

"Yes, Gabriela is very upset."

"I'm sure. I was wondering if she was here. If so, I'd welcome the opportunity to extend my concern to her."

"I'm sorry," she replied in a not very sorry way. "She's not here today. I can let her know you inquired about her."

"Thanks, that would be great. I'm disappointed I couldn't see her."

"You're not alone."

"I bet," I said, giving her a smile of resignation. "I'm off to the gardens."

I was a bit confused with myself. I'd just tried to meet Goodst's executive assistant. Being in her presence might cause me to melt while I was committing a felony for another woman.

Like a moth to a flame, I seemed to be drawn.

# CHAPTER NINETEEN

# BREAKING AND ENTERING

I HEADED OUT a side door that opened onto a patio from which various paths stretched out. I looked out over the palm trees and vegetation that seemed to be without boundary. The mountains were a few miles away and there were plenty of benches and chairs where people could sit and just take it all in. There were also a couple of pools for people to swim in, and hot tubs to do whatever in. The place had a tropical Polynesian feel to it despite sitting in what was basically the desert.

I tried to look like I was having a serene back-to-nature moment as I casually glanced at the side of the building, where a series of French doors marked different rooms.

I was on a parallel path to the building. There were some foot-worn trails where people had headed off the main path to the patios outside each set of French doors. Every patio had some inviting chairs, a small table, and an umbrella.

I tried to amble toward the patio. As I got closer I could see into an office that might very well belong to the good doctor. It was empty.

What the hell. I turned the handle.

The office reeked of success. The décor was expensive, impressive, yet tasteful. A bookshelf framed the doorway and held leather-bound books that beckoned me, but like Ulysses I bound myself to the mast at hand. Plaques, photos, and trophies lined the wall behind his desk. The facing wall held some paintings that cost more than I'll ever make. There were no spaces that might have held a file or tape.

I stood scanning the room and felt the blood running through my heart and the knot that was my stomach. While I was glad I'd gotten into the office, I wanted out as soon as possible—perhaps a feeling some of my, and maybe his, clients felt now and then.

I decided to check the file room but the adjoining door was locked.

*Why make it easy?*

I went over to the door leading to the hallway and put my ear to it. I couldn't hear anything, though I imagined it was as close to soundproof as you could get. I'd have to open it, stick my neck out, and hope there wasn't a noose waiting.

I turned the knob slowly, inched open the door, and tried to look purposeful as I stepped out. My luck was holding up. I took a few quick strides when it ran out.

My stomach jumped out of my throat when I heard a man's voice say, "Why, hello."

I was afraid to turn, but equally afraid to make a run for it. I gamely turned to face the voice, but it wasn't there. Then I heard Jordana from the front desk say, "It's so good to see you," and I exhaled.

I promptly ducked into Goodst's file room.

There were wood filing cabinets stacked along a wall alongside a built-in bookcase with a lot of candles and a TV. In one corner stood a tripod and video recorder. A couple of Polaroid cameras sat on a small table. And there was the circular bed and mirror over it.

I searched but saw no videos. Maybe they were in the filing cabinets. I'd only repeated *Pearson, Pearson, Pearson*, Britt's last name a few hundred times so I swiftly headed for the middle cabinet. I opened a drawer and saw Manila folders lined up against each other, but no videos. The first file said Madison, F. It was either to the left or right. I went right. Lily, B. I went left a bit more. Oscar, S. Pearl, K. Peter, J. Peter, W. No Pearson. I didn't know what to do. My mind started racing a mile a minute but I wasn't getting anywhere. Was her name Pearson? Pierce? Purse?

No. No. No. It was Pearson but it wasn't here.

I tried to take a deep breath and focus, but I was too scared. I wanted to get out but I didn't have what I'd come for. Either the file was missing or something else was wrong. Had the Johnny Trombone guy taken it?

I looked back at the Peters. There were two. I looked more closely at them. Peter Lerner and Peter Werner. It took a moment before I realized the filing was by first name. Not the usual, but neither was anything else.

I opened the other cabinet. There it was—Britt, P. I snatched it, tucked it under the back of my shirt, and headed for the hallway door. I took a moment. Almost breathed, opened the door, and went out.

That was when I almost bumped into the person who must have been talking with Jordana.

"Why, hello," he said again, although this time definitely to me. "What are you doing here?"

"Hi. I was trying to find the bathroom. Obviously, that's not it."

"Obviously," he sneered. "It's across the hall on the left."

"Great. Thanks. Kind of in a rush," I said, gesturing toward the part that needed to rush and moving hastily across the hallway.

Safe inside the bathroom, I didn't want to linger lest he decide to speak to Jordana, but I had to wait a justifiable amount of time. I tried to breathe slowly and deeply. I was too wound up to use the facilities. I flushed the toilet, took a look in the mirror so I'd remember what I looked like before I'd gone to jail, and stepped out.

I could hear Jordana talking but couldn't make out the words.

Then right before I turned the corner, I heard her say, "Well, fuck you too," and hang up.

I waited a moment for propriety's sake and then assumed a casual stroll. As I rounded the corner, I could see her writing on a piece of paper. I angled a little sideways so she couldn't see my torso, as if I were admiring the walls.

She looked up and before she could speak, I said, "Thank you for all your help. I didn't realize the time. I have to go now. Hope to come back when things are up and running."

And with that I tried not to run out.

CHAPTER TWENTY

# ONE DOWN, ONE TO GO

As I HURRIED toward the car, I thought about taking a peek at Britt's file. I was curious. I did, however, still have some bearings on my ethical compass. I'm a therapist and value confidentiality. Sneaking a look at her file wasn't just intrusive. It was disrespectful to her and my profession. Still, I thought about it.

Approaching the car, I could see her staring expectantly at me. Gauging my slight strut, a smile broke across her face. That smile made everything good in the world. Seeing her so happy lit me up in a way I'd not expected. I knew I didn't love Britt but I sure loved her in that moment. I'm a sucker for making someone happy.

I managed to get my enlarged self-satisfaction into the car.

"So?" She beamed at me.

I wanted to milk the moment. Take in all the goodness. But the moment was hers, not mine, so I reached behind me and pulled out the file.

I thought she'd grab it from me, but she just stared at it in disbelief. "Did everything go okay? Did they suspect anything? What happened?"

"Yes, no, maybe. Basically, I was able to get it without any trouble, aside from my blood pressure spiking. I did bump into someone in the hallway outside the file room but said the thing about asking for the bathroom. He looked at me a little funny, but I turned my back on him and went directly to the bathroom. I stayed there a while and then got out as quickly as I could."

"Right on," she said as she took the file and put it in the back seat. I could tell she wanted to look at it but she said, "What about the videos?"

"I couldn't get into the real file room, but they weren't in his office or his personal file room."

"Too bad. The videos wouldn't be in the real file room as it's too public, so don't worry about that."

"Okay."

She started up the car.

So much for languishing in my moment of glory.

"I'll tell you a secret," I said. "This robbery stuff is better than drugs. My adrenaline is pumping so much, if I wasn't scared shitless I'd be enjoying myself."

"There you go. Just keep it pumping for a little while longer."

When we turned up at Goodst's street, I knew right away I wouldn't have to be practicing my second-story skills. There were two cop cars parked in front of his house. A yellow strip cordoned off the driveway. There was no way I'd go in there now and I didn't think Britt would ask me to.

She confirmed my assessment. "Shit."

"Too bad," I said, trying to hide my relief. Stealing the records had given me an adrenaline high, but it was starting to slip away and I was happy to have it leave entirely.

"We have only one chance now," she told me as we drove past his house and headed back into town. "We have to go back to Johnny Trombone's and see if some of the tapes he stole were mine."

"What? No. There's no way we should go there. It's one thing to steal a file from a shrink; it's another thing to steal from someone who steals things."

"You don't have to steal them. You can buy them."

"Buy them? What are you talking about?"

"It's a video store. They sell videos. Just go in there and tell them you heard they had some videos of teenage girls and you'd like to buy some. I'm sure they've heard that a thousand times."

"Yeah. A thousand times this week, but how will I find yours? I'm sure they have plenty with teens or would-be teens."

"Look in whatever section they point you to. Usually they have pictures of the participants on the covers. Go look and see if you can find one of me—just a younger version."

"Maybe. But those are commercial videos. If they're selling Goodst's tapes that would be an under-the-table deal."

"Start with the commercial ones. Then tell them nothing is doing it for you and ask whether they have some that aren't on display. I'm sure they've been asked that a thousand times too."

"What if he says he doesn't have any other videos?"

"Be persistent."

"You want me to be persistent with a criminal?"

"You can push him a little. I'm sure you'll know when to back off. But don't give up easily."

"Okay, so let's say he does show me some tapes. How do I know it's you? There isn't a cover picture, but even if there is, it was a while ago and it might not be easy to recognize you if they printed up a frame from the video."

She gave me a don't-be-stupid look. "I basically look the same except my hair was half way down my back."

"What if he shows me a video with a cover picture that might be you but might not? Can I ask him to show me some of it so I can tell him I like it and want to buy it?"

"Yeah," she replied reluctantly. "You can do that, but you can't like watching Goodst molest me."

"I'd prefer not to look but I don't want to buy it and then have it turn out to be somebody else entirely."

"Okay, I get it. But just look long enough to know it's me and then forget you saw it. I don't want you seeing me that way."

"Fair enough. I don't have any interest in carrying that picture with me. But one more thing—what if he gets suspicious?"

"He's a businessman. Just tell him you heard a rumor at the conference there were videos of Goodst and young women and you'd really like one—but only with a certain kind of woman that turns you on—redheads with long hair."

"Or redheads who used to have long hair."

She smiled at that.

I smiled at that.

"Oh, one more one more thing. How much do I pay?"

"As much money as we have," she said. She went into her straw pocketbook, took out a yellow wallet, and started to count her money. I opened my wallet and took out the forty-five dollars I had plus the hidden hundred I kept for a rainy day. She had eighty-five so that made two hundred and thirty in total. I didn't know the going price but figured we ought to be well within the ballpark.

As I grabbed the door handle, I looked back at her and asked, "Any chance of a good-luck kiss?"

She blew me one.

# CHAPTER TWENTY-ONE
# THE HOUSE OF SEX

**Wednesday afternoon**

JOHNNY TROMBONE'S HOUSE of Sex wasn't exactly the kind of shop I'd want people to see me in, although, to be truthful, I didn't mind doing a little browsing.

By the front door there was a twenty-foot-long counter with all manner of sexual paraphernalia. Dildos seemed to be the popular item—numerous forms and sizes that expanded my knowledge of the depth and breadth involved in dildoing. I wondered how to include that information in my class.

Why not take them all on a field trip to a sex boutique to help expand their knowledge base? I could do that. Two classes down; eight to go.

A lanky guy with slicked-back black hair was sitting behind the counter, focusing on a magazine cover with the title *Intercum.* He gave it the kind of attention I wished my students would give to their texts.

"Excuse me," I said.

He didn't move.

"I was wondering if there's a man here who's about six two, two hundred pounds, with brown hair. Drives a Mustang."

As soon as I said it, I realized I'd gone off-script.

"Who wants to know?"

"My name is Dr. Unger and I heard someone at the conference I'm attending talking about him. I'd like to ask him if he has some particular videos for sale."

He looked up from the magazine. "Hold on."

He picked up a phone and after a minute said, "There's some preppy-looking guy here who wants to see you about buying some videos."

There was a slight pause.

"Nah! He looks legit."

Another pause.

Then, "Yeah. Okay."

"Johnny will see you now. He's upstairs in the back room on the left."

Orders relayed, he went back to *Intercum* and I headed up the stairs.

So far so good. I went down the hallway toward the same door where I'd seen him watch a video. I could feel my heart racing and stomach rumbling. The door was ajar again. I knocked and managed to let out a fairly clear "hello."

"Come in."

I did. He was sitting at a desk, his feet resting on a corner, facing a television set. He was dressed in black with a big golden pendant that looked like a penis hanging from his neck. A video was playing soundlessly with three girls and someone who wasn't Goodst actively using some of the marital aids I'd seen downstairs.

"Whaddaya want?" he asked without offering me a seat.

"First off, I want to thank you for seeing me. I don't want to take up much of your time," I said, probably taking up too much of his time already. "I'm attending a sex-therapists conference in town and I heard you were the man to see when it comes to videos."

"I repeat. What do you want?"

"Well, to get to it, I heard you might have some videos featuring Dr. Goodst. If you do, I'd certainly like to buy some. I'm a big fan of his."

He raised his eyebrows, gave me a nasty look, and swung his feet off the desk. "Who sent you here?"

"No one sent me here. I overheard a couple of people at the conference talking about you and how you have the best collection of videos. I figure that means you might have some of Dr. Goodst. If you do, I'd like some of him with young women. I'm into young women."

"There's a problem with that. Not many people know about my private collection. It's not the kind of thing people talk about when others are eavesdropping."

"You have to understand, this conference is all about sex. I wouldn't be surprised if a bunch of people from the conference have already dropped in. Everyone there is involved in the business of sex in one way or another. I imagine some of the local people attending the conference know all about you and were just chatting you up."

"I don't know," he said. He took out a cigarette, lit it, inhaled, and slowly let the smoke out. He was taking a break to think about it, which was fine by me.

"You're full of shit," was where that cigarette break got him.

"You aren't the first to say that."

"I may be the last. But, you got balls," he said, and grabbed his own to show me where they were located. "Or maybe you're just stupid."

"I've heard that before too. Well, maybe not the balls part."

He looked at me the way some people do.

"What do you want me to do? You want me to leave or do you want me to buy some of your videos?"

"To tell you the truth, I don't even know if I got any with Goodst and young stuff."

"What would it take for you to know?" I asked.

"For one thing, it would take me finding out more about you."

"Okay, what do you want to know?"

"I want to see your driver's license."

"Why? You don't think I'm old enough to buy videos?… Sorry. Just joking. Here it is," I said as I reluctantly handed it over while trying to look enthusiastic.

He looked at the picture, then me, and began to write down some of the information. I wasn't happy about that.

"Where are you staying?" he said, wanting to know more of what I didn't want him to know.

"The Sofia Hotel. The conference ends Sunday but I'm thinking of heading out sooner. Could you check me out and see if you have any Goodst videos with young girls, especially redheads, please? And let me know before I leave?"

"Don't worry. If you're legit and I can find them, they'll be worth waiting for." He handed me back my license.

"Do I call you or will you call me?"

"We'll be in touch."

I got back to the car and told Britt. She was visibly disappointed. She was also audibly disappointed. "Dammit" was her response to the heroic efforts that had returned me safe but without the tapes.

"I'm sorry. There doesn't seem to be much we can do but wait and see if he reaches out to me."

"That sucks."

"Indeed. I don't like having him know my name and address. It's not exactly the kind of information I like to share with purveyors of porn."

Not overly concerned with my concern, Britt said, "Let's go back to Goodst's house and see if the police are still there."

"I'd rather not. I've had my fill of this stuff for today. I wouldn't mind sitting in on one of the afternoon sessions so I can take a nap and let my adrenaline settle down."

"All right," she said in a not very all right way. "But I want us to go back to Goodst's place soon."

# CHAPTER TWENTY-TWO

# COMEUPPANCE

By the time I got back to my hotel room to collect my thoughts and freshen up, the hotel phone was blinking. I called the message center and was told Lieutenant Arnie Golk wanted to see me in the Beachside room. Whatever momentary relief I'd felt in the safe confines of my room quickly disappeared as my stomach did the tighten-up.

I tried to calm myself down before heading out. I've learned a fair number of stress-reduction techniques, which, truthfully, have marginal effect in times of aggravated stress. I breathed slowly and deeply. I lay down, closed my eyes, and tried to think of a serene place. I pictured myself talking with Lieutenant Golk and everything being fine. After five minutes I gave up and went to find out what was in store for me.

There were half a dozen folding chairs outside the Beachside room. Two were occupied by guys who nodded at me. I remembered, with some relief, that many of us would be interviewed about the kidnapping. I nodded back. Just a routine interview, I told myself.

A relieved woman came out of the door followed by a uniformed San Diego police officer. The officer saw me and came over to me.

"Who are you?" she asked.

I gave her my name. She looked down at her clipboard. Asked me for my driver's license and for the second time in less than a few hours copied down the information. I wasn't sure who I wanted to have it less. Then she asked one of the other guys to come with her and off they went.

Five minutes later, the door opened, the guy left, the other guy went in. I waited. It wasn't long before a woman I recalled seeing earlier in the audience came and took a seat. She said "Hi" and I nodded.

"You here to see the detective?" she asked. When I said yes she seemed relieved, and for some reason that reassured me. Just another cog in the machine.

The door opened and the other guy left. The officer asked the woman her name, got her license, and wrote down the information. Then she motioned for me to follow her.

The room was set up with a small row of folding tables. Lieutenant Golk was sitting behind a stack of papers in the middle beside another person in an underwhelming suit. There were also two uniformed cops sitting in chairs between the table and the door. There was no chair for me.

I quietly stood there until the ill-suited person looked up, looked me over, looked back down, and mumbled, "I'm Sergeant Nunn. This is Lieutenant Golk. We want to ask you some questions about your relationship with Dr. Goodst. First, what is your name and when did you first meet Dr. Goodst?"

"My name is David Unger and I've never met the doctor."

They both looked up.

"How come you got a ransom note if you don't know Dr. Goodst?" Nunn asked.

"I didn't really get a ransom note."

"We've got you on the list," Nunn said, checking.

"I cheated," I replied, and realized that was not the best choice of words.

I quickly continued, "I wanted to find out what was going on. Lots of people had gotten notes and the place was abuzz about the kidnapping. When the meeting was announced, I wanted to go and the only way I could think to get in was to create a ransom note. You can check at the front desk. I asked to use their typewriter but they had me rent one. It's up in my room."

"So how come you're willing to go to all that trouble?" Lieutenant Golk wanted to know.

"Professional and personal inquisitiveness. Don't you like to know what's going on around you? I didn't really think I was doing anything wrong. I was just curious about all the commotion."

Lieutenant Golk looked at me and then over at Nunn. "You ever go to all that trouble and expense just to go to a meeting? That doesn't make sense to me. Frank, you ever sneak into a meeting?"

"No. I can't say I have. Although I've tried to sneak out of meetings. I got to tell you"—he paused to look at his list—"Dr. Unger, something isn't right here."

"Let me explain. I work at a graduate school. They paid me to come to this conference so I could learn more about human sexuality because they want me to teach a class about it. I'm sorry but it seemed to me the most important thing going on here had to do with Dr. Goodst so I decided to go to the meeting. I know it might sound a bit peculiar but it's the truth."

I wondered how many times they'd heard that from people who were lying.

"You want us to believe the only reason you went to that meeting was professional curiosity?" Golk said, incredulous.

"Okay, I admit I've spent a good portion of my life reading whodunits. And here I am, minding my own business, and all of a sudden there's a kidnapping. That's never happened before in my life. So, yeah, I was curious, professionally and personally. It seemed innocent enough when I did it."

"You're a weird one," Nunn said, then leaned over and huddled with Golk for a couple of minutes. "You better make sure you don't leave the hotel until we get this whole thing sorted out."

"I was originally planning on staying till the end of the conference on Sunday but I was thinking I might go home Friday. I haven't made up my mind."

"Let us do that for you," Golk said helpfully. "Don't leave until the end of the conference unless you check with us first."

"If you say so."

"He does," said Nunn.

"So, Doctor, what exactly did you get out of going to the meeting?" Golk inquired.

"That's a good question," I replied, trying to kiss up to him. "I learned everybody was very concerned about Dr. Goodst but that there was no consensus on what to do about it."

"That's all?" Nunn asked.

"That's all I can think of now." Or at least all I was willing to tell him.

# CHAPTER TWENTY-THREE
# CALL ME INEPT

I WENT BACK to my room. My shirt had a certain *eau-de-nervous* about it. If I continued to get into anxiety-inducing situations, I'd have to invest in the hotel's laundry service. I didn't think the school would spring for that.

I hadn't told Golk about Britt or the Institute. Even as a teacher and therapist who likes to be open with his students and clients, I've learned in certain situations if they don't ask, you don't tell. I didn't think Lieutenant Golk had any way of finding out how I'd spent my morning. If he did find out, well, after our next meeting I might not have to think about having the hotel launder my shirt. I might be thanking my lucky stars I'd gotten the job in the laundry at the big house.

A little before five I followed the carpeting to the central meeting area where the Sunset room, Beachside room, Ocean room, and Grand Ballroom met. There were a lot of people hanging out. Scanning the crowd, I recognized familiar faces and groupings.

I overheard a group talking about their last workshop on why people like to have sex in public. Growing up, most of us have been naughty and wanted to get away with it. You don't have to observe kids long, or think back too hard on your own youth, to know the joy children find in fooling their parents or stealing a cookie. Some kids feel guilty and confess the misdeed, others hold it in delight. I guess we know which ones grow up to be the kind of people wanting to have sex in public.

As intrigued as I was to learn more about the subject, I could see Britt and my attention instantly shifted. She was with Astrid and the annoying woman I'd met earlier whose name I'd forgotten. I tried not to rush over too quickly but was relieved and excited to see her. They were talking about tomorrow being the deadline for the ransom to be paid. But I wasn't really interested in that.

"Boy, am I glad to see you," I blurted out, totally interrupting their conversation.

They all looked at me like the lout I was. I immediately wanted to go back and listen to the public-sex conversation.

"I'm sorry," I said. "Please forgive my interruption. I've had a rather trying day and I was just so relieved to see Britt, I butted in to your conversation. Please continue. I'm sorry."

The backtracking didn't seem to do much good. They turned their disgusted looks into smirks as they faced each other and continued talking. As much as I like to listen in on others' conversations, my head was too busy reprimanding me.

*David*, I told myself, *be considerate. It's not all about you. Yes, you've had an unusually drama-filled day but that doesn't mean other people's lives are not equally important. Wait your turn. Your time will come. Don't go rushing into things.*

As I'm wont to do, I started singing the words to an old song about fools rushing in where wise men never go.

"So, what do you know?" I heard someone ask.

"What?"

"What's so important you had to come barging in?" Britt asked with an exasperated yet inquisitive look.

"I'm sorry," I said to the group.

I don't like it when people keep on apologizing but I felt my behavior warranted at least a couple of rounds. "It's nothing all that urgent. I just spoke with Lieutenant Golk and I wanted to share that with you."

"Oh, I spoke with him earlier today," said the woman whose name I couldn't remember. "What do you think of him?"

I have to stop here. The woman with no name asked me a question. I imagine most of us were raised such that when someone asks you a question it's polite to answer. While I mostly do that in day-to-day life, I've found, as a therapist, all questions come attached to a statement that may or may not be given.

In therapy mode, I'd start by asking her what *she* thought about Lieutenant Golk. Once she'd shared what was on her mind it would be easier to respond. If she said, "Lieutenant Golk was overbearing and threatening. I thought he'd arrest me," I'd respond one way. If she said, "He asked me if I knew some guy named David Unger. They suspect he's one of the kidnappers' inside people," I'd have answered differently before I bolted.

I wasn't that paranoid yet, and I was out of the office, so I said, "Lieutenant Golk is smarter than he dresses."

"Well, then hopefully he'll be able to find Dr. Goodst. For myself, I thought he was kind of cute."

"Really? I guess we have different tastes. Or maybe I wasn't viewing him through that lens."

"I really don't care," said Astrid emphatically. "But I'll tell you, they're wasting their time talking to us."

"I heard," said Britt, "the police were over at the Institute and his home so they're just being thorough."

I couldn't help but notice there was a chill between Britt and Astrid. Evidently, their difference of opinion about how to deal with the situation hadn't entirely healed.

I tried to catch Britt's eye and let her know I wanted to talk with her privately, but after my stumbling start I wanted to tread cautiously. Whether she was upset with Astrid or could sense my need to speak to her, she said, "I'm feeling a bit tired. I'm going up to my room for a little rest. I'll see you all later."

Startled, Astrid said, "What about dinner?"

"I'll have room service. I'm going to skip the evening presentation, write some notes, and go to bed early."

"Are you all right?" said Unknown.

"Sure. I'm fine. Thanks for asking. I'm just tired. The jet lag caught up with me and I could use a night off."

Britt tried to convince Astrid it would be best if she and Unknown went out to dinner with me, but Astrid, Unknown, and I agreed that wasn't going to happen. It was time to go our separate ways, so after a round of goodbyes we split up. I saw Britt heading one way alone, waited to make sure I wasn't being watched by Astrid and Unknown—or anyone else—and headed after her.

# CHAPTER TWENTY-FOUR
# FOLLOW-UP

I KNOCKED ON her door. She let me in straightaway. I liked that she knew I'd be coming and hadn't kept me waiting.

"It's been quite a day. Are you really tired or were you just saying that?"

"I'm tired. I've had it with Astrid bothering me about Goodst. I just need some time alone."

"I'm sorry to barge in. I'm happy to leave soon. I just want to touch base with you." I'd considered saying I was sorry about Astrid bothering her but didn't think I could pull it off.

"It's okay," she said reassuringly. "I know you didn't want to talk about anything downstairs. What's the matter?"

"When I got back to my room after I left you, there was a message to see Lieutenant Golk. I was scared he might have found out something but, fortunately, he just wanted to see me to ask some general questions about what I knew about Goodst."

"Just like he did with Rhonda."

"Yeah, just like he did with Rhonda." I was relieved to have a name to call Unknown but had a hunch the memory synapses weren't firing sufficiently for me to remember.

"Except there was one big difference between Rhonda's

experience and my own. Golk asked me how I knew Goodst. I said I didn't and he asked me why I had a ransom note—"

"You had a ransom note? You never told me that."

"That's because I didn't really get a ransom note."

"Stop," she said, holding out her hand like a traffic cop. "You're confusing me."

"Yeah. Well, I was confusing Golk too."

"But, you told him?"

"Yeah. I told him. It's not that I didn't tell you. It's just it wasn't really worth mentioning."

"But now it is?"

"Yeah. Now it is."

It wasn't that what I'd done was that big of a deal, but I could tell Britt felt that not telling her but telling the police was a basic affront to team building.

"Remember the meeting where everyone was asked to come to the ballroom and bring their notes? I didn't have one but I wanted to go. So I got a piece of paper, an envelope, and a typewriter and wrote myself one. Nobody was checking them so I didn't have to show it to get in, but at the end of the meeting the police took all the notes. Mine included."

"That was stupid."

"I'm starting to feel that way myself. When Golk called me in and asked how I knew Goodst, I told him I'd written the note."

"He thought you were stupid too."

"Yeah. He did. But he might have me pegged as a suspect."

"Just because you forged a ransom note?"

"For standing out; it made him look at me a little closer than your friend what's-her-name."

"I wish you'd told me about this earlier," she said, the exasperation in her voice not totally unfamiliar.

"Yeah. Well, so do I. It wasn't really anything I wasn't sharing with you. It just never occurred to me to share it until I got called on the carpet."

"That's when most men think it's time to fess up."

"Wait a minute. That's not fair. It's not like I was deceitful."

"Wasn't it?" Her exasperation was growing. "You didn't tell me something that might affect me. Did you also tell him you went to the Institute and Goodst's house?"

"No no no. I didn't do that. I'm not that stupid. He didn't ask and I didn't tell. I felt I had to explain the note, but that was it. He didn't ask me anything else and told me not to leave the conference before Sunday unless I checked with him first."

"Okay," she said, calming down a notch. "Maybe there's nothing to worry about. Just make sure you keep a low profile."

I was about to explain the low profile I wasn't keeping was because of her but figured my stock was depreciating enough already.

"I certainly don't want him to find out about my visit to the Institute. If Jordana or the guy there describes me, and Golk thinks I fit the bill, I could be in trouble."

"Don't overreact. There's nothing distinctive about how you look."

Ouch. I wanted to be distinctive to her. And though my ego was taking a tumble, I took some comfort in being lost in a police lineup. Not sure where to dwell, I said, "You wait till Golk talks with you. Talking to the police makes you nervous. I kept remembering they could put me in jail if they wanted to."

"Usually you have to do something first," she replied, cute and snide all at the same time.

"Well, I did trespass and steal a file. Does that count?"

"They'll never find out and they're not going to throw you in jail for writing up a fake ransom note. Relax."

I wasn't quite there yet but it seemed her frustration had diminished.

"Okay, I'll try," I said, breathing deeply. "I'm just going to take your advice, keep a low profile, and everything will be fine."

"Everything is almost fine," she said. "The only thing that's not fine is my not having those tapes. If I had them then everything would be fine."

I didn't like the sound of that. Somehow or other it felt threatening to my low profile.

"I can understand that. We'll likely be hearing from Johnny as soon as he figures out if he has the tapes and how much he wants to ask for them. In the meantime, the deadline for Goodst's return is tomorrow so hopefully enough money will have been paid, he'll come back, and things will settle down."

"It must be nice to be a dreamer."

She stood by the window and stared out into the early-evening light. In another hour the sun would set and the night-blooming jasmine would be making its presence felt. Her figure outlined against the window was alluring. Her back to me was less so.

"There's another thing I didn't tell you," I began.

She spun around. "Yes?"

"Hey, it's nothing. Just that the receptionist at the Institute said someone had stolen the ransom money."

"You forgot to tell me that?" she asked, her exasperation returning.

"I got caught up in the moment. She said she thought some people would give again and they were trying to get in touch with those who'd donated."

"Nobody's contacted me."

"Did you give them your address here at the hotel or at home? Maybe they called you at home and left a message. Do you have an answering machine?"

"I do but I haven't checked in since I've been here. I'll have to do that."

# CHAPTER TWENTY-FIVE

# BAD NEWS

**August 25, 1977**

**Thursday morning**

THE SEARCH FOR Goodst was no longer above the fold. Elvis's death, followed by Groucho Marx's, was capturing people's attention. Both had broken barriers and taken their art form to new places, only to see time move past them. Below the fold was an article about Goodst and some unsubstantiated rumors about the goings-on at the Institute. The writer had interviewed conference attendees, who'd shared their own sexual escapades at the Institute and some of the workshops they'd attended. No one knew for sure about Goodst's own sexual activities, but they'd all heard he had plenty.

There was a brief reference to the police investigation, and speculation about possible outcomes, but little new information. Everyone was waiting for the deadline—now just a few hours away.

I sat at the table and looked over the workshops for the day, hoping I might actually attend some. With my best intentions in place, I headed off to "Talking About Your Sex Life: Past, Present, and Future."

The presenters—a man and a woman—were speaking about

the stages of sexual interaction: During the onset of a relationship we're exploring how the other person feels, touches, and moves. We're learning what excites our partner and what doesn't. Some people are comfortable talking about these matters but most are silent or indirect.

Listening to the presenters, I knew protecting my fragile ego wasn't a winning formula for an ever-expansive sex life. If I wanted more out of life, I'd need to put more in. Phooey.

I was giving myself a good pep talk when a man hurried to the front of the room and whispered into the male presenter's ear. The woman was telling a story about the thrill of joining the mile-high club when the man said, "Excuse me. There's some tragic news. We've just found out Dr. Goodst was shot dead in his home. I'm so sorry to have to tell you this."

The room was silent. The co-presenter cleared her throat and haltingly said, "I don't feel it would be appropriate for us to continue. Let's support each other and share a moment of silence for Dr. Goodst."

Most people bowed their heads. I could hear sobbing. I wanted to feel sorry for the doctor, but mostly I was worried about myself. I knew I hadn't killed him, but my behavior, if it were to become known, would certainly make me even more of a suspect in the police's eyes.

I was sorry he was dead. I'm sure he'd neither wanted nor deserved to die, and his death would bring a lot of pain to those who'd known and cared for him. I could say those words but I wasn't really feeling it. I hadn't known the man; I'd just stolen from him.

I apologized to the doctor, offered my wishes for whatever peace he and his family and friends could find, thanked the fates for keeping me intact, and expressed my hopes the police would solve the murder without discovering my involvement.

Lieutenant Golk, his sidekick, and some conference officials came onto the stage. Golk stepped to the podium and said, "We're all sorry about the news. We'd like you to stay at the conference until we get more statements. If you plan on leaving before Sunday, talk to Sergeant Nunn so he can set up an early interview. We will find the responsible person or persons."

With that, he left the stage. One of the officials came to the podium and asked if anybody had anything they wanted to share. There was silence for a moment, then people stood up and started talking about the tragedy of it all, the inconvenience, refunds, ceremonial services, and how and why he'd been killed.

I half-listened, half-watched, and felt a wave of anxiety begin to work its way through my body. If Lieutenant Golk found the responsible parties, might that mean he'd find this irresponsible one as well?

Bit by bit the crowd began to leave. I made my way to the aisle just as Astrid passed by. "Hey," I said.

She nodded slightly and kept moving.

Before I could get out of the room, Chet and Layla were by my side.

Chet reached out his hand and said, "Howdy," without much enthusiasm. I stopped and looked into his eyes. I could see the sadness and it took me away from my own self-interest.

"I'm sorry about Dr. Goodst," I said. "Looks like you're pretty upset."

"To say the least."

"It hasn't been a good week for you," I said. "Yesterday it was Elvis and now Goodst."

"Don't remind me," Chet replied, sinking even lower.

"Yeah, it's really too bad on so many levels," Layla said.

"I'm sure lots of people have reasons to miss him and Elvis," Chet said. "But it really makes me angry someone would kill Goodst right now on the eve of one of his biggest parties ever."

"Biggest parties ever?"

"Yes." Layla stared at me in a way that felt sexy and uncomfortable all at once. "It was rumored he was going to blow everyone's mind."

"I can see why you'd want to go to a party like that. But you seem more upset about missing the party than about his being killed."

"Listen," Chet explained. "The guy was an asshole. Anybody could have killed him for any number of reasons. But why the hell do it now? He had this big blowout of an event planned and everyone, and yes, especially me, was looking forward to it."

"I guess anybody can be an asshole, but not everyone can throw a great party. Do you think someone might have killed him because of the event?"

"Could be," Layla said. "His parties have upset people. You know, if someone is for something, someone else is going to be against it."

"There's that. But you'd think if someone killed him because of their convictions, they'd come out with some manifesto."

"That could happen too," Chet said. "I'll tell you what—I'm thinking about packing it all in and going home."

"What? Really? It's only Thursday."

All of a sudden I didn't want them to leave. I'd enjoyed my time with them and wanted to get to know them better. Especially Layla. She had an overt sexual energy that attracted me. While I was unsure about Britt's relationship with her sexuality, it seemed Layla was all in.

I couldn't tell what kind of a relationship she had with Chet. They were together, no doubt, but I wasn't sure what that meant.

I felt a tinge of guilt as I was also attracted to Britt. I didn't have any promises of fidelity with her but I still felt being attracted to and flirting with another woman was, once again, hovering close to my ethical boundaries. But evidently not over.

"I hope you two stay. I've enjoyed our time together and would like to have more. There still are a lot of workshops you can attend. Why not sign up for some of the more experiential ones? There might be a level of involvement there that could hold your interest. That 'Feeling Your Way: A Sensual/Sexual Journey' workshop sounds pretty inviting."

They both took a moment. I took my own to scan the auditorium. Most of the crowd had dispersed. My spirits lit up when I spotted Britt talking with Astrid and Feel Me. Then I felt guilty and hoped she hadn't seen me with Layla. At least Chet was there.

*Boy, David,* I said to myself. *You have to work on being more open and expansive, but you also need to work on why you're so attracted to different women, feel guilty about it, and don't know what to do about it. When this whole thing settles down, you're going to have to do some therapy on yourself.*

I finished off that sermon with *So what else is new,* and moved on.

"I'd like to cheer you both up and convince you to stay but I've got to talk to someone. Maybe we can have a drink later and try to figure out how to convince the Institute to carry on Goodst's party ways. There ought to be a tribute party or some such thing."

"Now you're talking."

We said our goodbyes and I made my way across the auditorium to Britt's group, intent on not barging in.

I purposely stood on the fringe, a few feet away from the three of them, and could almost hear what they were saying. Astrid might have lowered her voice when she saw me heading their way. Or she might have raised it. I heard "Goodst," "son of a bitch," and "crime scene."

None of them looked distraught; if anything, pleased.

I caught Britt's attention by angling myself directly across from her so Astrid and Feel Me had their backs to me. I took a step closer but got no response that beckoned me any further.

I tried to look understanding and cool but wasn't sure whether I was pulling it off. Hearing the words "crime scene" had tweaked my nerves. I was innocent, I reminded myself. Yeah, I hadn't killed him. I'd just stolen from him. But what if they didn't find the killer? Would they find the thief?

So much for gracefully and slowly entering a gathering. "Hi." I nodded to Feel Me and Astrid as I stepped in between them. "How's everyone doing?"

"Better than Goodst," Astrid said.

"Yes," I replied. "I guess we all can say that. Unless, of course, you believe there's a better life yet to come."

They looked at me to see whether I was joking or they were going to have to find a way to tolerate my religious beliefs. As is my wont, I decided to move things along. "What do you think happened to him?"

"Who cares," said Astrid.

I couldn't tell if she was just being her ornery self or was upset with me for barging in.

"It's horrible he was killed," Feel Me added. "But you reap what you sow."

Evidently this wasn't the sobbing group I'd heard when the announcement had been made.

I looked intently at Britt. "How are you?"

"I'm fine," she replied in a less-than-convincing tone.

"Glad to hear that. Whaddaya say we all go get a drink or some coffee/tea/fresh air?"

Nobody responded.

"Let me be blunt. Do you have any plans in which I can accompany you or would you all rather be alone?"

Astrid stared at Britt. Feel Me smiled weakly at me. Britt turned to me and said, "Why don't you meet us at the café in an hour? We have an errand to run."

Astrid didn't look happy. Feel Me didn't look one way or the other. Britt turned away and the three of them headed off.

CHAPTER TWENTY-SIX

# COMPLICATIONS

LEFT TO MYSELF, I didn't feel much like doing anything. I had to cool my heels for an hour before I could talk with Britt. Even then, who knew when I'd get her alone.

An hour is not that long, though in high school I had to take driver's ed after lunch. That hour lasted way too long. At the end of the school year, one of my friends had written this in his student evaluation: "If I had just one hour to live, I'd want to spend it in this class as it felt like an eternity."

I sat in the lobby, watched the world go by, and thought about whodunit.

A lot of people had known Goodst and some had reason not to think highly of him. The only people I knew who had any significant relationship with him were Britt and maybe Johnny Trombone. Not exactly the most thorough suspect list.

I didn't want to think Britt had it within her to kill Goodst. They say we all are capable. I suppose under certain circumstances it's mostly true. Was Britt under those circumstances?

I preferred to think a purveyor of porn would be more predisposed to consider murder. Of course, I had no data to back that up;

maybe porn-shop owners are the salt of the earth. They do provide a service.

Goodst had business acquaintances, friends, lovers, ex-lovers, ex-clients, and family members, along with any number of possible sordid relationships. Any one—or more—of which could have had motive to kill him. It was likely those who'd kidnapped him had also killed him, but why would they do that?

He'd been found murdered on the day the ransom was due. What had prompted the murder? Had his kidnappers found out the ransom money was short and killed him as they'd promised? Or what?

I was trying to put the pieces together but everything I was thinking was based on something I didn't know. I just hoped the police knew more than enough to find the guiltier party.

After checking my watch too many times, it was finally time to meet the group in the café. Unfortunately, it wasn't time for them to meet me.

For the first fifteen minutes I read the menu, overheard a family of four talking about their trip to the zoo, and was considering if the guy who looked like he might have been up all night also looked like a killer. Not that Goodst's killer would want an early lunch here, but they had to eat somewhere and right now I was checking everyone out.

For the next fifteen minutes I wistfully checked out the hostess. She had those natural good looks that seem a prerequisite for a beach hotel. She also belonged to a different dating age group. She had absolutely no interest in me. Not that she was alone in that, but slowly over the last few years I'd noticed myself becoming more and more invisible to younger women. Where once there'd been a momentary pause to consider eligibility, now I was no longer even in the pool. Like other aspects of aging, this didn't make me overly happy.

Of course, to be truthful, she too was no longer in my own eligibility pool. I know some people date and marry others substantially older or younger, but I tend to be comfortable with people who share cultural reference points. I wasn't sure if she knew who Groucho and the King were. So, while the hostess was attractive, she didn't attract me.

On the other hand, seeing Britt hurrying into the café did. Before I could slide out of the booth and stand up, she slid in.

"Hey, it's good to finally see you," I said with enough emphasis to generate a weak apologetic smile from her. "I see you're alone. Is everything okay?"

"Sorry to be late. Things took a little longer than expected. Marie and Astrid are still busy."

I refrained from cheering. "I'm glad you could make it and we can have a little alone time."

"Me too."

At that moment any irritation over being made to wait disappeared.

"I don't know if you're ready for an early lunch, but if you are, I recommend the garden salad," I said as I handed her the menu. She gave it a quick once-over and put it down. The waitress came over and asked if we wanted coffee or anything. Britt ordered iced tea. I ordered coffee.

Britt straightened her silverware and took a moment. Then she looked me in the eye and said, "You have to go back to Johnny Trombone's."

Suddenly my feeling good didn't feel so good.

"I do?"

"Yeah. You do. Sorry, but you have to go back and tell him you want the videos right away. I really don't want them circulating around now that the investigation has heated up."

"What makes you think he'll sell them to me now? And what do you mean, heated up?"

"I don't know. You know, the media and the police. Just tell him if he doesn't give them to you now, you're going to tell the police he has them."

"You want me to threaten him? Are you out of your mind? He knows where I live."

"Don't get overworked. Don't threaten him. Just make a business deal with him. Maybe blackmail him a little. Tell him you don't want to cause trouble for him but if the police found out he had videos of Goodst with underage girls, he could be in trouble. You're doing him a favor and taking some off his hands."

"I don't think that's going to work and I'm pretty sure he won't like me talking to him like that."

"Not everybody has to like you. He just has to accept it, take the money, and give you the videos. It's business as usual."

"It's not a matter of me wanting people to like me, which I admit I do. It's more that he really won't like me—enough so to take me out in the alley and beat me up."

"There's nothing to worry about. He won't hurt you. There's too much risk for him. He'll be happy to unload them."

"I'm not sure."

"Don't worry. You're a therapist and teacher of therapists. You can do this."

She was playing to my ego and it was working.

# CHAPTER TWENTY-SEVEN

# JOHNNY'S HOUSE

WHILE I MIGHT read whodunits and fantasize about being a tough guy, as you've noticed, it's not really my thing. When I hear comedians telling how, growing up, they developed their sense of humor to handle challenging situations, I can relate. Try to disarm them with humor was my preferred method. When that didn't work I relied on foot speed.

Approaching Johnny Trombone's, I could feel a now familiar tightening in my stomach and an itching in my feet. Here I was, the knight without his armor, taking on the dragon.

I was hoping Johnny wouldn't be in, but before I could check out the Wet Women in the August edition of *Playboy*, the clerk called him and a few moments later told me to go on up.

Not one for pleasantries, he said, "What are you doing here? I told you: 'Don't call us we'll call you.'"

"You did, but that was before Goodst was found dead."

"What's that got to do with anything aside from the price?"

"That's what I was thinking. I figure the price ought to be less now and you'd be more willing to let go of it."

"You got a screw loose, Doc. Goodst ain't going to be making any more movies so now the price goes up."

"Well, I was hoping…"

Before I could share my hopes, the phone rang and he picked it up. I tried to look like I wasn't paying attention as I took a closer look at the surroundings. Videos with suggestive titles and the kind of pictures you wouldn't show your mother were strewn all over the place.

"Listen, Trixie," he said, "this is the kind of business you don't talk about on the phone. Besides, I got a customer here." Then there was a short pause before he said, "Okay. Hold on. This won't take long."

He put the phone down on the table, turned to face me, and impatiently growled, "Now, I ain't got time for any more bullshit. What do you want?"

"What I want is to remind you we both know you have those tapes. Now, I don't care that you have them. In fact, I'm glad you have them so I can buy some of them. But I'm not so sure everyone would see things the same way."

I could see that was a mistake.

"I was hoping you could sell me some tapes and I could forget where I got them, and we both could go on with our lives."

I looked at him and gave him a twisted smile. He didn't smile back. I could see his wheels turning and it didn't look like they were turning well.

"I want to give you some advice. I can tell you don't know what you're doing or what you're messing with so I'm going to be lenient. Don't you ever threaten me."

He leaned over, glared at me for too long, and slid back into his chair.

"If you want to walk out of here on your own two feet, I suggest you apologize and get the fuck out of here before I cut off your balls and stuff them down your throat."

He started to get up.

"No need," I said. "I didn't mean to upset you." I took a step back toward the door. "I'm sorry. I clearly hear what you're saying. It's just that I very much want those tapes and thought you might be more motivated to get rid of them now."

"Are you getting the fuck out of here?"

"You bet," I said en route.

Bravery in the face of castration is not my thing. It's a bit embarrassing, telling you I hauled ass out of there, but at least I can adjust myself in the process. Telling Britt was another matter. While she might be glad I'd left with my package intact, not bringing hers wasn't going to win any praise.

As I approached the car, I could see the look on her face shift from expectation to frustration to resignation.

"What happened?"

"I almost got my balls cut off," I said, hoping to salvage some points.

She didn't seem to appreciate my narrow escape.

"He wasn't pleased to see me. When I suggested it might be in his interest to sell, he promptly let me know it would be in my best interest to leave with my manhood intact. If he hadn't been on the phone with some trixie, he'd have changed my sex life way more than this conference is doing."

"Did you say trixie?"

Here we are a decade into the women's movement, and being a relatively sensitive man I knew better than to call a woman a trixie. But I had and she'd called me on it.

"I don't know why I said that. I didn't mean to be a chauvinistic pig. It was just when he was talking, he said 'Listen, trixie,' and I guess I said what he said. I didn't mean to imply the person he was talking to was a trixie."

"Shut up," she said. And I did. For a moment. Until she said, "Trixie is the name of Goodst's ex-wife."

A wave of relief swept over me. While there are certainly

remnants of my narrow-minded upbringing lurking about, I wanted to believe my consciousness-raising had helped me dispatch sexist name-calling.

"Wow. Do you think that's who it was? The way he was talking, it did sound like they knew each other. I wasn't really listening but I'm pretty sure the call wasn't about getting a video. He said he couldn't talk to her while I was there. Then he told me it was time to leave."

"Did he sound chummy?"

"I don't think that's a word I'd use to describe him. He was more matter-of-fact with her. Like you might be with someone you know."

"Maybe she has business interests with him." I could see her eyes moving up, the left side of her brain, searching. "I wonder what kind of business interests the two of them might share. As I remember it, she wasn't exactly a shrinking violet. She was a porn star when they married—Trixie Alot."

"That could be the connection. Maybe she's going to do a video signing."

"Or maybe she wants the private ones of Goodst and her."

# CHAPTER TWENTY-EIGHT
# GOLK AND NUNN

BRITT DROVE US back to the hotel. While she was disappointed about not getting her videos, Trixie's entrance into the picture had lifted her spirits. Conspiracy theories filled the time on the drive.

When I got back to my room, the phone light was blinking. Like a call in the middle of the night, that light wasn't welcome. Nor was the message. Lieutenant Golk wanted to see me ASAP.

A wave of anxiety made its way across my body. Anticipatory anxiety is what they call it in the business. In reality, it's worrying about the future and it has few redeeming values.

Any way you cut it, worry is its own worry.

A few other people sat outside the Beachside room along with a uniformed officer. My turn came soon enough and I knew right away that my worry wasn't for naught. Sitting next to Lieutenant Golk and Sergeant Nunn was Gabriela Barbosa, who was as striking as one can be in a hotel room with florescent lights. There wasn't time to admire her as beside her was Jordana, the woman from the front desk at the Institute.

"That's the one," Jordana said.

All my life I've wanted to be the one, but when I finally was,

I wished I wasn't. Golk and Nunn looked at me with newfound curiosity. I tried to not look as displeased as I felt.

"Oh, hi," I said as warmly as I could. "It's good to see you again."

"You recognize him?" Golk asked.

"Yes," she replied. "He's the one who came to the Institute. He came after the robbery. He wanted to come to one of our events but when he heard they were all canceled he roamed around the gardens, then took off. Or, at least, I think he did."

"You seem to be the one, Dr. Unger," Nunn said.

"I suppose sometimes it's better to be the one than the many. Just which one am I?"

"You tell us," Golk told me.

"I guess I'm one of the people who went over to the Institute. That would make me one of the many. Not sure what would make me the one."

"Think real hard," Nunn suggested.

"Well, I was curious since I'd heard so much about the place. It's kind of a shrine for some people. The place was mostly empty. I saw maybe one other guy."

Nobody was buying that.

"And the real reason?" Golk asked.

"This is kind of embarrassing."

"You're a big boy," said Nunn. "I'm sure you can handle some embarrassment."

"Well, it's nothing new." I paused and looked at Gabriela Barbosa, who sat erect and looked disinterested. "On Monday I'd seen Ms. Barbosa speak about Dr. Goodst and, frankly, I wanted a closer look."

The side of Gabriela's mouth rose just slightly.

"How quaint," Nunn said. "What did you see?"

"I didn't see anything. She wasn't there."

"Ms. Handler," said Golk, gesturing toward Jordana, "says a regular at the Institute came up to her while you were there and

told her someone was lurking near Dr. Goodst's office. Would that
have been you?"

I smiled at Jordana to let her know how much I appreciated her
ratting me out. "Well, I was in the hallway, looking for a bathroom.
I don't know where Dr. Goodst's office is but I may have passed it
on my way. I don't think I was lurking. I had a more urgent need.
There was someone else in the hallway; I asked him to point me in
the right direction."

Nunn looked at Jordana. "Is that so?"

"John did mention someone asked him about the bathroom."

Nunn looked over at Gabriela and said, "Do you have anything
to add to this?"

She turned her attention my way and I felt my brain cells
disconnect, no longer sure the synapses would fire in any meaningful way. If she'd asked me to confess to killing Goodst, I'd have
just bobbed my head. I don't enjoy being intimidated, but in that
moment I was happy to be the object of her attention, such as it was.

"Not really," she said. "I don't know this man and his interests. Perhaps Jordana and I are being a bit paranoid. After all, it's
been a harrowing week. First, Wilhelm was kidnapped. Then someone broke into the records room and stole a substantial amount
of money. Then, yesterday, Dr. Unger wandered in. It just feels a
little off."

"Agreed," Golk said to my dismay. "I can understand how dis-
tressing this all is and Dr. Unger's story reeks to me."

"Listen, Doc," Golk said, staring at me. "You're a bit of a wild
card in all this. I don't believe what you're saying, except maybe the
part about wanting to meet Ms. Barbosa."

He obviously wasn't a detective for nothing.

"I don't think you know what you're doing. I can't put my finger
on it yet but you'd better keep your nose clean. As Ms. Barbosa says,
there's something off about you and I aim to find out what it is."

I doubted even if I'd known what to say I'd have been able to communicate it coherently, so I kept my mouth shut.

"Just don't leave the hotel without checking with us first," said Nunn.

"Okay," I replied.

Great. Now I was a wild-card suspect. If Golk found out about my visits to Johnny Trombone's or Goodst's house, I could be wearing an entirely new wardrobe.

Nunn had grounded me. I couldn't leave the hotel without telling them. I could tell Britt any more forays were off limits.

If I did, would she listen? Would I?

All I had to do was stay put, go to some workshops, and keep a low profile.

It seemed so easy.

CHAPTER TWENTY-NINE

# ME & YOU

**Thursday afternoon, later**

As GABRIELA LAID out the events in order, a thought popped into my head. Britt had told me when she'd gone into the Institute she'd seen Trombone steal the files. It was entirely possible the money and the files were in the same area, and Trombone could have taken one or the other, or both.

But so, too, could Britt.

I had no idea what she'd done in there. I remembered she'd taken a large purse in with her, and she could have easily put another file and/or money in it.

I didn't like that I suspected Britt but suspect her I did. She'd had access and motive. And she'd had me doing her dirty work such that I was now a suspect.

I didn't like that either.

All told, Britt could be a kidnapper, thief, murderer, and big-time manipulator of me.

So, what did I do?

I knocked on her door.

She didn't look happy to see me. I wasn't sure if I was happy to see her. I couldn't see Astrid so that made me happier.

"Hi," I said. "If you're not too busy, I thought I'd tell you about my afternoon." She didn't seem too excited by that so I threw in a tease. "I learned something of interest."

"I was about to meet some people for a drink but I have a few minutes. Come on in."

"Thanks. This ought not to take long. It'll be of journalistic interest to you, but I need to ask you some questions first."

"Go on," she said as she took a deliberate look at her watch.

"I'll be quick. There are two things. First is a you/me question; the other is a fill-in-the-details one."

"Let's do the details first," she said, sitting down and crossing her legs. I tried not to look.

"Okay. Can you tell me what happened when you went into the Institute?"

"Nothing happened."

"What exactly is nothing?"

"Nothing is nothing. I was at the receptionist desk. Jordana—she's the Girl Friday—left after I gave her the money and told her my name. When she went down the hallway, I saw movement in the file room next door. It was a man I didn't recognize. For a few moments I couldn't see him. Then he opened a cabinet, took a file, and rushed out. That's it. End of story."

"Did it look like he was searching for a specific file or was he just grabbing what he could?"

"I only got a quick glimpse. He wasn't just grabbing anything. He knew what he wanted. What's this about?"

I ignored her question. "So how come you suspected him and didn't think he just worked there?"

"It was a hunch. It didn't feel right… Wait a minute. I know what it was. He was wearing an overcoat. If he'd worked there, he'd have taken it off. It wasn't a cold day. You and I weren't wearing coats. Maybe it was the way he scurried out of the room. He was rushing. Way more than you would if you worked at the place."

"So you didn't have time to go into the records room?"

"Why the third degree?" she said, somewhat defensively. "What's the matter?"

"There are some things I don't understand. You went there for your file. Wasn't that the priority? Why didn't you just go back in there and get it?"

"I told you—it was either follow him or get the file. I wasn't sure he hadn't caused a disturbance that might get us both caught. I didn't think it all out. I just reacted. I must have figured the records would still be there another time whereas he wouldn't."

"Okay, I guess that makes sense. It's just that things have been moving so quickly, I haven't really had time to digest anything. He might have stolen more than files."

"What do you mean?"

"I mean, someone stole the ransom money. There probably wasn't all that much there but it was taken and he's the likely suspect. We just didn't know the money had been stolen when we followed him."

"And you suspect me as well?"

"No, not really. But, yes, you were there. You could have. I don't like thinking that or saying it, but it crossed my mind."

"Fuck you," she said, her irritation rising to anger. "You have no reason to suspect me. I've done nothing to earn that. I'd be really upset with you if it weren't so ludicrous."

"I'm sorry. Hey, I don't really suspect you. It's just that Lieutenant Golk now has me as a suspect. He had me meet with him again and Jordana was there and pointed a finger at me... said I was acting suspiciously."

"Were you?"

"I don't know. That was my first robbery since the candy bars I stole in seventh grade."

"So now I'm going to suspect you." A little smile accompanied that.

"Hey, fuck you too. Let's drop the suspect thing and move on if that's okay with you."

"It's fine with me, but you started it."

"Okay, let me finish it. I no longer consider you a suspect and I hope soon Lieutenant Golk will no longer think I'm one as well. Or you."

"Hold on. Does Golk know about Trombone?"

"I don't know. I hope so but I sure didn't say anything. Do you think Trombone might have stolen the money when you couldn't see what he was doing?"

"Could be."

"What do you say we find a way to tell Golk about Trombone? That would make me feel a lot better."

"We can't do that. Trombone might tell them about your wanting the videos and pressuring him."

"Oh, yeah. I forgot about that part."

"Don't worry," she said, trying to comfort me and maybe herself. "If Trombone's involved, Golk will find out. It's better for us not to be connected to him in any way."

"Okay. I'm just going to follow Golk's advice—keep my nose clean and stay out of trouble."

"You do that," she said, and took a close look at me. "Don't get all mopey. If worse comes to worst, I'll tell them you stole the file for me."

"That's good to hear. Thanks. They'll give me a year off for that."

She gave me a poker face that didn't make me feel any better. I couldn't get a good read on how things stood between us. I'd hoped I was headed for an innocent conference romance like the one I'd overheard being discussed in the reception line. Now I was worried about being a poster boy for the *Police Gazette*.

Britt broke my reverie. "Was that the me/you stuff?"

"Sort of. I keep running around, getting all sweaty and nervous, and I don't even know if I'm ever going to get to first base."

"Come on," she said as she stood and beckoned me to the door. It wasn't the direction I'd hoped for.

I was a few feet down the hall when she opened the door and waved me back. A wave of excitement came over me and I tried not to saunter on my way back.

"Listen," she said, "why don't you call Trixie and pump her?"

"I beg your pardon?"

"You know what I mean. Call her up. She's probably in the phone book. How many Trixie Goodst's can there be? Call her and see if you can wine and dine her... find out what she knows about Trombone."

"You want me to call her out of the blue and ask her out? I have enough trouble trying to wine and dine you."

"This should be easier. Just make up some excuse. Or better yet, hint about the videos."

"Oh, great. That went so well with Johnny Trombone. I'm not inclined to use that approach again."

"If at first you don't succeed... Come on—it'll be good for you. Maybe you'll even get to touch some bases."

I didn't rush off and call Trixie. I figured I didn't need to; I'd see her in the morning at the memorial service.

Instead, I had a delightfully uneventful evening in the company of room service and the new Lawrence Block book—*Burglars Can't Be Choosers*.

I was learning that myself.

CHAPTER THIRTY

# TRICKY BUSINESS

**August 26, 1977**

**Friday morning**

GOODST'S MEMORIAL SERVICE was scheduled for 10:00 a.m. at the Institute. Given the mixed responses I was hearing about his death, I was curious how people would react.

I signed my name in a book by the entrance and followed some signs through the gardens. We were in a big open meadow surrounded by eucalyptus trees. A recycling stream cut through the meadow and deposited its waters in a hand-crafted, football-field-sized lake. Poor Goodst. He'd really had it good.

A well-robed New Age-type speaker explained to the large crowd how death was life's partner and Goodst was now fulfilling his destiny. Although to cover his bets he was having his body frozen so perhaps someday he could be revived and renew the other side of his destiny.

There were a few designated speakers scheduled after which everyone else was invited to share their thoughts. Soon there was a long line and I wondered whether lunch would be served.

People thanked Goodst for saving their lives and joked about their newfound sexual freedom. All in all, he'd have been proud of what was being said. The naysayers seemed to be deferring for the moment.

When all was said and done, it was announced that lunch was being served in the dining area and the crowd dispersed. I asked a few people if they knew Trixie and was pointed in the direction of three attractive women all wearing black leather miniskirts. Maybe the skirts were homage to Goodst's preferences. I was informed they all were exes and the one with the Farrah Fawcett hairdo was Trixie.

I watched as various people came up to them and offered their condolences. There didn't seem too much emotion on display. I imagined Goodst had picked his women for their good looks rather than their emotional availability.

I watched and waited. I recognized some faces from the conference but didn't see Britt, Astrid, Feel Me, Chet, or Layla, although they could have been there as there were well over five hundred people in attendance.

Eventually the exes broke up and Trixie began to step away. I angled my way toward her and intercepted her with a weak smile and a perfunctory "I'm sorry for your loss."

She thanked me and I quickly added, "If I had a wife who looked like you I'd never die."

She liked that. Heck, I liked that too. She took a moment to size me up.

Before I could produce more flattery, a couple came up to her and offered their condolences and a conversation ensued. I drifted off. It hadn't been quite the start I'd wanted. I kinda peaked too early. I hoped I'd intrigued her enough to warrant another chance.

However, first things first. Food. I kept an eye on Trixie as I made my way to a very healthy buffet. I was scooping up some avocado and shrimp salad when I nearly bumped into Gabriela Barbosa. "Oh!" I said.

She gave me an icy look, then asked, "Checking out the exes?"

"Not anymore," I said, stabbing an artichoke heart with a toothpick. "I can see a similarity among them. But you're certainly the class of the group."

"Perhaps that's because I'm not an ex."

"Could be," I said, glad anything resembling a sentence was finding its way out of my mouth. "It could also be you aren't wearing a leather miniskirt. Although I'm sure you'd look great in one."

That earned me minus points—I wished I could take it back as soon as it was out of my mouth. At least I was able to talk; I just wasn't able to be as cool as I wanted to be. But I'm used to that.

Before I could further jeopardize myself, I noticed Jordana at Gabriela's side. She didn't seem happy to see me.

"That's no way to talk. This has been a horrible time for us, and today is not the place for sexist flippancy."

I couldn't argue with that so I hung my head. Shame is not my favorite emotion. I don't feel it often but when one of my flippancies makes a nuisance of itself, I feel exposed as a low-life scoundrel. I very well may have been that in another life but like to think I've mostly left that aspect of my being behind. Though obviously not entirely.

I apologized awkwardly and Jordana guided Gabriela away. I guess they'd had enough of the buffet.

I suppose as a teenager it's more acceptable, or expected, to be ruled by your sexual drive, but here I was, thirty-one years old and flirting at a memorial service. I could point a finger at the sex convention priming me but, the truth was, my sex drive still wanted to be in the driver's seat.

I didn't think my attraction to Britt, Layla, Gabriela, and now Trixie had much to do with my overactive sex drive, although it certainly had gone into high gear this week. I just happened to be in the company of some very attractive women. Any way you looked at it, I wasn't making much headway. Before I could lament my fate, I saw Trixie making moves to leave.

I hustled over to her.

"Excuse me again."

"Yes?" she said, barely acknowledging me as she kept walking.

"I know it's not appropriate on such a day, but since I may never see you again, I wanted to take a moment to introduce myself."

"Hello," she replied but didn't slow down.

"I realize you're getting ready to go but I'd really like a chance to speak with you. Let me introduce myself. My name is David."

"Nice to meet you but I have to get going."

"Can I escort you to your car?"

She paused for a moment. Looked me over again. I must have passed the test because she said, "All right," and started walking again.

"How did you know Wilhelm?" she asked me.

"I didn't really know him. I'm attending the sex-therapists conference and was eagerly anticipating his presentation. Since his disappearance I've been swept up in the events and I wanted to come today and pay my respects."

"That's very kind of you."

At this rate we'd have nothing more than a very nice exchange. I needed to take a leap. We all know to get ahead you eventually have to take some risks—step out of your comfort zone and be prepared to deal with whatever comes your way.

"I also really wanted to meet you."

She stopped. "How come you say that? Didn't we just meet earlier? You'll have to forgive me; it's been a difficult week."

"Of course. Totally understandable."

It's a strange thing, sincerity. It's easy to fake. And in that moment, I was mostly faking it. I knew it had been a horrible week for her and I wouldn't wish it on anyone, yet I was on a mission.

"Some people were talking at the conference about you, and after all the things they said I was hoping we could meet."

"Well, we have," she said, moving forward again.

"I want to apologize for being so pushy. It's not usually my style but since we're almost at the parking lot I'd like to ask you a personal question."

"Yes?" she said, not stopping.

"I know you and Dr. Goodst are no longer married. And although his passing must be difficult for you, I was wondering if you'd consider going out with me."

There it was. Vulnerable step taken.

She hesitated, assessed me again, and said, "That's very nice of you but I'm already involved with someone."

She was on the move again.

"Oh," I replied with measured disappointment. Trying to salvage a lost game, I said, "Would a platonic lunch be out of the question?"

"For the time being, yes. Thank you, though. It's very sweet of you. Now here's my car." She took out a key to a magenta Corniche Rolls Royce. "I really have to go."

I wasn't all that disappointed. She was a very attractive woman, and the Rolls didn't hurt, but life partner she was not. Hot date, that was another thing. But Trixie was destined for the memory bank of what-could-have-beens, where she'd be in good company.

I'd been reluctant to ask her about Trombone directly. I'd hoped if we went on a date we might get on better footing and I'd find a way to bring him up. As it was, we weren't on any footing.

# CHAPTER THIRTY-ONE

# THE HEALING POWER OF PARTYING

**Friday afternoon**

I WAS WAITING for the hotel elevator when I got tapped on the shoulder.

"Howdy." Chet extended his hand and gave me a hearty smile.

"Howdy," I responded, but the word didn't sound as natural coming from me.

"It's good to see you," said Layla.

"You too."

"You just get out of the S&M workshop?" asked Chet in a way that made me kind of leery.

"No. I missed that one. But I'm guessing you didn't."

"You're damn right. Wouldn't miss that one for anything. Layla and I have been talking about it, haven't we, honey?"

"You bet. We heard some things today we didn't know before."

"Yessiree." Chet chuckled. "But let's be clear, Doc. We're into consent. Consent and partying."

"It looks like you got a little riled up."

"Chet's a big one for extending the boundaries. Hard to rope in this cowboy," Layla said, giving him a knowing look.

"Oh, I can see that," I said. "I can go for extending boundaries as long as we're talking about consent."

"Don't worry, Doc," said Chet. "I haven't compromised anybody. But there's a whole new aspect of S&M I knew nothing about and it's starting to light a bulb for me."

"That's right," Layla went on. "Mostly it's about crossing a boundary of engagement. Which in the S&M world is a big no-no. Unless, as you say," she said, staring directly at me and making me blush, "there's consent."

I couldn't tell whether she was flirting or just had a naturally evocative way about her. Either way, it felt good.

"Yeah," Chet said, kind of bubbling. "There are some glimmers of light up here"—he pointed to his head—"that if I can put together will just shimmy up to that line, but not cross over it. I'm starting to see a way."

"That's exciting. Seeing a way is usually a good thing. Just as long as everyone's on board."

"The presenter said the country has a growing conservative population," Layla said. "And get this. When conservative movements have grown, there's been a concomitant growth in kinky sex. He said it's a personal rebellion against social oppression."

Layla was starting to impress me. Heck, my vocabulary is in the B/B+ range, but concomitant is definitely an A word. To be truthful, I didn't know what it meant when she said it. I had to look it up later. Kind of a cool word that doesn't get called forth often, but when it is, it fits the space nicely. As did Layla. Initially I'd been attracted to her beauty and sexiness, but her intelligence was starting to make its presence felt, and that was also a turn-on. A triple threat.

"I never thought about kinky sex as rebellion against the constraints of society but it makes some sense," I said. "I guess if you cross a boundary, be it sex in public or anything else, it's exciting, scary, and rebellious."

I didn't know if I'd scored any points with her but I was

definitely flirting. Not faux flirting, but real flirting. Sort of like I was also doing with Britt, and maybe Trixie. And let's not forget Gabriela. Hmm.

"Hey," Chet said. "I've been thinking we ought to talk to Dr. Goodst's executive assistant about holding a memorial bash. Sort of a New Orleans send-off for the doc."

"You mean Gabriela Barbosa?"

"Yeah. She's a babe. I'm sure she likes to party. What do you say we ask her?"

"It's a great idea," I said. "Although there are a lot of people in mourning. I'm not sure 'party' is the best word."

"Come on, Doc. I know it's been a rough week for everyone but, if you ask me, Goodst would want us to be partying. He wasn't one to pass anything by."

"Nor, it seems, are you."

"Doc, please. Don't hurt my feelings. There's nothing wrong with wanting to party. People don't become sex therapists and surrogates because they don't like to party. We're professional party people."

"Good to know I'm among professionals."

"We don't mean any disrespect," said Layla. "We have—I have—a lot of respect for Dr. Goodst. But you know as well as I do there's nothing we can do to bring him back. But we can celebrate the spirit of him in the same way he'd have celebrated."

"I have no problem with the healing power of celebration. I just know people don't always feel like partying, as therapeutic as it may be. But celebrating a life, that's another thing."

"Now you got it," said Chet.

"I don't want to ask Gabriela. You two do it"—I looked directly at Layla—"and I'll be happy to celebrate alongside you."

"Great," she said, which made me feel great.

"Sure," said Chet. "But don't say we didn't invite you to join us in talking with her. Who knows? We may go ask and she might just want to start the celebrating right there and then."

"In that case," I said, "I have total faith in your being able to carry on without me."

Chet gave me a thumbs-up and Layla winked.

## CHAPTER THIRTY-TWO
# TALK ME INTO IT

**Friday afternoon, later**

By the time I got back to my hotel room, the phone was blinking again. My chest tightened. Was Lieutenant Golk after me? Did he know about my recent excursion to the memorial service without his permission? I didn't want to find out. But not knowing was worse. Better to deal with reality than let my imagination drive my blood pressure to places it needn't go.

A soothing wave of relaxation came over me as I listened to the message. It was from the front desk, asking if I was still using the typewriter. I called them up and asked them to take it. Whew! Nice to have ordinary happen.

Of course, as soon as I thought that, I wondered whether Golk had asked them to retrieve it so he could match it with up the damming evidence of my fingerprints on Britt's envelope.

*David, take it easy*, I said.

When that didn't work, I turned on the radio. Jimmy Buffet was in Margaritaville and I was wishing I could join him. Before I could go, there was a knock on the door. Things suddenly looked a lot better—it was Britt, looking like she could have been the woman to blame for Jimmy's arrival in Margaritaville. She wore a sparkling white top and black jeans that made her look extremely inviting.

"Why, hello," I said, and kind of gasped.

"Mind if I come in?"

"How could I mind? When you look like that you can go anywhere you like."

I stepped aside and watched her move in. She had a strong stride yet it had a little sway. She must have known I was watching but gave no indications she cared. I forced myself to look away as she slid onto the sofa.

"Can I offer you something? A glass of water, a bedside Bible, a romp in the hay?"

"Quit joking. I want to talk to you."

"I'm sorry. It's just not easy to stop myself from coming over there and, ah, well, reaching out to you," I said, angling for a seat next to her.

She pointed at the chair. "Sit down. I'm dressed like this because it's almost Friday night and there's a sex-theater show tonight that's supposed to be outrageous, and then there's going to be dancing."

"Sounds great. It's just when you look like that—"

"Enough of that. We need to talk."

"Okay. What's going on?" The therapist's best opening line.

"Did you see Trixie?"

"Yes, I did. But don't get excited. Although I have to tell you she, too, is a very provocative dresser and has about as much interest in me as Astrid has."

At that point Jimmy left Margaritaville and Fleetwood Mac started singing about going your own way.

"That's all very nice and I'm sure Astrid won't be surprised to hear others share her opinion."

"Ouch."

"Come on—did Trixie say anything helpful to us or just hurtful to your ego?"

"She didn't say much of anything at all. Yes, I did try my charm on her but, as you pointed out, some are immune to its effects."

"Okay, wounded warrior, what happened?"

"There actually were three ex-Mrs. Goodst's there. All I can say is, Doctor Goodst had a proclivity for beautiful, sexy women. Their idea of memorial-appropriate dress made me think they might get a rise out of the doctor."

"Very funny," Britt said in the way that said it wasn't funny at all. "Now, aside from your voyeurism, did you learn anything of value?"

"I don't think staring at beautiful women qualifies me as a voyeur. If so, just line me up with everybody else."

"Okay, admirer of beauty. Anything of use?"

"I tried to talk with her but she wasn't interested. She was one of the first people to leave. She wasn't visibly upset, but you never know."

"I wonder…"

I wondered as well. Why had the music stopped? Just then a newscaster came on and announced that the body of local porn entrepreneur Johnny Trombone had been found in his store with bullets though his heart and his personal parts. No suspects. More to follow.

Britt and I looked at each other. The radio played "Time in a Bottle" by Jim Croce.

"What do you think?" I asked.

"I don't know what to think. I'm shocked."

"Yeah. Me too. I'm afraid to think what this means. But my first thought is Golk is going to find out I was there. Sorry, I know I should feel bad for Trombone but I don't. I feel kind of relieved and worried at the same time. I'm sure my fingerprints are there, although I was kind of careful about touching anything. I just hope he was killed while I was at the memorial."

"Calm down. I'm sure you don't have anything to worry about. Given his business interests, there are plenty of people he'll have rubbed the wrong way."

"You're right," I said. "But I'll spend some time worrying about it anyway."

"Suit yourself. If you want to worry about someone other than yourself, you might focus on what's going to happen if the police find my videos there."

"I'm sorry. I have a tendency to put myself first. But you're right—you have way more to worry about than I do."

She didn't like that. It wasn't exactly soothing.

"I don't want to worry about it and I don't want those videos to be seen," she said.

"I don't blame you."

A moment later, she said, "I want you to go back to Goodst's house with me and see if the videos are there."

"Give me a break. Bad things are starting to happen and you want us to go break into his house? No way!"

"But I'm really afraid. If the police find the tapes, they might suspect me."

"Join the club. What's the big deal? You told me we didn't have anything to worry about."

"It's not a good thing for those videos to be seen. I'm going to his house, and if there's no one there I'm going to break in and look for the tapes. Are you coming or not?"

"Why do I feel like you only like me because I do what you ask? I don't want to be an accessory to a crime just to have you like me."

"Does that mean you're coming?"

"Yes, but couldn't you throw me a bone so I think I'm more than a pawn?"

"Don't you know I want to do what you want to do?"

"You do? Really?"

She got up off the couch and stood in front of me. She leaned over and lightly touched her lips to mine. Gently but firmly she kissed me. I felt my built-up passion rising but steadied myself. *Slowly, David, slowly. This doesn't have to be over before it starts. Stay in the moment.*

I slowly put my hands around her. Her body was strong; I could feel her muscles as I slid my hands down her back to the base of her spine. Abruptly she pulled out of arm's reach, took a couple of measured breaths, and said, "We have to go to Goodst's."

"Let's do this first and that later."

# CHAPTER THIRTY-THREE

# A CROWBAR, A VIDEO, AND YOU

DURING THE DRIVE to Goodst's house, I got to thinking. I haven't always been my best self with the women I've pursued, but I was about to cross a line I'd never really even approached before. While I could say I was doing this because there was a greater good involved, I knew better. Or did I?

Was I doing all this just so Britt would like me? Have sex with me? Be a life partner? Was she a real contender? How attracted to her was I? Hadn't I also flirted with Layla earlier? And I couldn't forget Trixie and Gabriela. If I was so attracted to Britt, why would I flirt with someone else? Maybe my juices were flowing and I'd had a heightened sense of arousal ever since I'd stood in line and heard those two women talking about their sexual adventures.

Yes, I was very attracted to Britt. How she carried herself drew me to her. I liked being with her. And, yes, I liked looking at her. But I didn't really know much about her. Or Layla, Trixie, and Gabriela for that matter. All I knew was I was caught up in the action and when Britt kissed me, I'd gotten a little light-hearted. And maybe light-headed.

She stopped the car at a hardware store and I followed her through the aisles as she bought a flashlight, rope, glass cutter, and crowbar. I was fine with the flashlight. Not so fine with the rope. Not at all fine with the glass cutter and ready to resign when I saw the crowbar. Unfortunately, she wasn't done. She got a Swiss Army knife, bolt cutters, goatskin gloves, and two red bandanas.

By the time we were back in the car, I was sure there was no good reason for me to continue to be with this woman.

We were now two well-equipped burglars with a receipt to prove it. I was waiting for Golk to drive up with his lights a-flashing. In the meantime, the bag with our gear was sitting on my lap.

*I have a voice in this*, I said to myself as we drove to Goodst's house. *I've not done anything illegal—today—and as long as I continue not to cross the line, I have nothing to worry about.*

Except I didn't tell Golk I was leaving the hotel to rob Goodst's house. If he found me now, even just sitting in the car with all our newfound, um, camping gear, I'd rocket up his list of suspects.

No reason I couldn't be one and done. No reason at all, I thought, as we drove down Goodst's street. Unfortunately, there were no police cars to be seen.

"What do you say we put all this gear in the trunk and just go up to the door and see if we can't find an easy way in. Otherwise I'm staying in the car. I'm not going to get caught in someone's house with our beginner's burglar kit."

"I get it," Britt said. "You think I want to go in there all packed up? Of course not. But here's the deal. You need to go."

"What? No way. Well, I'll go ring the doorbell and ask if I can see if Goodst still has the videos I lent him. That I can do. That sounds pretty fair."

"That's very sweet. But you know that won't work. First, we'll watch the place and make sure no one's there. Then, once we're certain, I'll keep an eye out here while you go and try to find the videos. It shouldn't be that hard. Johnny Trombone was in and out in no time."

"That's because he—and I'm guessing here—was a professional in these types of matters. My professionalism doesn't extend into this realm. Why can't you go in while I stand guard?"

"I don't want to get you in trouble," she said in a comforting way. "I'd rather go in there than have you go. I'm not asking you because I'm afraid to go. Far from it. I want to go. It's just that it's not the smart move here."

"We've obviously gone beyond smart. I'm glad to know you're not just throwing me in there because you don't want to go. But why exactly is it better for you to be out here and me in there?"

"Because, worst-case scenario, if you get caught it'll be easier for me to get you out than if I get caught and you try to get me out."

I took a moment, trying to digest that. When I couldn't, I said, "I still don't understand. Why don't we both not get caught and forget about the videos? There are probably hundreds of Goodst videos with him doing all sorts of things. What makes you so worried about yours? I know it's personal and I shouldn't ask, but if I'm putting myself in serious jeopardy here, I ought to know everything. And, yes, I'm very excited about the possibility of our having some kind of relationship that doesn't involve the police, but I need to have a somewhat higher cause than that. Just somewhat. Help me out here."

"I understand. I've told you all you really need to know. I don't want the police or anyone seeing my videos. I don't want to share the details with you or them. I just want to have what is rightfully mine."

"I get that. I want to do it for you. I just don't want to get in any trouble because of it, and this could lead to big trouble. I'm not saying no, but I'm not quite ready to say yes."

"Okay. You stay here and I'll go. It'll be fine. We haven't seen anyone even driving on the street. It's almost dinner time. People are either on their way out for their evening or they're hunkered down. I'm going to go."

I was out of it. I felt my body relax. She was sensitive to my concerns and had acted on them. I've learned there's a point of no return once someone comes to a hard decision. And she was good to go.

I could have let her. I could have asked for a good-luck kiss. But once I'd made my mind up, I opened the door and got out. I was afraid if I didn't move I wouldn't move.

"Honk the horn if there's trouble," I told her as I hastened up the street. *You're an idiot, Dave*, I told myself. There could be any number of alarms, patrols, or who knows what ahead to scare the shit out of me and provide me with a horny muscle-bound neo-Nazi roommate for the rest of my life.

And why? Why do this to myself? What could be so incriminating in a video that Britt didn't want the police or anyone to see it? Yes, he was fucking her, and while that's not exactly how I'd want to earn my fifteen minutes of fame, it's not going to set the world against me.

Britt was the victim, right? What could she have said or done that would warrant this risk? And if what she'd done was so outside the box she didn't want the police to know, why was I helping her?

What if she was the perpetrator? What if she'd blackmailed him? Or they'd planned a kidnapping years into the future and she'd come back to execute the plan … and then him?

Relationships need a high level of trust to survive. At the moment, despite my thoughts, I needed to believe Britt had her good reasons, was indeed the victim trying to retain her good name. Unfortunately, that train of thought wasn't coming too easily.

As I approached the house I put on the gloves. No sense leaving a fingerprint even on the front-door buzzer. I pushed the buzzer. Nothing happened. I tried again and gave the doorknob a little twist.

I went around back. Needless to say, the back door was locked as well. *Why be easy?* I asked the universe. I looked for the French door Trombone had broken in through. Either I couldn't find it or it had been fixed. I chose a door and checked for a wire that might indicate a security system. Not that I'd know what one looked like, though I knew what a wire might look like.

Nothing.

I took out the glass cutter. The guy in the store said to trace the shape and bear down hard with a steady hand. Sounded simple enough. I tried. There was a lot of slipping and squeaking. Finally, I said fuck it, took out the bandana, wrapped my fist in it, did an Ali shuffle, and stung the window like a bee. I'm proud to say I knocked that windowpane out with one blow.

Glass was protruding from the edges. I carefully put my hand, then my arm through the gap and tried to twist my wrist enough to open the latch without donating any blood to the crime scene. I slowly turned the latch, the door opened, and, voilà, I was breaking and entering.

I was in a formal dining room with a large table that had a big, expensive gold centerpiece. I wasn't sure where to search for tapes but I figured it wasn't here. If it were me, I'd keep my tapes near my TV, so I went hunting for TVs. How many could he have? There was one in the living room that didn't look lived in, and the bookcase held books not videos. The den/family room had a TV, but no tapes. Same with the kitchen and pantry. Every room was slightly askew and there were remnants of what must have been fingerprinting dust. I figured the police must have given the place a good going over and hadn't left things exactly the way they'd found them. The outline of his body on the floor by the steps gave me an eerie feeling I didn't really want to dwell on.

I headed upstairs. The master bedroom had the usual stuff. That is, if you consider a giant circular bed in red satin with a gold-plated mirror on the ceiling above it usual. Velvet pictures of satyrs chasing and mounting nymphs decorated the walls. A twenty-five-inch TV sat in a custom-made black lacquer bookcase. No books. Just a small statue of a boy peeing and a collection of ropes and handcuffs, a couple of random videos, and some old Marlene Dietrich movies. I opened the closet doors and entered a space bigger than my first apartment. There were a lot of blue suits and white shirts.

Next door to the master bedroom was another large room I'd call a study. An eight-foot mahogany desk was surrounded by books, awards, plaques, photographs of Goodst with famous people, and another large TV. There were mostly empty shelves that had probably held the videos. I knew Britt wasn't going to like hearing that.

I opened some doors down the hallway and found what looked like a couple of generic guest rooms. Then I was done. Nothing more to be gained here. I hurried back down the hall and was about halfway down the staircase when I heard the front door open and footsteps. It sounded like a pair or heels but the tat-tat-tat might have been my heart pumping.

Speedily, yet oh so noiselessly, I made my way back up the stairs. I headed for the farthest guest room, slipped in, and closed the door. I put my ear to the door. It didn't seem likely they were headed to this room, but I could dart into the closet if required.

I heard footsteps coming up the stairs, then down the hallway, and stop. The person had either gone in the bedroom or the study. I waited… and wondered why Britt hadn't honked the horn.

Soon I heard the steps retreating down the hallway and stairs.

I was headed back down the hall as I heard the front door close.

I went into the bedroom. It looked just as I'd left it. I went into the study. Something was different but I couldn't tell what. I scanned the room and noticed the empty spot on the wall. I couldn't remember what had been there; all I could see was an empty picture hanger.

It was time to leave while the going was still good. I hurried downstairs and out of the house.

I sensed a little swagger in my step as I made my way down the street. This thievery business was playing havoc with my adrenaline and blood pressure, but it was helping my strut. It must have been a little deceiving because when I got back into the car, Britt said with a gush, "You got them."

"I wish. All I got was a good case of the jitters and this video of *Charade* with Cary Grant," I said as I tossed it to her.

"And Audrey Hepburn."

"And Audrey Hepburn."

"What about the tapes. Did you find any others?"

"Trombone or the police cleaned him out. There were some mostly empty bookcases so they could have taken them from there. They might be hidden somewhere I didn't discover or at the Institute."

"You saw Trombone go in with an empty bag and come out like Santa Claus. I have to think there were more videos than just the ones he stole. Although that bag was pretty full."

"The police likely took the rest."

"Let's not go there," she said with a disdainful look.

There was a chilly silence. She started up the car.

"Thank you. I know that was a scary thing to do and you didn't want to do it. So thanks again. I have to tell you, it wasn't easy waiting in the car."

*Maybe not easy but easier*, I thought, but was wise enough not to say. "Speaking of waiting, how come you didn't honk the horn? Did you see who came in? They almost caught me."

"I'm sorry. I wanted to warn you but I couldn't. She parked real close to me so I had to duck down. I didn't want to draw attention. And I don't know who she was but her miniskirt couldn't have been any shorter. She looked like she might be a working girl."

"Did she have a Farrah Fawcett hairdo?"

"To the nines."

"That sounds like Trixie. I'm sorry I missed seeing her."

Britt gave me a nasty look.

146 | David Unger

"Did she have heels on?" I asked, oblivious to her disdain. "I could hear footsteps and it sounded like someone in heels."

"You don't wear an outfit like that with flats," said Britt.

I couldn't help myself. I looked at her feet. She also had black heels on. I didn't know what to say. Neither did Britt.

"Whoever she was, and I'm betting on Trixie, she came in the front door, went up to his study, and took something off the wall. I don't know what it was but it was approximately eighteen inches by twenty-four so it was probably a photograph, plaque, or an award."

"Maybe he didn't want to give it up in the divorce," Britt said.

"Maybe. Most of the pictures were of him and other people. I can't imagine he kept pictures of the exes on the wall but maybe he did. It could have been anything."

"It could have been a picture of him and Trixie and maybe someone else as well," Britt said.

"Someone like Trombone?"

"Maybe. But as interesting as that might be, it's just a guessing game. All we know is, we don't have the tapes and they aren't there. But maybe they're at the Institute."

"No no no. Let's not go there," I said. "The police most likely have them or maybe Trixie told Trombone where they were and he took them. Who knows? But let's not go back to the Institute."

"We have to. While it's a long shot, right now, it's the only one we have. If it's not there, we'll let it go, but I really don't want to do that just yet."

"You don't understand. When I heard those footsteps coming up the stairs, I lost a year of my life. I don't know how many I want to put on the line tonight. My blood pressure either saps my life away or the police take it. I don't think it's worth all the risk. We know Trombone got the tapes at the house not the Institute."

"Goodst did not have all his tapes at the house. He told me there were some special ones he kept in the file room."

"I know. You told me, but they weren't there."

"We have to look again. Check the other file room. Give the place a second going over. It's Friday evening," she said, putting the car in drive and moving out into the street. "No one is going to be there. Let's drive there and check it out."

*Oh, David,* I thought. *This is not what your parents had in mind when they raised you to help others in need.*

# CHAPTER THIRTY-FOUR

# YOU NEVER KNOW

**Friday evening**

ON THE DRIVE over to the Institute, I tried to think of what I'd tell my parents if I got caught stealing. I couldn't think of anything they'd understand and support. While I don't always use this tactic as my moral compass, it has served me well. This would have to be one of those things I didn't tell them. Unless, of course, they read about it in the newspaper.

Britt and I had a redundant conversation about who would go in and look for the tapes. By this time, my moral compass no longer knew its way north and wasn't going to be rectifying itself any time soon.

It was weird. What I was doing was wrong on most levels, but it seemed to be right for Britt. And for reasons I couldn't totally fathom, I was doing what she asked.

We made our way up the driveway. I was disappointed to see there were no cars in the parking lot. The place looked deserted. Had there been a cluster of cars we'd—hopefully—have to go back. With no cars in sight, it looked like I was about to put the family name at risk.

The evening was unfolding into a picturesque sunset. I didn't care. We agreed Britt would drop me off in front of the Institute, drive off the property, and park on the side of the street so she could see any car entering. If she did, this time she'd honk the horn twice after they turned; hopefully, I'd hear it and protect myself. Just how, I'd need to find out.

I checked the flashlight for the tenth time, put on the gloves, checked the bandana for glass shards and stuffed it in my pocket, and left the glass cutter and crowbar.

I asked for a goodbye kiss and got one that made me want to stay. Of course, any decent kiss would have done that. As she drove off, I remembered a sign I'd once seen in a California ghost town: *Kiss my ass goodbye. I'm going to Bodie.*

Britt and I'd decided if the tapes were here, they'd be in one of four places: Goodst's office, the file room, the office supply/file room… or somewhere else. I'd re-check his office and his file room and then the official file room. Unless inspiration found me, I'd leave the somewhere else to someone else.

I went to the back of the Institute where I knew Goodst had his office. The dusk provided enough light to see and almost enough dark to hide. As before, the door wasn't locked. Somehow or other that was reassuring. Breaking a window and entering seemed a bigger crime than entering through an open door, I heard myself telling the judge.

Once inside I pointed the flashlight toward the floor and turned it on. Even in the shadows the office still reeked of success. I stole a quick glance at the pictures to see if there was one with Trixie or anyone else I'd met in the past few days. It seemed odd that none of the pictures were personal. Just a lot of shaking hands with officials and notorieties at noteworthy events.

There was no closet. Just bookcases, pictures, and plaques. I checked the desk drawers but they were full of papers, dried fruits, assorted nuts, and some Polaroids of Goodst in what looked like a schoolboy outfit. I wondered who'd taken the pictures and where.

I checked the doorknob to his personal file room but it was still locked. I peeked out the door, saw the coast was clear, and scurried next door. So far so good. I gave his file room another good going over, but no tapes.

I opened the door. The hallway was still clear. I headed for the front file room. Once inside, I checked the filing cabinets but they were all administrative paperwork. No person files or videos.

I wasn't liking this. But I wasn't not liking it either. I could check a few more drawers and get out of there.

I was intent on finishing up when my focus shifted to the door. It was opening. There wasn't time to hide and there was no place to do it. Like a deer in the headlights, I stood frozen as Trixie entered the room.

"What are you doing here?" she asked as she opened her purse, took out a gun, and pointed it at me.

The moment called for something… just not the truth.

"Hey, what a pleasant surprise. Good evening, Trixie."

"Oh, yeah. I remember you. What are you doing here?"

"I have a very good explanation for this I'm more than happy to share, but could you put the gun away? It makes me very uncomfortable."

"Your being here makes me uncomfortable. The place is closed. How did you get in here? What are you doing here?"

"All very good questions and ones I'm happy to clear up for you, but could you at least lower the gun? We don't want there to be a mistake—like you sneeze and the gun goes off just as we're getting to know one another."

"Shut up," she said, keeping the gun uncomfortably still. After a moment of silence that didn't do anything for me, she asked, "Are you alone?"

"Well, I'm with you. But otherwise, yes, I'm alone. How about you? Are you alone? Do we have the place to ourselves? That could be fun."

She didn't seem the least bit interested in changing the focus of our interaction.

"Shut up. We're going for a walk," she said, and waved the gun in the direction of the French doors.

"That's great. I like walks. Where are we going?"

"You'll find out."

# CHAPTER THIRTY-FIVE
# KINKY IS AS KINKY DOES

**Friday night**

LIVING IN LA you develop a distorted relationship with nature. You trade seasons for mostly sunny days, forests for tree-lined medians, and clear days for cool nights. A nature walk could easily be making your way through Dodger Stadium parking lot.

Most times I enjoy any walk outdoors and discovering what lies ahead. I wasn't feeling that way now. We headed toward the foothills on a path that wove through gardens full of native bushes and trees. The further we went, the denser and darker it got. After about fifteen minutes a fence appeared with a *No Trespassing* sign. Trixie opened the gate and I added trespassing to my sins.

I wondered what Britt was doing. Had she not seen Trixie driving up? Why hadn't she honked? This was the second time she hadn't warned me.

Maybe Trixie had been here before me. But we'd seen no cars parked in front of the Institute when Britt dropped me off. Still, the place was big enough for cars to be parked someplace else and Trixie would know those places.

So how long would Britt wait before she came to find me?

Would she? Would she call the police? Why worry about what she'd do when I could just as easily worry about what Trixie would do? I worried for another five minutes. Then I saw the outline of a small cabin in front of us. As we approached, I realized this wasn't the kind of dwelling where neighbors would be calling the police and complaining about the noise.

"Stop," she ordered a few feet from the entrance. "Put your left hand out."

She noticed my gloves and raised an eyebrow. She put a key ring in my hand. "Open it up."

I did.

"Go in."

I did.

"Welcome home," she said as she locked the door behind us.

It was too dark to see anything. I heard her strike a match, then step over to a table and light a hurricane lamp. The room started to take shape. The lamp was on a coffee table next to a couple of chairs and a sofa clustered facing a stone fireplace. While the Institute spared no expense, this place was basic. And very tidy. Everything—although there wasn't a lot of everything—was in its place… including a tripod, video camera, and a Polaroid camera. You just can't have enough of that stuff.

She lit another lamp on the other side of the room. What it revealed gave me a greater level of concern. The far corner looked like a replica of the Marquis de Sade's country torture chamber. There were whips on the wall, a saddle, and a chair that looked like it might have spent its youth at San Quentin but had been spruced up with black leather and a hole where I didn't want to see one.

She gave me a knowing smile. "You got it, buster. That's for you."

"I'm comfortable standing."

"I'm sorry to hear that. It's not nice to reject hospitality. And take it from me, you want to be very, very nice to me." Then she pointed the gun in the vicinity of where I thought my body might match up with the hole and motioned me to take a seat.

I sat.

Slowly she came over and, with a dexterity born of experience, clamped my hands and feet to the chair. I began to hope Britt had called the police.

"Now, isn't that better?" she asked as she put the gun on the table. "You just sit there and think about all the things you're going to have to do to make up for having been a bad boy. I'm going to get a drink and change into something more suitable for the occasion."

"Do I need to gussy up for the camera?"

"I don't think we'll be using it tonight, but you never know." Sauntering to the door she said, "Don't go anywhere. You're going to remember tonight for a long time."

At least I'd be alive to remember it for a long time.

I tried to wiggle my way out of the restraints, but like those who must have come before me, I failed. I didn't see any bloodstains on the chair, which was somewhat reassuring. Maybe she was just going to do some mild Spanish Inquisitioning and/or some non-consensual sex.

I tried to picture myself calmly resting by a gentle stream, but that wasn't getting any headway.

S&M wasn't an area I had any real experience in so I'm sure the school would be happy to know I'd be broadening my knowledge base. I'd had some experience with spanking when a librarian I'd met had decided my books were overdue and I needed to pay a fine. I hadn't really enjoyed that payment system and had resisted her invitation to settle my overdue account.

The black leather miniskirt and outfit Trixie had worn at the memorial was replaced by a black leather corset and a leather thong that had some nasty spikes on it. Her black leather boots came up above her knees and she was carrying an oversized black leather doctor's bag I hoped had a bottle of wine and some crackers in it. She strutted over to the table and opened the bag. On the positive side, she took out a bottle of Patrón tequila and two shot glasses. On the negative, I didn't see any crackers. Yet there was still a lot of room in that bag for other things. She put the bottle and glasses on a small black lacquer table next to my chair. She filled up the glasses, lifted one, said, "Here's to discipline," and downed it.

She lifted the other, raised it a foot over my head, and slowly tipped it. A drop fell on my cheek. She seemed amused and tilted it a little more. A few more drops hit my eyelids and cheek and fell to my lips. My eyes stung.

I wanted to drink as much of the tequila as I could, figuring whatever was in store for me would be better experienced anesthetized.

"Now don't be a bad boy and flinch," she said. "I'll have to punish you for that."

She slipped her free hand into my shirt and pinched my left nipple hard enough to make me want to cry out. If wincing wasn't tolerated, I doubted screaming would be so I kept it to myself. I couldn't tell if that pleased her or not. Neither was I sure whether pleasing or displeasing her was the better approach. I just knew I'd not be talking about this part of the conference to my students.

She raised the glass again. The next drop hit my nose and ran into my mouth. It didn't taste as good as I remembered but it didn't taste that bad either. Perhaps I was entering the pain–pleasure zone where it's hard to tell when one leaves off and the other begins.

"Do you like that?"

"Yeah," I replied. "It tasted good."

"Not that, you idiot," she said, putting her boot on the end of my shoe and lifting herself up so that her weight was resting on my toes. She put her face close to mine. "I want to know if you liked my twisting your nipple."

With that she jumped up a little and landed back down on my toes. It wasn't a scream-worthy event, but it got my attention.

"It was a little rough for foreplay."

"Good," she replied, somewhat miscalculating my response. "Because it's only going to get rougher. If you continue to be a bad boy, I'm going to have to teach you to behave."

"Yeah," I said. "My parents had difficulty with that too. But I'm sure there's a lot you can teach me. And I'm certainly motivated to be a good student."

"That's very wise because as we both know, you've already been a very bad one."

"I'm sorry I've been bad and certainly want to make it up to you and be as good as I can be."

"Now that sounds better."

My mind flashed to a former client—a very successful salesperson. He'd told me: "I kiss ass so well they never feel my lips."

I was hoping my own ass-kissing would allow me not to have to kiss her actual ass, although the prospect wasn't entirely unpleasant and certainly better than some other alternatives.

Never one to savor any small win when I could push another boundary, I put on my best boyish smile and told her, "I'm a quick study. I bet I could show you just how good I am if I could get out of this chair."

"You don't like it?"

"I feel it's constricting my ability to show you how good I can be."

"Maybe if you're a very good boy we can let you out of the chair. But first you're going to have to prove it to me. Words are cheap. Actions speak to me."

"I'm with you there," I replied, doing my best to make my client proud.

She trickled a little more tequila down my face. This time it hit me above the eye, causing me to flinch again.

Unfortunately, she saw the reflex. So much for being a man of action.

She lowered the glass and with a look any poker player would find hard to decipher, she unbuttoned my shirt. When she was done she put her middle finger in the glass and wiggled it. Then she lifted her hand in front of my face and rolled her finger and thumb together. When she'd had enough of that, she slipped her hand inside my shirt and revisited my nipple with some gentle circling that wasn't at all bad.

When she bit me things shifted. The momentary pleasure was replaced by an injection of pain. I couldn't tell if her teeth were grinding together or my teeth were chattering. When she'd extracted all the pleasure she could from the moment, she moved away and admired her work. I felt a drop of blood running down my chest to my belly. There didn't seem to be that much, but it was more than I wanted.

She smiled at me and then put her finger back in the glass and repeated her performance on the other side. There might have been a little part of my OCD that was glad she'd balanced things out, but mostly I wished one had been enough.

I was learning one was not enough for Trixie.

She probably hadn't gotten enough of her mother's milk, and I silently cursed her mom. While she was admiring her work, I scanned the room for anything that might help me.

Unfortunately, nothing I saw translated into an escape route.

# CHAPTER THIRTY-SIX

# BAD BOY

I WAS SCANNING the room for an escape route when Trixie took my head and thrust it between her breasts. I must admit, I found this pleasing. That is, until I felt her lean over, grab something, and then, with the grace of a skilled practitioner, crack a whip. This was getting to be an old, bad B movie. I nestled my head a little deeper into her cleavage in hopes of finding some solace there.

That didn't work. She pulled away from me and straddled the chair. Then with a satisfied sigh, she leaned over, poured herself another shot, and downed some.

"You'll like this," she said—as much to the whip as to me—and cracked it in the air a few times.

"I'm not so sure."

"This was always Wilhelm's favorite," she said, taking a few steps back. She cracked the whip inches from my chest.

"Oh, yeah," I muttered. "What exactly did Wilhelm like about this?"

"This." The whip caught the leg of my pants.

While that was helpful information, it hadn't really explained what Wilhelm particularly liked about it. Before I had time to ask for a clearer explanation, the whip caught my other calf.

"This is what he liked? Being whipped on his legs?"

"He liked the anticipation of the discipline… while I like the execution," she said as she artfully moved the whip up my leg. It wasn't hard enough to really hurt, but I wasn't feeling the pleasure.

"I agree with Wilhelm. The anticipation is the best part. Perhaps in deference to him we should just anticipate and not execute."

"Wilhelm understood his anticipation was so high because he valued the glory of being punished." She tried to prove her point with a lash across my thigh. I wasn't convinced Goodst had known best.

"Tell me how bad you've been and how badly I need to punish you."

"Can't we just sit outside in the cool evening and discuss this under the moon? Don't you think that would be a lot better?"

She flicked me another one—a little too close to the part that had been responsible for most of my bad behavior. "It's a long story. I've been bad for quite some time."

"Good." She swallowed her drink. "I want to hear it all."

It's what every teacher wants their students to say, what every parent wants their child to say, but only the lucky get to hear. And I wasn't feeling particularly lucky in the moment.

"I'm just like Wilhelm. My bad behavior goes all the way back to my childhood. I used to steal chocolate bars from the local candy store, along with comic books."

I got another lash on the thigh with a bit more snap to it. Her whips so far had been more for show than for purpose. I wasn't sure if I was getting closer to the glory, but I wasn't feeling it.

"I used to sneak smokes when I took the dog out, steal money from my dad's wallet, and slip downstairs when my parents went to bed so I could watch TV."

"Yes, I'm sure you were a naughty little boy but you can move the story along." She encouraged me with another shot to my stomach, causing a wave of relief to wash over me as she bypassed some sensitive territory.

"Of course, when I started to get interested in girls, the naughty factor shifted."

"You had better tell me."

Suddenly I felt like I was in a confessional. Was that what was at the core of S&M?

My thoughts often allow me to drift away from the moment but Trixie had a way of keeping me on task. The whip was an effective tool but one I ought not bring to class.

"Now!" the whip called out as it made its presence felt right below my exposed nipple.

"Well, when I first started dating, I did a lot of talking and a lot of scheming in order to cop a feel."

For that I got a shot on my forearm. I couldn't tell if that was where she'd been aiming or whether her mark was off. Either way, the pace seemed to be picking up. I wasn't sure what to say. I knew I was stalling as for once I was in no hurry. Maybe this is how I could break my urge to rush ahead and stay in the moment.

How did what I was confessing relate to the whipping? Was I being good or bad? Did it make a difference? What's a guy to do?

"If I was getting what I wanted I stayed. If I wasn't I left. Now that I say it, it sounds awfully shallow and narcissistic."

I got a couple of good ones on my shoulders. Certainly, it had been bad that I'd been so shallow and thought only of myself, but was she punishing or rewarding me? If the whipping was such grace for Wilhelm, had he received more of it for being worse or better? I was scraping the barrel of my being and not sure how I felt about it. Or she felt.

"Truthfully, I was afraid to ask for what I wanted. I tried to sweet-talk my obscure way into things and when that didn't work I left. It took me quite a while before I could be more honest."

She downed her drink. I could have used one but wasn't sure I was supposed to ask. I hoped she was getting drunk, but then I wasn't sure if she was a happy or not so happy drunk.

I went on with the confessional. "I suppose one of the worst things I've ever done with women is to romance them when all I really wanted was to have sex. I acted real loving and pretended to like them more than I did."

"You're a sick puppy," she said as she crisscrossed my stomach.

"In my defense, some of that pretending I did to myself. I fooled both of us."

"Quit sniveling," she demanded as she hit me way too close to my crotch. I hoped her aim was good and her mark had been deliberate.

"I'm sorry. It isn't easy talking about this stuff. Is this the kind of sexual-healing therapy they do at the Institute? It's very intense."

"This therapy is only for special cases."

"Like me and Wilhelm?"

"Wilhelm and I spent many happy hours here." That thought seemed to take her away for a moment.

Therapists learn when a client gets emotional, you don't back off. You seize the moment of their vulnerability and try to escort them as they probe a little deeper and expose a rawer nerve.

"I'm sure you two cared for each other very much," I said, trying to steer her away from me and into her affection.

At first, I couldn't tell whether she'd heard me. Then she glared at me.

I'd interrupted her reverie.

One therapy rule overruled another: Go for the gusto versus don't interrupt the client's reverie.

I had picked the wrong one.

## CHAPTER THIRTY-SEVEN
# THE DEEPER IT GETS

TRIXIE POURED ANOTHER shot and downed half of it. One thing I've learned about people who drink a lot is they can drink a lot. I'm not a big drinker. If I'd drunk as much as she had, I'd be in the bathroom puking, but it didn't seem to be making all that much difference to her.

For no particular reason I could discern, she snapped the whip close to my shrinking but not forsaken privates. I got to thinking she might be an ugly drunk.

"I suppose Wilhelm sat here, just like me, and confessed his bad behavior to you."

"He could be very bad."

"Was he bad to you?"

She was still. She had that look in her eye clients often get when they see a path they could take but it looks scary.

"Why do you want to know?"

"Because I can tell he hurt you and you're still hurting."

She wanted to whip me for that but her heart was elsewhere.

"You wouldn't understand."

"Try me."

"I can't trust you."

"Come on. What can I do? You have me tied up."

"You know I'm going to eventually let you go. Then you could tell someone."

"What am I going to tell them?" I said, breathing more freely. "You caught me in the Institute, took me to a cabin, tied me up, and told me your ex hurt you? That's not a story I'm going to tell."

"You know what I'm talking about." I didn't but kept that to myself.

We were silent. Therapists learn silences broken by clients are more beneficial than those broken by the therapist. This wasn't exactly that but it was close enough.

However, true to form, I barged in. "Listen, if I tell anyone, you can bring me back here and punish me for that. Now there's something to look forward to."

She dwelled on that for a moment. So did I. I didn't really like being tied up but Trixie did have a certain way about her that sparked my battery. Although I'd prefer she not hurt me and skip the whip.

"You know," she told me, "this is all just a game."

"If you say so."

"Wilhelm liked to play it. He taught me everything."

She seemed self-conscious in that moment. "I don't always dress like this but I'm missing him more today. It's sad actually. Wilhelm begged me to wear this outfit and now he isn't here to see it."

"Yes. It's sad."

She looked at me with suspicion, as if I might be mocking her. I wasn't. On the other hand, I wasn't all that sad.

"We did have fun here before he was killed."

"What do you think happened?"

"I don't know. The whole thing confuses me. And that's where you come in. Now that we're not playing games anymore, tell me what you were doing at the Institute. And no funny crap this time."

"I was trying to find out who killed him."

"Bullshit!" She lashed out the whip again against my chest. Just when I thought we were moving forward.

"Hey, it's only partial bullshit. I'm here because I have a natural curiosity about mysteries. They engage me and keep me involved. And, to be a little more truthful," I said, lying some more, "I figured Dr. Goodst, Wilhelm, must have had some special secrets about sexuality that would be helpful to know. Just like he taught you, I was hoping he could help me."

Slick as I thought I was, she replied, "You came to steal his soul, his secrets? That's such crap."

"I don't know exactly what I wanted to steal. I came to the convention to listen to him talk. I wanted to learn from him. When he was killed, it didn't kill my interest. I still want to learn and came here. And," I added, smiling slightly, "you've taught me a thing or two."

Flattered as she might have been, it didn't stop her from saying, "I don't believe you," and following it up with a couple to the thighs.

I pressed on. What I lack in restraint I make up for in fortitude. "I really wish you'd believe me. This whole week has been very charged for me. First off, the week has been about sexuality and, while sexuality plays a decent role in my life, this is the first time I've been to a conference devoted to sex. Usually people just go to a conference and fantasize about having an encounter, but this week all the workshops and conversations are all about sex. The people at the conference make their living as sex therapists or surrogates. It's all a little much for me."

She seemed to be listening, although I couldn't really tell. Either way, I carried on. "Then there's the kidnapping, the murder of your ex, my seeing you at the service and being attracted to you. And then there's this chair, your outfit… and I don't know what to tell you. It's arousing, disturbing, and confusing all at once."

She filled her glass and looked at it in the kind of way people who've had too much are able to peer into the core of the universe. Or maybe she was just lost in her own recap of recent events.

"Suppose I told you"—she came up toward me and put her face awfully close to mine—"that the person who kidnapped Wilhelm didn't kill him."

"I'd say you know a lot more than I do. Do you?"

"Of course I do. We already know that."

"Of course. But if you know the person who kidnapped him didn't kill him, are you going to tell the police? Have you told the police? Have you told anyone aside from me? What are you going to do?"

I could tell my rapid-fire questioning wasn't helping and tried to shut up. It was too late.

"If you tell anyone I will cut your balls off."

First Trombone had wanted to shove them in my mouth and now Trixie wanted to cut them off. If this kept up, I'd be able to get a job guarding the harem at the Palace.

"Hey, I don't need to tell anyone. I was just curious. Do the police know?"

"Fuck the heat."

"Right. Fuck the heat. But why this time?"

"Can I trust you?" she asked, her face now even closer to mine.

I could smell the tequila and see the speckles in her eyes, which looked quite nice.

"That's up to you. I suppose that's not very reassuring. How about of course you can. I can't think of any reason why I'd betray your trust."

She didn't like my answer. I didn't either. Part of me felt a responsibility to explain the existential impossibility of ever trusting anyone to do anything other than what they want to do. Trust isn't so much about other people; it's about you. You trust that whatever happens, you'll be able to take care of yourself. That's the best kind of trust.

I knew better than to launch into a mini-lecture but I needed us to be on the same page.

"Tell me and I'll do whatever I can to make things better. That's what I do for a living. If you don't give me a chance, I can't do anything."

I could tell she wanted to be talked into it but was torn. She had no reason to trust me or tell me anything. But neither does that stranger on the plane who decides to unload their life story on you while you'd prefer to sleep.

"If you want me to trust you, you can't keep giving me bullshit reasons why you were in the Institute tonight. If you don't tell me the truth, I sure as shit am not going to tell you. Remember who's in control here." She drove the point home with a series of lashes.

It was time to be a little more honest.

"To tell you the truth, I have women problems."

She whipped me good for that in an area that again bordered too closely to a pleasure/pain center.

"I'm a classic case of chivalry gone amok."

"What are you talking about?" She raised her voice but, thankfully, not the whip.

"I met a woman at the conference and she asked me to help her out—specifically to get some of Dr. Goodst's tapes out of his office. So I went to find them and that's when you found me. There, I've said it. That's the truth."

I admit, I felt a little better for the confession.

"Go on. Let's hear the rest."

"That's basically it. I liked her and thought if I helped her out it might further my cause. And then, when I saw you at the service"—I stared hard at her—"I got confused. I'm attracted to both of you."

I wasn't sure she was buying that but I didn't think it had hurt me to add it. And it wasn't completely untrue.

"Why did she want the tapes?"

I didn't want to tell her, but she flicked the whip a little too close to my head and I lost my resolve. "She was a former client and from what I gather she and Wilhelm had sex. She wanted the tapes before they got out in public."

"Why did she think they would?"

"Maybe she thought with all the publicity it could turn into a circus. She just wanted to protect herself."

"Who is she?"

I'd been afraid of that.

"Do I have to tell? I don't think it's relevant. She's just one of his old clients."

She stopped to think about that and poured another drink. She'd consumed a lot but I still couldn't detect much softening.

"I'm still not sure I believe you. The whole notion of your trying to steal just because you wanted to get in someone's pants is very outdated. On the other hand, it's romantic. Maybe I'll have you steal for me... although you're not very good at it."

"You're right. For better or worse I don't have much experience."

"What do you have experience with?" she asked in what I thought was a flirtatious manner. Maybe the tequila was taking effect.

"A few things. And one thing I might really be able to help you with is figuring out who killed Wilhelm. Why don't you share your suspicions and let's see if we can deduce whodunit."

"I'm still not sure I trust you," she said, but it had lost some of its edge.

"You'll never be sure. Why don't you just go ahead and tell me anyway?"

She pirouetted away from me and stood still. I admired the view. I could let her thoughts run their course—that was the therapy thing to do—but not one to stay silent for long, I thought I'd pitch my case one more time.

"Listen," I said to her back. "There's no way I can prove my trustworthiness unless you give me the chance. I'm not a threat. You caught me breaking into the Institute. I'm the one at greater risk here. Believe me, I'm not going to want to tell anyone about our time here together."

Still facing away, she asked, "What about your girlfriend?"

"She's not my girlfriend. She's only interested in getting the videos. I don't think she'd want to hear about any of this."

She spun around. I could see a new level of concern on her face. In case I'd misjudged her look, she cracked the whip in the air.

"Damn!" She strode right up to me and her nose almost touched mine. "Okay, buster, time to be honest. Where is she? Is she waiting for you to bring her back the tape? What was the plan? Tell me!"

"She's waiting back at the hotel," I said. "I told her I'd come over here tonight and take a shot at getting the tape for her. There wasn't much of a plan."

"What time did you tell her you'd be back?"

"I didn't. I just told her I'd drop by her room. I guess if I'm not back there soon she'll become concerned, but we had no set times."

She stared into my eyes for a moment, then turned, strode over to the table, and grabbed the lantern. "In that case, we have enough time to finish talking and find out what kind of man you really are."

# CHAPTER THIRTY-EIGHT

# TRIXIE SHOWS AND TELLS

**Friday night, later**

TRIXIE PUT THE whip down, sat on the edge of the table, and talked. She made me promise not to tell anyone and I was glad to do so—confidentiality is my stock in trade. She told me the kidnapping had been Goodst's idea. The two of them had set it all up. Some months ago, he'd told her he loved her and it had been a mistake to leave her. He only wanted to be with her. He wanted to run away with her but to do that they'd need to stage the kidnapping, grab the money, and take off to a getaway house in Argentina he'd secretly bought years ago.

Evidently between the alimonies, high living, and bad investments, he had more debt than fame. He'd thought his clients, supporters, and fans owed him one last cash-out. He'd planned the whole thing strategically—thought about each person and how much they could pay. He and Trixie would collect the money and take off. People would just assume the kidnappers had killed him and disposed of the body.

Except for the getting killed part, it was a pretty good retirement plan.

The two of them had shacked up in this very cabin and enjoyed some tension-filled sex while the pressure mounted. They'd fine-tuned their getaway plans as she snuck back and forth between the cabin, the Institute, his home, and her own.

She left out any conversations she might have had with Johnny Trombone. I figured her truth, like my own, hadn't quite made it out in full.

On Tuesday night she'd come to the cabin to tell him the safe had been broken into and he'd gone berserk, saying his life had been ruined. She'd calmed him down and said they'd just announce the money was stolen and ask people to contribute again. She'd convinced him the robbery would make everyone even more worried and upset, and they might get more money. She'd told Gabriela and Jordana to notify everyone on the mailing list, the police, and the press in that order. Then she'd gone home to take care of some personal business she didn't feel inclined to tell me about.

She'd come back to spend the night and found him face down on the floor. She'd rushed to him but she needn't have hurried.

She hadn't known what to do. Her fingerprints were all over the cabin so she'd be a primary suspect. She was innocent but wasn't sure anyone would believe her. Plus, she had no solid alibi. I had a hunch there were other reasons why she didn't want the police looking too closely at her life but I continued to listen.

She'd gone to the Institute's garden shed and gotten a wheelbarrow. She'd worked a good part of the night wrapping him up in sheets and blankets and carrying him in the wheelbarrow back to her car. Then she'd returned the wheelbarrow and cleaned up the cabin as best she could. She knew if the police inspected the place she'd be in trouble. She'd hoped when they found him in his house, even if they discovered he hadn't died there, they'd have no reason to search the Institute's outer grounds.

She'd driven back to his house and dragged him in. He'd been too heavy to move upstairs so she'd left him in the entry hall. Then she'd grabbed the sheets and blankets and left.

When she was done, I asked her a flurry of questions.

"Who else knew about the cabin?"

"Just me, Wilhelm, Gabriela, Jordana, and anyone else Wilhelm brought here. And, of course, the people who built it years ago, and the long-time cleaning and maintenance people who have worked for Wilhelm since the place opened."

"Who would want to kill him?" I said.

"I don't know. He was an SOB sometimes but not so you'd want to kill him."

"Are you sure no one saw you?"

"I hope so. It was late at night when I left the Institute."

"Did you collect any more money after the first lot was stolen?"

"Close to a quarter of a million," said Trixie.

"What happened to it?"

"After people found out he was dead, they wanted it back."

"So?"

"It's still in the safe, I think."

"Who has the combination?"

"I don't know. Certainly Wilhelm, Gabriela, Jordana. Possibly some others."

My mind was racing and I had a lot more questions, but I could tell she was done talking. There's a certain emotional release that follows the revelation of a significant secret. I'd felt it earlier when I told her why I'd been trying to steal the videos. Now I could see that relief in her face. I've logged enough client hours to teach me there's a point when you've gone as far as you can go and pushing is counterproductive. It was time to give it a rest.

But that's not what she had in mind. She poured two drinks. Evidently our secret-sharing had brought us closer together. She tilted my glass and this time let it cascade into my mouth. It had a revitalizing effect.

She downed hers, then picked up the whip, snapped it a couple of times to get my attention, and informed me she was about to find out how bad a boy I could be.

Since there's sex in the title of the book, I ought to try my hand at conveying what happened next. To tell you the truth, I wouldn't mind getting more into it, but that's all I learned from Trixie that directly related to the matters at hand.

Let's just say I left the cabin with some regret. We made our way back to the Institute. I told her I'd taken a cab, told them to wait, but guessed they had left. She stayed with me as I called another cab. I asked if it was okay if I looked for the tapes and she gave me a threatening look and the finger.

When the cab arrived, we had a moment of eye contact that drew me closer to her. Then she said, "Ciao." I don't know what she did after I left but when the cab got out on the street, I noticed Britt's car was no longer there.

# CHAPTER THIRTY-NINE
## GOOD NEWS–OF A KIND

**August 27, 1977**

**Saturday morning, very early**

I MADE IT back to the hotel room a little after 1:00 a.m., swallowed some aspirin, and called the hotel operator and left a message for Britt to call me in the morning. Even with all the thoughts and images that went to bed with me, it didn't take long for my mind to switch off and I fell gratefully to sleep.

The trill of the phone jolted me awake. I figured it must be early morning as the sun still wasn't up. I turned on the bed light, looked at my watch, and answered the phone. I'd been in bed for thirty minutes.

Britt's voice broke through the fogginess. She was worried about me and had been calling the room on and off. Was I okay? Did I have the tapes? What had happened?

I gave her the bottom line—I didn't have the tapes. I was tired and wanted to sleep. How about we talk in the morning?

I did want to know what had happened to her and why she hadn't come to find me but knew if I asked for her story I'd need to tell mine. Before I did that I needed some sleep, distance, and breakfast.

She wasn't happy to wait and I got a little grumpy. It got us off the phone and though I'd pay for it later, at least I'd get some sleep first.

I had a restless night. I kept waking up, wondering what to tell Britt. I'd have to say Trixie had caught me and questioned me. I felt uncomfortable about sharing Trixie's part in the kidnapping because I'd promised not to tell, but my word hadn't exactly been given freely. I certainly didn't want to share the details of where I'd been sitting at the time or what Trixie had been wearing and doing.

I nodded off about the time I decided to tell her truth. Minus a lot of the details.

I bought a newspaper in the gift shop and made it to the café. I was hoping Britt wouldn't be there. I wanted to eat, read, drink some coffee, and get my game face on. Fortunately, Britt wasn't there. Chet and Layla were, and they beckoned me over to join them.

I need to make a small confession. Some people have sex, eat a pizza, go to a movie, and get it out of their system for a while. I can do that with pizza and a movie. Trixie had charged up my batteries… and depleted them. But they were still sparking when I saw Layla. She looked tantalizing, even first thing in the morning. Chet looked okay, too, but he didn't quite attract my eye like she did. Her hair was pulled back, making her eyes and cheekbones stand out. Her tight Rolling Stones T-shirt—the one with the tongue hanging out—caught my eye.

I slid into the booth and we shared our hellos. They looked in good spirits. I doubted I did.

"Well, it looks like we might get our wish," said Chet.

"Oh, yeah? What wish is that?"

"We didn't see you last night at the sex theater," Layla said with what might have been a trace of disappointment. "We bumped into Gabriela, Goodst's 'executive assistant,' and Jordana, his less luscious yet very competent director of operations."

"While I was happy to handle all the action," Chet said, "I coulda used you."

"Get out of here," Layla said, gently shoving his shoulder. "There was no action for him or you to cover, but the show was a blast."

"You're right, as always," Chet said. "I'm not sure what's going on with those women but they didn't really give me the time of day."

"Or me," Layla added.

"Their loss, I'm sure," I said. "They're pretty upset about Goodst and even though you two could easily get people interested in other matters, we all might need to wait."

"They reject you too?" Chet asked.

"Pretty much. I'm not sure I could hold my own with Gabriela but I wouldn't mind trying. Of course, she's not the only one I feel that way about."

"Hey, Lay," Chet said. "He's flirting with you."

Those of us not named Chet blushed.

"She's a free woman," he informed me. "If you and Lay want to do your thing, I got nothing against it. Lay and I have a very open and fluid relationship."

I was intrigued. Still, whatever open and fluid meant, I wasn't comfortable openly flirting with her.

"Open and fluid," Layla said. "I guess you could say that. We've certainly covered all the bases with each other."

"And a few others too," Chet said, beaming.

"Still, even with all the fluidity, it sounds like Gabriela and Jordana aren't wanting to run the bases," I said.

"Well, Dave, that's where you got it wrong," Chet said.

"Yes," said Layla. "We had some drinks with them and Chet wore them down."

"Chet, you dog, you. What did you do?"

"Well, I can't take all the credit. Me and Lay just told them how much the soirées meant to us. We explained it would be a fitting tribute to have a proper send-off while all the convention people were here to honor and celebrate the man. We laid it on pretty thick. They took it all in. We didn't know if our words had any effect until after the show."

"What happened then?" I asked.

"There was an announcement about a gathering/happening tonight to honor Dr. Goodst."

"Cool."

"Yeah, fella," Chet said. "We looked for you to share the good news but we couldn't find you."

"I got detained."

"Whatever you were doing last night I hope it was good," Chet said. "But don't you worry. You just missed the announcement. You didn't miss the party."

"Well," Layla said, "there was a spontaneous shindig that followed the announcement. And the sex-theater show was pretty interactive and fun. It would have been great to have you there."

"I'm sorry I missed it. I got tied up."

"Too bad," Chet said. "But we can make up for it tonight. Everyone will be truckin'. Unforeseen things are gonna happen."

"That sounds exciting," I said, hoping I could catch a nap beforehand.

"Yes, it will be quite the night," Layla said, beaming. "Although it looks like you already had quite a night."

I could feel the blood rushing to my face. I probably looked as ragged as I felt. I couldn't tell whether Layla was teasing me or just stating the facts.

Shortly after that they got up to leave. We said our goodbyes and see you laters. I watched Layla as she walked away. I certainly was attracted to her. But this week that didn't mean much. I was also attracted to Britt, had some residual feelings and welts about Trixie, and was smitten with Gabriela.

Sitting there in my reverie, I saw Britt, Astrid, Feel Me, and the other woman whom I'd seen with them on the first night enter the café. They got seated but didn't see me. I'd had my breakfast, coffee, and distance so figured now was as good a time as any to say hello.

I tried to look chipper as I made my way over to the group and offered a general hello. A few nods as they continued their conversation. I stood there awkwardly while they exchanged views on sex and menopause. I didn't think any of them had firsthand experience with menopause but they were concerned about their futures. Evidently, the previous day a presenter had spoken about research into female sexuality and determined it peaked in the mid to late thirties. There was some debate about that but they all seemed to agree that men's sexuality peaked in college.

I listened for several minutes and was tempted to join in but I had enough social awareness to know when I wasn't welcome.

"I guess I'll see you all later," I said.

Britt gave me a weak smile, Astrid ignored me, Feel Me gave me a little wave, and the other woman tilted her head and gave me a nod.

I headed out.

# CHAPTER FORTY

# FESSING UP

**Saturday morning**

I WAS ON my way to the lobby when Britt caught up.

"Sorry about that," she said. "We were in a very vulnerable and open space and didn't want to break it."

"I understand. Talking about dwindling sexuality is not an easy subject. Of course, since my sexuality peaked years ago, it's hard to have a lot of compassion."

"Don't be a jerk," she said. "We were having a serious conversation and your would-be levity wouldn't have been welcome. Besides, what happened to you last night? Let's talk about that."

I seemed to be losing ground with Britt while picking some up with Layla and who knew what with Trixie. It was too bad as I was leaning Britt's way as she seemed to be taking a step back. And I hadn't yet mentioned what happened last night.

Still, they say the best defense is a good offense.

"Yes, let's talk about last night. What happened to you? Where did you go?"

"I asked you first."

"Really?"

"Really," she said with a bit of a smile.

"You sure you want to get into this before the presentation?" I said as I looked at my watch. "It begins soon. I was hoping I could go to my room for a few minutes and then go the 'Building to the Ultimate Climax' workshop."

She gave me a look that was both disapproving and enticing. Although I may have been imagining the latter.

"Come on," she said as she took my hand and led me to an empty sofa in the lobby. "You know, I'm not very pleased with how you conducted yourself on the phone last night."

"I'm sorry. I was whipped and needed to sleep." I couldn't believe my unconscious had come up with that explanation. It was close to a Freudian slip and a confession all at once.

"Still, you could have been more courteous."

"You're right. I was rude. Sometimes when I'm tired and hungry some of the polish comes off."

"Apology mostly accepted. So tell me what happened."

"I got in okay, but couldn't find the tapes and was about to give up when I got caught."

"Who caught you?"

"Trixie."

"What was she doing there?"

"You'd have to ask her. I wasn't exactly in a position to start asking questions. She is—was—very close to Goodst. There's more there than meets the eye."

"If you want to go learn about that Ultimate Climax," Britt said with what might have been encouragement, "you'd better hurry up and tell me."

"Yeah, well, it's not an easy story to tell. It's a bit strange."

"Strange can be okay. Tell me."

"Well," I said, stalling, "she caught me in the front file room. There wasn't much I could say. She knew I was up to no good. I could have tried to run away but she had a gun pointed at me."

"A gun? What was she doing there with a gun?"

"Maybe she thought there was an intruder, which there was. That might explain it. Her ex and Johnny Trombone have been killed; she needed to protect herself. All I know is she found me and had me hike into the foothills till we came to a small cabin in a clearing. The place was isolated. When we got there, she had me sit down and tied me up."

"Why did she do that? She had a gun."

"Maybe she was tired of holding it. I didn't ask. I was just worried she'd call the police. Turns out she wanted to play twenty questions. She asked me lots of questions about what I was doing there."

"Did you tell her?"

"I told her I was at the convention, that I was curious and decided to go to the Institute and look around."

"Did she call the police?"

"No, but I kept worrying she would."

"Did you tell her about me?"

"Of course not," I replied, perhaps too quickly. "I told her I wanted to find some tapes. But I didn't say whose."

"She didn't ask?"

"Yes, she did. But contrary to your experience, I can say no every now and then."

"So go on. Why didn't she call the police?"

"That's a discerning question with an intriguing answer."

"Yes?"

"Okay. Here's the thing. I can only tell you if you promise not to tell anyone. I gave Trixie my word. While keeping my word with her is not my highest priority, I like to think I keep my promises. This must be off the record or whatever else you want to call it. Just between us."

I recalled what Walter Winchell, the original Hollywood gossip columnist, had said about keeping secrets—*I usually get my stuff from people who promised somebody else that they'd keep it a secret.*

Maybe Britt would be a better secret-keeper than me.

"What's the big deal?" Britt said in a less than reassuring way.

"She'd be very upset with me if she found out I'd told anyone. This is a big-time secret. If you want to hear it you need to reassure me you won't share it. Really. She took a chance with me and I'm taking a chance with you, but only because you deserve to know and aren't going to write about it."

"Okay, I promise. But I won't promise how long I'll keep it under wraps."

"Then forget it. That's no promise."

"All right. I promise."

"What do you promise?"

"I promise I won't tell."

"How about until I tell you it's all right to tell. How does that sound?"

"Okay."

"So we have a deal?"

"Yes."

"No crossing fingers."

"Come on."

"Okay," I said, and apologized mentally to Trixie and my integrity. "She told me she and Goodst had arranged the kidnapping themselves."

"Wow. That's crazy. Are you sure?"

"I'm sure that's what she told me. She said they were holing up at the cabin until someone did him in."

"How do you know she didn't do him in?"

"She told me she found him dead and I believe her. She was pretty upset."

"We need to tell this story!" said Britt. "What we know could assist the police in trying to apprehend his killer."

"Let's not go through this again. I'm a little surprised you want the police involved."

"Of course I want the police involved. The sooner they find his killer the less need there is to go scrambling through all of his belongings."

"That makes sense. But we're not going to tell… at least not until I talk to Trixie so maybe she can lawyer up, get immunity, then tell the story herself. I know you want the scoop, and for your tapes to remain hidden until you can find them. But we're going to keep our word. Well, you are and I mostly am."

"You're getting too wound up in this and losing perspective."

"You're right. I'm totally losing perspective. Although I find it hard to believe you're accusing me of being too swept up in the action when it was your idea for us to go out there. I was just following along."

"Calm down. Let's not be blaming," she said, and quoted the therapist's mantra: "Let us each take responsibility for our actions."

"Yeah. Right. But I'm no more swept up in anything than you are. I just happen to be more wound up at this moment."

"Very well. But can we focus?"

"I'll try. If we take what Trixie said as truth, she also told me Goodst was short on money. He was ready to collect one more payday, then take off to a distant hideaway and live naughtily ever after with Trixie."

"Why would she want to run away with him? I thought they'd had their chance, divorced, and moved on."

"They moved on and came back. People do that. The way she tells it, after being apart they both realized they were each other's true mate. It didn't sound like they'd been reunited that long ago. When he shared his getaway plan she cast her fate with him."

"That's a trip. I'm not sure where it gets us but some of the pieces are coming together."

"Speaking of pieces coming together," I said, "what happened to you? I thought you were going to warn me or rescue me. Help me in some way."

"I never saw anyone drive in. I waited and waited. I got concerned and considered going in but didn't think it was wise. I even thought about calling the police but decided against it. I didn't know what was taking you so long, but nothing was happening and I didn't know what to think."

"So?"

"So I anguished over it. Then after a couple of hours I decided to come back to the hotel and wait to hear from you. I was worried and upset but thought that was the best thing to do."

"I can understand not calling the police and kind of get why you didn't come in to find me. It's the leaving that bothers me the most."

"It wasn't an easy decision. My stepdad was a Marine so I know you leave no man behind, but my mother was a cop and she told me sometimes you need to take a step back before you leap. I wasn't quitting on you. I was just relocating."

"That's reassuring," I said. "We're in this together and, as it turns out, it was better you didn't come in. Trixie got to talking to me. And using my vast therapeutic skills, I was able to get her to feel comfortable enough to share her story with me."

"Okay, Doc. Let's not get too full of ourselves. We still haven't found my tapes."

"Yeah. Sorry about that but it's time to give it up. Let's go learn a thing or two about having the ultimate orgasm."

"Don't rush it," I heard for maybe the umpteenth time in my life. "We still have work to do. If you really don't want me to take this to the papers, the least you can do is help me find out more. After all, I'm a journalist and if I can't use this exclusive yet, you can help me discover the rest of the story."

"I'm not so sure there's anything else we can do," I said, seeing the ultimate orgasm slipping away.

"Come on. You're a teacher. You have to publish or perish. You can write about this too."

"Well, there is that. But it would really help to have some ultimate orgasm kind of ending to make it really satisfying."

"Just like a guy. Rushing to the ending. I'm sure whatever they're dispensing at that workshop is going to include a lot of foreplay."

"Yeah, but—"

"No buts about it. If you want to have the ultimate orgasm, you're going to have to work for it. Those things don't come easy."

"Ha ha. Okay. More foreplay it is. But can I ask one question?"

"I'm not so sure."

"Me either, but here it is. I just want to know if, from your point of view, do things look promising for me? I hope they do but I can't tell."

"Is that your foreplay? What happened to sweet-talk and romance?"

"That wasn't sweet-talk and romance?"

"Not really. Once again you're rushing."

"Okay." I took a breath. "How about this. What do you say we go find a quiet nook and whisper sweet nothings to each other?"

"I hate to say this to you but be here now. Just be with me. Be nice. Be engaging."

"Oh, sure. Have the higher consciousness."

I don't particularly like it when I get busted but she was right.

"You're right," I said. "Let's just be here together. How are you?"

"That's very nice. I'm fine," she replied. "But now we're going to leave here and go find a quieter nook."

"All right! You were so right about that being-here-in-the-moment thing."

"Thank you. But before you pat yourself on the back, we're going to go find that nook and do some brainstorming about what might have gotten Goodst killed and where my tapes are."

We sat out on a patio under an umbrella that shaded us from the sun. There were a few people nearby but no one close enough to overhear us. Britt took a pen and pad of paper from of her purse and started making notes.

*Trixie—planned kidnapping. Probably knew Johnny Trombone. Was at the Institute at same time as David.*

*Gabriela— "executive assistant"? What's her real relationship with Goodst, Jordana, and Trixie?*

*Jordana—long-time director of operations. What's her relationship with Gabriela and Trixie—amicable/competitive?*

*Johnny Trombone—shot dead. Stole from Institute and house. Involved with Trixie? Did person who killed him also kill Goodst? Or had Trombone been hired to kill Goodst, then been whacked to keep him quiet?*

*Clients/associates past and present?*

*Other?*

Britt thought we now had a leg up on the police and could solve the mystery ourselves. Especially if we looked into Johnny Trombone and Trixie's relationship and found out more about Gabriela and Jordana.

We brainstormed about the best course of action. I mentioned a concept I'd learned while writing my dissertation. She, like others, had little interest in hearing it but that didn't stop me from explaining concurrent time. It meant both our clocks were ticking simultaneously. To accomplish more we needed to split up the tasks.

I was assigned to go back to the Institute and see what I could find out about Gabriela, Jordana, and maybe Trixie. Britt would look into Johnny's demise and the Trixie connection. We agreed to meet for dinner. She gave me a goodbye kiss that held some promise.

I didn't like the idea of leaving the hotel and was sure Golk wouldn't like it either. On the other hand, that goodbye kiss had indicated good things upon my return.

# CHAPTER FORTY-ONE

# FOLLOWING UP

**Saturday morning, later**

While I drove back to the Institute it occurred to me I had no idea what I'd run into there. If one of the people who worked there had killed Goodst, why was I going back there and riling things up? It's a time-honored mystery tradition that the criminal returns to the scene. And here I was, a criminal returning to the scene of one of my own crimes.

What if I bumped into the killer like I'd bumped into Trixie? Could I convince the killer I was a bumbling teacher needing class material? They might buy the bumbling part but it sounded pretty weak to me. I didn't think someone who killed would fall prey to my verbal powers of persuasion. No one else had—well, maybe Trixie, but who'd been persuading whom?

Driving alone in the car, anxiety was running through my core. Therapists say knowing why we feel anxious is better than not knowing. I knew exactly what was bothering me… and that's what was bothering me. It was hard to take solace from the knowledge I'd feel even worse if I didn't know why I was so nervous.

I didn't know what lay ahead at the Institute, but the closer I got the more jittery I became. Then a wave of relief swept over me. I didn't have to do this. Britt reminded me I needed to take responsibility for my actions and now I could. I could go back to the hotel, catch the last of the orgasm workshop, and endanger myself no further. And I could lie—tell Britt I'd found nothing. Trixie, Gabriela, and Jordana hadn't been there so I'd come back. I could do that. Probably even get away with it. Heck, I'd already evaded telling her the truth about my night with Trixie. I could pair my lie of omission with one of commission.

It's one thing to lie about your sexual history to someone you're trying to court. Heck, most everyone does some of that. It's quite another to lie about what you agreed to do. If I was ever going to have a serious relationship with Britt, I'd need to be more fully aligned with my integrity. I just didn't feel compelled to do so now.

I did feel compelled to tell her I was unwilling to go to the Institute. I could face her and tell her I just hadn't felt comfortable going there. I'd wanted to help but there were boundaries. She might not like it but I hoped she'd respect it. If not, at least I would.

Over the course of the week I'd had other self-talks along this line. At some point I was either going to have to give them up or pay better attention.

I drove onto the property and down the road toward the Institute. The parking lot was empty but there was one car in front of the entrance. A black jeep. I wasn't a hundred percent sure but I thought it was one of the cars that had been here on my first visit.

I took a couple of deep breaths and threw caution to the wind. Or at least I opened the front door. There was no one in the lobby. I thought about yelling hello but decided to take a peek down the hallway first. The file-room door was ajar and as I inched closer I heard a woman's voice. I recognized it but couldn't associate it. In an exasperated tone she said, "Fuck them."

I could have stood still, stepped back into the lobby, and yelled out hello but instead I went into the room. Her back was to me but I knew it was Jordana. She was throwing bundles of money from a wall safe into a bag.

"Hi, Jordana."

I don't think she jumped out of her shoes but she spun around awfully fast.

"What are you doing here?"

"I might ask you the same, but, to answer your question, I came to see you. Hi."

"I remember you," she said, staring intently at me. "You were 'roaming' here before. And now you're back."

"While there's some truth to what you say, I came to straighten things out. I was hoping I could speak with you."

"There's nothing to straighten out. I told the police what I saw, and what I saw was you."

"Fair enough. You did your civic duty. I just wanted to introduce myself to you so you can understand why I was here and why I'm back today."

"I'm not interested. Thank you but I'm very busy." She started to turn back to the safe.

"Very well. Just one question before I go. Who do you think killed Dr. Goodst?"

She stopped to look me over a little more closely. "Who are you? What are you doing here? And will you please leave now?"

"Happy to oblige. I was just going to introduce myself and leave anyway," I replied, not moving. "It's just that I was wondering what your insight is into the events of this past week. You were very close to Dr. Goodst. You have as much of an idea as anyone about what happened and I'd really like to hear it."

"Once again, you need to leave."

"You're right. Do you think Gabriela did it? I'm guessing they had something going on and maybe it went south."

"Shut up."

"Maybe she found out he planned to dump her. Isn't the jilted lover always the prime suspect? That ice-queen demeanor is disturbing."

"You don't know what you're talking about."

"Maybe, but I suspect the whole kidnapping thing was a setup just so Goodst could grab a big payday and head for the hills. And I bet he hadn't planned on taking Gabriela with him."

"You have a lot of crazy ideas. Wilhelm wasn't going to run away," she said defiantly. "He's at the pinnacle of his success. He has everything he needs and wants right here."

I could tell from her use of the present tense she was upset. I wondered if she meant she was right here. If he'd only noticed. Or had he? It didn't seem much had escaped him, aside from the killer. Perhaps Jordana was the jilted lover.

"Maybe he was going to run away with you. You're the trusted ally. You've been through everything with him."

I could feel her composure slipping a notch. As I said before, that's when we therapists bore in.

"Obviously this is a very emotional issue. I don't mean to pry. I just really want to help and find the person that did this horrible thing to him and you, and the Institute."

Her lip quivered a little.

"It's okay. I really am here to help," I said in as soothing a voice as I could muster.

She recomposed herself and said, "It's time for you to go now." But there'd been a moment. I wasn't sure what that meant but we therapists like to ascribe meaning to everything. So I chalked it up to the bond between her and Goodst and its disposition when he died.

"All right. I'll leave now," I said. "One last thing. Can you tell me what the connection is between Wilhelm, Trixie, and Johnny Trombone?"

"Who are you? Why would I tell you anything? Unless you're the FBI, you'd better go."

"I know. But, you know, I came in here and found you unloading the safe and saying, 'Fuck them.' I thought maybe we could help each other. I can forget I saw you taking the money and you can tell me about Goodst, Trombone, and Trixie."

"I have a perfectly legitimate reason for this."

"I'm sure you do. Why not just tell me anyway?"

She turned away from me and cleaned out the remaining contents of the safe, stuffing everything into a black gym bag. When she was done, she closed the safe, and turned.

"All I know is what everyone knows. Wilhelm dumped Trixie when he found out she was messing with Trombone. He didn't really care—he believed in open relationships—but he didn't like the criminal element. To be truthful, though, he was jealous. He might have wanted his own thing with Trombone. Wilhelm was very progressive when it came to these matters."

"Everyone likes bad boys," I said, trying to see if she'd be included in everyone. "Well, except the parents of the teenagers who like bad boys. They worry. But, otherwise, there's an attraction there that can't be denied. Rule breakers have their own magnetism."

"Thanks for the lecture but Wilhelm, as liberated as he was, was still influenced by the rigidity of his upbringing. He liked breaking the rules of society but didn't appreciate others doing it. He said it didn't bother him when his women were with other people, but it did. It was okay if he was part of the group and in charge but he didn't want his wives finding pleasure away from him."

"Who does?"

"Trixie was his sex goddess," she said with some disgust. "All his wives have been beautiful showpieces but she was the sexiest. It tormented him that he couldn't tame her. She'd rub his face in it and then, I imagine, they'd act it all out."

Jordana was definitely checking to see how I reacted but whether she was scanning for arousal or disapproval I couldn't be sure.

"I can see that too. Do you think when he finally kicked her out she and Trombone could have plotted to kill him?"

"That could be. They're all passionate people," she said as she began to move toward the door.

I wondered if she was trying to find out whether I, too, was a passionate person. For once, I opted out and said nothing.

"Now, I really have to go," she said. She motioned toward the door and nodded for me to join her.

"One last thing." I picked up the bag. It was heavy. "How much money do you have here?"

"Why would I tell you that?" she said, grabbing for the bag.

I kept it out of reach. "Well, it looks like a fair amount of money. I thought the thief had cleaned you out."

"Obviously, more people pitched in to try to save Wilhelm. He is… was a great man," she said, still reaching out.

"I'm sure he was. How come the police didn't take the money?"

She grabbed for the bag. I spun away. She fell on the floor and rolled over. While she was rolling, I looked inside. It was pretty full.

She got up. I handed over the bag. "Looks like there was a good second round."

She snatched it and opened the door. "We have to go now."

She escorted me out, locked the front door, and took off in her jeep.

I had two thoughts. The first was that given a chance to flirt with her I hadn't. I wanted to think of that as maturity on my part but wasn't sure. What with the sexually charged week, flirting just seemed to be a way of being. My not flirting made me wonder—was she an also-ran who didn't get much attention, surrounded as she was by all those very attractive women? Certainly she was attractive and if you'd put her in any other place she'd have stood out, but here she didn't light my fire. Working in a place like this for a long time could chip away at your self-esteem and build resentment.

That thought led directly to my second—I'd better follow her.

CHAPTER FORTY-TWO

# FOLLOW ME

SHE DROVE AT exactly the speed limit. Unlike when I go for a drive, she didn't seem very concerned with the rear-view mirror. I guess you can do that if you're doing the posted speed. She took the Mission Bay exit. I figured she wasn't going to Sea World; instead, she drove through some marshlands between the city and the built-up coast. Late Saturday-morning traffic in an area like this isn't the easiest; people are beginning to migrate to the beaches. We passed some palm-lined streets with apartment complexes and small businesses. She pulled into a parking lot next to Vince's Health Facility.

I found a space a half-block away. As I pulled in, I saw her going through the front door with her bag. I got out of the car and followed her.

In for a penny, in for a pound.

*She could be going in for a workout*, I said to myself. *But she took the bag*, I replied. *You're not sure. It could be her regular gym bag.*

I approached the front door and could see the facility catered to a fit crowd. Pictures of well-tanned and oiled women and men were featured in a display case.

I sucked in my gut, pushed my shoulders back, and tried to

look like I was there to lift some weights and sweat out the toxins of a life not wholly lived.

I was about to saunter behind some swinging doors when a cluster of muscles with a very white smile beamed at me. "Hey, this is your first time here, right? I'm Joe. Can I help you?"

"Thanks, Joe. It's good to meet you. You're right. This is my first time here. I'm actually here to meet a friend. Perhaps you know her. Jordana?"

"Sure, she just came in."

Moving toward the doors to what seemed like the workout area, I replied, "Oh, that's great. I'll just go in and find her."

"She isn't in there," Joe said, pointing the other way. "She went down the hallway."

"Oh. Thanks," I said as I changed direction and headed down the hallway.

"What the hell are you doing here?"

"Hi. I just came by to talk some more with you."

"How did you get here?"

"It's a long story and one I'd be—"

"How did you know I was here? Have you been following me, you fucking creep? You follow me, threaten me... who the fuck are you?"

"I've been wondering that same thing myself this week. It's the kind of existential question that's hard to answer."

"FUCK YOU! Hey, Joe, Rory, come here quick."

I had a slight epiphany: it might be time for me to go back to my day job. I didn't dwell on the insight because Joe and Rory quickly brought their musculature over to us.

"Help me get this pervert out of here," Jordana said.

Before they got to display the benefits of their gym work, I showed myself out.

I hightailed it back to the car and drove till I saw a payphone.

I called 911 and gave them an anonymous tip that the Goodst's ransom money might be found at Vince's Health Facility.

I wasn't sure if it was the right thing to do.

I hoped it wasn't the wrong thing.

# CHAPTER FORTY-THREE

# BEST-LAID PLANS

**Saturday, early afternoon**

I COULD UNDERSTAND Jordana's alarm at my showing up at the Institute and then at Vince's, but whether her yelling for help had been an indicator of her innocence or her guilt I didn't know. Had she been stealing the money? I figured the answer to that fell under the umbrella of police work.

While I couldn't put my finger on what was up with Jordana, I knew what was next up for me. I found Trixie's address in the phone book and took off for Del Mar. On the way, I stopped and got a couple of fish tacos, which picked up my mood. Like most people from LA, I've developed my driving and eating skills.

I'd never been to Del Mar but driving down to San Diego from LA I'd seen the picturesque racetrack speeding by in the distance. I didn't know about the neighborhood but the racetrack spoke of a bygone era when racing had been known for its leisurely gentility.

As I drove closer to the water, I saw real-estate values climbing. I passed house after house I couldn't afford. I know happiness doesn't have anything to do with having a lot of money. You need an adequate amount, good health, caring relationships, a half-full orientation, and the gratitude to go with it to find true happiness. Of course, being an American, I was raised to believe whatever you have you ought to have more. That's a lesson it takes time to unlearn and I still have some work to do.

Trixie's house was on a lane lined with the purple blossoms of jacaranda trees. They alone elevated home prices. I didn't know whether being Goodst's ex had bought this house or she'd had her own resources. If Goodst had helped pay for the place, along with providing support for the other exes, I could see why he'd had money problems. The house could have been in Cape Cod. The wood was bleached and looked like it had been built in the thirties and had several face-lifts to its name.

I don't know what I was expecting when I rang the bell but the hulk who opened the door wasn't it. Looking up, I asked if Trixie was home. He wanted to know who wanted to know. I told him. He closed the door. I waited, unsure whether he'd tell her who it was and come back or he knew who I was and had closed the door for good. Or maybe he'd come back and escort me to another realm of unwanted adventure.

The door opened and I followed in his shadow. He led me to the back of the house to what might have once been a library. Now, instead of books, videos lined the shelves. He left me and while I waited for Trixie to make her appearance, I did what I'd have done if there had been books: I stepped closer and scanned the titles. I remembered she'd once been a porn star and tried to find some of her videos. She had the classics—*Deep Throat* and *Behind the Green Door*—and a lot of titles I didn't know. I couldn't find any of hers or Britt's.

Trixie's skin-tight leopard-print tights caught my eye first as she strode into the room. Then I saw the sheer black wisp of a top that more than hinted at what lay beneath. Embarrassingly, my eyes eventually found hers, though I'm sure she was accustomed to such behavior.

"You look remarkable," Mr. Obvious said.

"Thank you."

"I thought I'd drop by and see how you're doing. I hope I'm not intruding," I said, realizing the outfit might be for someone else.

"That's sweet of you. While I'm certainly mourning the loss of my Wilhelm and Johnny, I am moving on."

"That's good to hear. It looks like you have someone here to keep an eye on you. That's wise given all that's happened."

"Drue has been with me a long time."

She smiled. I smiled. I changed gears. "I was wondering if we could kinda pick up where we left off."

"Yes?" she asked as she motioned me to sit down on the couch beside her.

I sat down and smelled her perfume, which might have been called Come Hither. She radiated a certain sexuality that was inviting but I had other things on my mind. "Aside from some of the stuff we did together that captured my attention, there are some things we talked about that made me curious and I want to follow up, if that's okay with you."

"What are those?" she asked in a less inviting way. My suggestion about picking up where we'd left off might have been a bit misleading.

"I know this is a difficult time for you, and I'm not sure I can help. But I want to. Ever since you told me about the kidnapping and your plans, I've wanted to help find the person who did this horrible thing and took away your future."

"That's very kind. But I really don't think there's anything you can do."

"That's probably true. But it helped us both last night when we talked and maybe if we talk some more, it'll be more helpful. I'm a therapist and have some skills to help people discover things that may have been hidden even from themselves."

"Could have fooled me."

"I'd like to ask you a few questions and see if maybe we can learn together."

Having finished with the foreplay, I dove in. "Who do you think killed Wilhelm? Do you think the same person who killed him also killed Johnny Trombone?"

She didn't seem to like my approach. "I don't know."

"Take a guess," I said.

"I've no idea. That's the police's job. They've already asked me all these questions."

"Maybe I can explain this better. You see, I need your help. The police consider me a person of interest."

Her eyebrows rose and her eyes widened a notch. Perhaps, once again, I'd not invested sufficient energy in gently guiding her down the path.

"Don't worry. It's all a misunderstanding that will be straightened out, but if I can help the police solve this it will save me a lot of aggravation."

She looked neither relieved nor happy. If anything, she seemed uninterested in me.

The tequila likely made me more interesting last night.

"Come on. Let's try to help each other. What about Jordana? Do you think she might have done this? I haven't really gotten much of a read on her but she seems to me like a middle child. Overlooked and willing to act out to get attention. What do you think?"

"I never trusted her," she said. "She was always prying into things. She did everything that was asked of her but she always wanted more recognition. She thought she was the power behind the throne but really she was just a tool."

"Yeah, that makes sense. Do you think she might have realized she was being taken advantage of and wanted revenge? She knew more than anyone what was happening behind the scenes."

While I thought that was an obvious statement, it seemed to upset Trixie. Her gaze got cold and faraway.

"I don't know when you last checked the safe, but she may have taken some of the ransom money for herself."

"What? That can't be. How do you know that?"

"I saw her take it."

"What?"

"It's a long story, but trust me. She stole it."

She was lost in her thoughts, and finally said, "I'll have to check."

"Was she jealous of you?"

"She was jealous of everyone. She kept all his appointments, filed his papers, and knew all the details of his life, including who he was and wasn't fucking. Come to think of it, she might even have known about our plans to get away, although Wilhelm assured me no one knew."

"I guess if anyone knew, she'd be the one. Was it uncomfortable for you that she knew so much about his private life?"

She didn't like that question and answered it with silence. So I asked an easier one. "Do you think she might have killed Wilhelm and Trombone?"

"She's a very ambitious, cold-hearted woman. She never liked being in his shadow but was afraid to go out on her own. It wouldn't surprise me if she'd wanted to kill Wilhelm so she could run the Institute in his stead." She paused, then added, "But I don't know about Johnny."

I tried not to look like I'd noticed she'd used his first name. I also hadn't thought about who'd benefit from Goodst's death. Certainly, the Institute was well enough established to carry on and Jordana very well might be the person who could pull it off. But, why kill Trombone?

"There are a couple of things I know about Johnny," I replied, using her words—it's part of the therapist's toolkit. "He and Wilhelm may have known each other, but the only person I know who links them both is you."

I watched her body language. Which wasn't that hard on the eyes. I wanted to see what her knee-jerk reaction would reveal. She was as blank as an analyst.

"What do you mean?" she asked with an innocence that belied her attire.

"Well, and I don't mean to overstep any boundaries, but there was a lot of talk at the conference about Wilhelm, you, and the other exes. A few people mentioned you and Johnny were an item."

"How would they know that? I don't know what you mean by 'item,'" she snapped. "If you mean Mr. Trombone helped console me through the breakup of my marriage, it would be true." I could sense her veneer slightly shifting. "He was a very sensitive man."

Obviously, she'd known a part of him I hadn't. "I'm sure. I would think he knew a lot of ways to be of assistance."

"I'm not sure I like your tone."

I agreed. I'd felt the mockery the moment it had escaped my mouth; whatever rapport I was endeavoring to build had just taken a backstep.

"I'm sorry," I said, realizing I'd said these words way too much all week. Maybe if I kept a closer eye on my behavior...

"I was trying to say I'm sure he was sensitive to your needs and wanted to help you as best he could. It's just that, from what I gather, he knew a lot about women in ways many other men don't."

"All the men in my life know about women in ways other men don't." She gave me a challenging look.

"Hey, I'm here to learn."

That seemed to comfort her.

"So why would anyone kill such a man?"

"Because shit happens and there are a lot of insecure, jealous assholes in this world."

I didn't think she'd seen directly into my soul when she'd said that but she'd heard my story and those words could apply.

"Insecurity and jealousy have lit many a fire. But is there anyone in particular you think might have been jealous of Johnny?"

Asking that question lit a bulb in the back of my head I'd need to revisit. It seemed I might get the time to do so when Trixie said, "I don't think we're getting anywhere. I have to go."

I'd been hearing that a lot lately and not paying much attention to it. This wasn't any different. Once again, I couldn't find a way to tiptoe into the question. "The hard part is figuring out why Johnny was stealing from the Institute and taking a bag of videos out of Wilhelm's house."

Her head jerked up as she involuntarily looked around the room at the videos surrounding us. Hmm, I thought. What did that mean?

"I have no idea what you're talking about. Have the police told you something I don't know? Why would they do that? How do you know Johnny did those things?"

Perhaps I'd overplayed my hand. I didn't know whether now was the time to be more honest or if I could partially truth my way out. I opted for the former... mostly.

# CHAPTER FORTY-FOUR

# THE TRUTH—SORTA

"HERE'S THE TRUTH. I'm telling you this because I trust you. You've told me secrets I'm honoring and I'm going to tell you one I hope you'll honor as well."

I looked earnestly at Trixie. I wouldn't say she returned the favor but it was reassuring enough. "Go on," she said, and I took that for as close to a pinkie promise as I'd get.

"I'm not going to go into details now as they aren't important." Especially since I was blending fact and fiction. "What's important is I saw Johnny rummaging through the file room at the Institute and I'm pretty sure he stole a file and the ransom money. Then he took off and went to Wilhelm's house, which he broke into and came out of with a bag over his shoulder like Santa Claus. I'm guessing he stole videos."

Trixie was attentive in ways I only wished my students were.

"How do you know he stole the money? And what makes you think the bag was full of videos?"

"Well, the timing seemed right. It wasn't that long after I'd seen him in the filing room—where, as you know, the safe is located—that I heard the money had gone missing. He seems to be the likely candidate but, certainly, someone else could have done it and he might have had an innocent reason for being there. But it didn't look that way. He was wearing an overcoat that could have been stuffed with money. And the reason there were videos in his bag is he was in the video business. And from what I gather, Wilhelm had a lot of videos that I'm sure are now collectors' items."

"What are you talking about? This all sounds so contrived."

It seemed like the pieces I had weren't fitting well with the ones she had.

"I don't believe Johnny would steal tapes. Maybe money, but even that seems farfetched. Certainly, he lived on the edge of society but if he were going to steal, he'd have had others do it for him. You've made a mistake. Maybe it wasn't Johnny you saw."

"I've certainly made mistakes. But this time I followed him back to his store. I went in and talked with him so I know it was him."

"You followed him to his store? Who are you? What are you doing here?"

"I've been asking that question all week. I'm just a guy trying to put a puzzle together so he can get back to his regular life knowing a bit more about human sexuality."

"What are you talking about?"

"Never mind. It's a long story. All I know is I spoke with Johnny about buying some tapes and he was going to get back to me. But a funny thing happened. While I was there he got a phone call. From you. Want to tell me what you two were talking about?"

"No, I do not. Are you insinuating Johnny stole the ransom money and videos and I was complicit?" she asked, her voice rising.

"Were you?"

We were quiet for an uncomfortable moment. I'd confronted her with a truth she hadn't known I knew. Were we now allies or enemies?

"Why should I tell you anything?" she asked.

"You know why. Just like you could tell the police I know more about Johnny than they think I know, I could tell the police about you and Wilhelm and Johnny. We either trust each other and work together or we don't."

I didn't like the silence that followed. She seemed to be measuring things out and weighing her options. On the one hand, as a therapist I wanted her to figure out what was best for her. On the other hand, not wearing my professional hat, I wanted what was best for me. I needed to tip things in my favor. For that I'd need to reach into the therapist's grab-bag of techniques.

I'd need to do a paradoxical intervention.

When I teach this to graduate students, they get very excited because they think it's the kind of high-grade tool that will empower them. And it is. However, no matter how smoothly you apply this technique, you can't get someone to do something they don't want to do; all you can do is help remove some of the obstacles.

Free will exists. So does free enterprise. While we're all ostensibly free to do as we choose, others are also free to influence us and get us to see things their way. That's where paradoxical intervention and advertising overlap. They're both methods to get someone to do what you want by telling them what they want to hear.

When a therapist employs paradox it's to reduce the client's resistance. If a client says they're afraid to talk, instead of coaxing or imploring, the therapist agrees.

"Don't talk about it. Maybe another time. It's a scary thing to talk about. I can understand that. Talking about it might upset the status quo. That's always risky so don't talk about it."

You'd think with that encouragement the client would breathe a sigh of relief and move on. And sometimes they do. But more often than not the paradoxical intervention—commonly called agreement—normalizes the resistance. With no pressure or judgment on them, the talker is left to wrestle with their own deliberations. Do I or don't I open up? If no one is pushing you to open up it's harder to focus on resisting; you're left to deal more directly with your desire to share and the fear of doing so.

As a therapist, I've learned to put my money on people wanting to share. You just have to help them with the fear.

I could tell Trixie was still grappling with which way to go. It was time to see if I could put the theory into practice.

"I know I'm being a pest. And to tell you the truth, I can understand your reasons for not telling me anything. We hardly know each other. Who knows what I could do with what you tell me. You're better off just keeping what you know to yourself."

She seemed unsure what to make of the shift, although I imagined she had enough experience with men to know they change their approach when they think they can make more headway coming from another angle.

I gave her a look of compassion. She looked away from me.

I doubled down. "I know this whole business must be horribly upsetting and off-putting. You just want to be left alone, and here I come barging into your life. Fate brought us together and we've forged a little bond, shared intimate moments. But, still, you don't know if you can truly trust me. There's no need to tell me. I understand. It's been a very difficult time for you and I don't want you to do anything you don't want to do."

"I don't know what to say."

I heard that as an opening and waited.

It's a manipulative technique but it really boils down to understanding and honoring the other person's reasons for doing what they're doing. Therapists like to put labels on things so they came up with paradoxical intervention, which doesn't sound very warm and fuzzy. But if you do it well, it really helps you and the other person share a compassionate, knowing space.

Maybe Trixie and I could do that.

"I'm just so scared," she said.

I felt the tears before I saw them.

I've learned enough about crying to keep my mouth shut most of the time. For Trixie, a tough-acting sex queen, to show me her vulnerability surprised me. Being vulnerable isn't easy, and when people open themselves up it brings me closer to them. I wasn't sure if it was doing the same for her but I hoped it was. It's difficult for me to cry in front of others but Trixie seemed to be past the point of constraint. Watching her cry reminded me just how difficult a time this was for her. I started to feel sad.

She sneaked a look at me and seemed surprised by what she saw. She became self-conscious and cleared her throat. "If Wilhelm hadn't been killed first, I'd have accused him of killing Johnny."

She struggled, trying to stay in control, but soon began to sob.

After a few minutes she got up, found some Kleenex, blew her nose, and sat back down.

"Thank you for sharing your pain," I said. "I'm sorry you're having to go through all this."

She gave me one of those are-you-fucking-with-me looks but her heart wasn't in it.

I was confused. Johnny had been the wonderful guy who'd been there for her. Yet, she'd been going to run away with Goodst. Who was the primary beneficiary of her tears?

When the tears subsided, the words came. She'd told Johnny where the safe was. They'd planned for him to steal the money and the videos, then run away together. Her story sounded familiar. Just different co-stars.

I reminded her she'd seemed surprised when I'd told her Johnny had stolen the videos. That was because she told him to get them, but he told her he couldn't find them. I asked why she'd wanted them stolen. Not surprisingly, her story wasn't much different from Britt's—she didn't want anyone else seeing them.

When she and Goodst had first met, the sex had been hot and heavy. He'd had her watch videos with him, then join in with him, and eventually make videos with him. It had all been very erotic and things had been good. Then they'd gotten married and slowly things had changed. He'd wanted more threesomes. But not just with other women. Men, too, everybody doing everybody every which way. It was more than she'd wanted and they drifted apart and finally divorced. Yet there'd been a part of her that was still very attracted to him and his boundary-breaking ways.

She was also attracted to Johnny. She'd been taken with his masculinity and sensitivity. I'd seen the former but would have to take her word for the latter. He could have killed me, though, so maybe there had been some human kindness there.

She and Johnny had a highly charged romance, and Goodst, even though he had ended their marriage, become very jealous. He'd call her constantly, drop by to demand she come back to him, and threaten to have Johnny "taken care of."

She'd wanted Goodst out of her life, and an idea came to her. She'd reconcile with Goodst and get him to run away with her. But to do that they'd need a windfall. Thus, the kidnapping plan had been hatched. Goodst thought it was his idea, but really she'd led him down the path.

Once the ransom money was collected, Johnny would steal the money and her videos as well as any others he could grab. They'd have the money and videos they could sell or blackmail Goodst with so he'd stay away. It was a reasonable plan and would have made for a happy ending… for everyone except Goodst.

Everything had been working out fine. She'd gotten back together with Goodst and they'd hatched their escape plan. The ransom notes went out and money was starting to come in. She and Johnny came up with the idea to steal the money early in the week so people might donate twice. After the theft, when they'd gotten together, Johnny told her there were no problems and handed over fifty thousand dollars he'd found in the safe. But he told her he'd not been able to find the videos.

She'd believed him then, but now was seeing things differently. Most likely there'd been more than fifty thousand in the safe. And Johnny might very well have made off with the videos for himself.

Not the best thing to learn about the man you loved and planned to run away with to distant lands. However, until he was killed she'd been ready to go.

Trixie was having a hard time relaying this but the more she said the more she seemed to want to unburden herself and make sense of it all. Like any client putting the pieces of their puzzle together and gaining greater awareness, her honesty would help cleanse her and allow her to move forward. It would also embarrass her and give her second thoughts. But her first thoughts would mostly be ones of relief and appreciation. Or so I hoped.

Hearing her wrangle with her conflicting emotions drew me to her. There's that damsel—or anyone—in distress flashing signal that brings out a certain chivalry in me. First with Britt, and now with Trixie. I wanted to hold her in my arms and tell her everything would be okay. Though when your ex-husband and new lover are killed in the same week, it's difficult to find relief in another's platitudes.

And, if I'm honest, if I'd given her that consoling hug, I might easily have tried to move things forward. I was supposed to come to her rescue, not try to seduce her.

When she was done talking, I thanked her for her trust in me. I knew what she'd told me hadn't come easy and I wanted her to know I'd respect her confidence and do my best to figure out what had happened and who was to blame.

We stood up, looked knowingly into each other's eyes, and shared an endearing hug. Then I left.

# CHAPTER FORTY-FIVE
# SUSPECTS APLENTY

**Saturday afternoon**

IT'S HARD TO solve a mystery when everyone you know is innocent. Of course, the killings could have little or nothing to do with what and whom I knew. But then we wouldn't have much of a story.

Perhaps I wasn't putting the pieces together correctly. Or I was still missing parts of the puzzle. I went to my room and wondered what Rockford or Columbo would do. I wrote a list of the suspects and a vague action plan.

The first and most likely suspect was:

Other.

Then came Jordana, Gabriela, Trixie, Chet, Layla, Astrid, and Britt.

While the odds favored Other, we know they didn't do it.

Jordana definitely fitted in somewhere. Her simmering resentment could have boiled. She'd taken/stolen the money. To my way of thinking, she'd overreacted when I'd shown up at the health club. If she really didn't have anything to hide, why had she acted so aggressively? Unless she really thought I was a stalker... and if that was the case, was there something in her history that drove her to that conclusion?

Gabriela was Goodst's Amazon goddess assistant who'd assisted in who knew what ways. She'd been close to him and had nothing to do with me. *Quelle surprise.* If she were a piece of the puzzle, I hadn't seen it yet. I'd need to make better sense of what I knew, or find her tonight and see what I could learn. A long shot but, hey, if I could string some sentences together, it wouldn't hurt to see her again.

Trixie. Certainly, there was more there than met the eye. And what met the eye was very pleasing and seductive. But she overdid it. Why? She'd hatched the kidnapping plot and agreed to run off with two men. And yet I trusted her. Goodst and Johnny had too. She'd been a porn actress; there must have been a lot of faking. She had a vulnerability and openness to her that made her appealing. Had the men in her life put too much trust in her? Or she them? She lived her life with a different playbook than mine.

Chet. A seemingly happy-go-lucky guy who'd found a way to make a living making love. Or at least going through the act. Like Trixie, there was a degree of faking involved in his work to keep his clients coming back. He'd traveled halfway across the country to get referrals and party at Goodst's place. I once dated a woman who lived two hours away so maybe Chet was on the up and up. But was I missing something?

Layla. Another highly attractive sex surrogate who was here to get referrals or for some other reason I'd yet to discover. What was their true relationship status? She'd been flirtatious with me, hadn't she? Or was that just her way of getting referrals?

Astrid. I wasn't sure what to make of her. Was she Britt's colleague, friend, lover? She didn't cotton to me, but she's not alone in that. She was a tough cookie. Who/what was she protecting?

And there was Britt. What was really happening with her and what was her agenda? Was there more to her story than she was letting on? Now that Goodst was dead what did she want? She wasn't exactly geographically desirable, but where there's a will there's a way. Was there a will for either of us?

I'd been going to add a column for motive and opportunity—a big thing in mysteries—but, for all I knew, everyone could have both. And, frankly, I'm not a list guy.

I was driving home in less than twenty-four hours, there was the big send-off at the Institute tonight, and if I wanted to do anything this was the time to do it.

I thought about taking a nap.

A wave of exhaustion mounted itself on the fringes of my body. I closed my eyes for a minute. I felt the muscles in my face slacken and my head fall to one side. I jumped up. If I didn't move, I'd be down for the count.

I stretched, went to the bathroom, and tried to revive myself with some cold water and an eye-to-eye in the mirror.

*It's the home stretch, David. Finish strong. Tomorrow you're on the road and the next day you're teaching human sexuality, seeing clients, and living a not-quite-so-exciting life. Make the most of the moment.*

I headed down to the lobby and passed the hotel bar. I took a look. There were two guys boxing on TV and a small crowd mostly ignoring it. Seated at the bar was Chet with a woman whose assets loomed large and looked store-bought. Chet seemed to be in the market.

"Hey," I said, coming up behind Chet and touching him on the shoulder. He turned and offered a most unwelcoming stare. True to form, I kept going. "So, what's new?"

"Not much," he replied. The fake smile told me now wasn't the time for us to talk. Before I could consider my next move, his new interest reached out and gave me an energizing handshake. "I'm Wendy. And who do I have the pleasure of meeting?"

"Well, the pleasure's all mine. I'm David. Chet and I are attending the conference together."

"That's so interesting," she said. "I didn't know that."

Chet gave me a get-lost look. And as much as I wanted to pepper him for answers, he seemed to have a different kind of seasoning on his mind. I figured even with Wendy in the picture, he'd still find a way to be at the party tonight with or without her. I'd get to talk with him then if he wasn't equally distracted.

"I'm sure Chet can tell you all about it. I'm sorry but I have to go."

I headed to Britt's room and knocked. Astrid answered. She didn't look any happier to see me than I did her. I gave her a weak smile, which was more than she'd offered me.

"Hi," I said. "I haven't seen you in a while."

"Let me count my blessings," she replied, keeping the door a full foot open.

"I suppose that's one way to look at it. How come you're in such a chippy mood?" I asked, smelling alcohol on her breath.

"What are you, the question man?"

"Sorry. It's an occupational hazard. It won't surprise you to know I came by hoping to see Britt. Not that I'm not happy to see you. It's just that I have something I'd like to share with her."

"I bet you do," she said, sneering.

I tried a winning smile but gave it up.

"I haven't seen her all day. Your guess is as good as mine."

"That's too bad. Any idea when she might show up?"

"We have plans to attend the 'Surviving Abuse and Flourishing' workshop at four. I imagine she'll be there."

"Thanks, Astrid. Do you mind if I join you?"

"Would it matter?"

That was the straw that pushed me into action.

"Can we be real for a minute? What's up with you? Every time you see me it's like I've rained on your parade. You wouldn't be the first... but what have I done to make you feel this way? I just don't understand."

"Look, I know you're a therapist and you like this I/thou stuff, but it's not my thing. Let's just say I don't like you nosing around with Britt. I don't trust you and I don't think you're good for her. So, yes, I'd prefer it if you stayed away. But it's a free country and Britt's a big girl, and if she wants you to tag along that's her decision."

"Okay. That's pretty clear. While it's not easy to hear, it puts your reaction to me in a certain context. So thank you."

"Good," she said, closing the door. "Now goodbye."

"Wait. Wait. Wait. We have over an hour before the workshop. Why not spend some of it educating me on my shortcomings? Consider it an act of kindness and a growth opportunity for me."

I could tell she'd prefer to be rid of me but the allure of berating me about my deficiencies seemed to intrigue her. Apparently, she was enough of a sadist to go for it and, I guess, I was enough of a masochist to ask for it.

"Go ask Britt. She knows you better."

"I can do that. But your observations are equally valid. And since you don't seem to have any great inclination to be nice to me, you might be more honest."

"How does 'Your pushy cuteness makes me puke' sound?"

"You're getting there. But that isn't really news. I know not everyone's going to like everything I do, including me, but I'm sure you can do better."

"You're very irritating, you know that? On the one hand I want to slam this door in your face and tell you to fuck off. And on the other I like telling you what an asshole you are."

"There you go. That was better. Not original but at least you're acknowledging a duality. That's encouraging."

"You really are annoying."

Feeling good about myself, despite Astrid's feedback, I thought I might try another paradoxical intervention.

"It doesn't feel good to hear you think I'm so annoying and irritating, nor that my cute pushiness makes you want to puke. I know it's kind of a waste of time for you to tell me more about my deficiencies and I'm sure there's more to it. But, really, if you don't want to tell me you don't have to."

Like Trixie, she didn't seem to know what to make of what I'd said. On the one hand I'd encouraged her to tell me more and on the other I'd said she could step away.

Her response summed up her takeaway. "Don't give me this sensitive therapist crap. I know all about that shit."

"Oh, yeah?" I said, going with the flow. "How come you know so much about it?"

"There isn't a woman at this convention who hasn't been abused by a shrink."

"Whoa. You were abused by a shrink?"

"Clear the presses. Newsflash. Me and most of the women here saw some opportunistic pig therapist who took advantage of our vulnerability."

"I'm sorry to hear that. Really." And then I recalled I'd done exactly that with Trixie. "At dinner the other night you said you met Goodst when you were doing some freelance work. But were you one of his patients too?"

"I had one session with him when I interviewed him. He tried his dirty tricks on me but they didn't work so I never went back. But many of the women here either were fucked by him and still want him, or were fucked by him and want to kill him."

"I take it you're in the kill group."

"Fuck off, asshole."

"I'm not saying you killed him. I'm just saying I can understand your anger. He betrayed your trust."

She seemed almost to hold me in some positive regard for a moment. Then she said, "That's enough for now," and closed the door.

Waiting for the elevator, I wondered whether Astrid had killed Goodst. She'd almost said as much. She had a motive and I could see how she might have confronted Goodst as Britt had done, and how her anger could have boiled over. She wasn't exactly your touchy-feely type.

Maybe she'd seen Goodst longer than she told me and he had made videos with her as well. Maybe Trombone stole her videos, gave her a call, and offered to sell them to her but she hadn't wanted to pay his price?

I went to my room to rest before the workshop. Given what I was learning, I was extra curious about the surviving-abuse workshop and wanted to go in with a clear head.

# CHAPTER FORTY-SIX

# SHE SAYS, HE SAYS

**Saturday, late afternoon**

BACK IN MY room, I was greeted by a blinking light on the phone. I didn't want to answer but, like a lot of things I don't like to do, I did it anyway.

Golk was telling me to see him ASAP.

I didn't exactly hurry. I told the uniformed officer outside the door who I was and sat down. Before I could warm to the seat, the officer returned and told me to go on in.

Golk, Nunn, and some other officers sat shuffling papers; Jordana looked smug.

"It's about time!" she said. "You're in a lot of trouble."

"Hi. It's good to see you too."

"Come on in," said Nunn. "Ms. Handler has been relating some very interesting information to us."

"I'm sure she has," I replied, trying to affect a carefree attitude I didn't possess.

"First, earlier in the week Ms. Handler thought you might have been snooping around the Institute. But as I remember it, you told us you were there chasing skirts."

"I don't think that's quite what I said. I can't be responsible for what Ms. Handler thinks but, as I told you, I was there to inquire about the Institute. I was curious. I wasn't snooping or looking for skirts."

"You told us you went there hoping to meeting Dr. Goodst's executive assistant, Gabriela Barbosa."

"That's not untrue. It was part of why I went there."

"Like I told you," Nunn said, "chasing skirts."

"Whatever," said Golk. "It doesn't matter, because then Ms. Handler says you returned to the Institute and again she found you snooping around."

"Once again. It's a point of view. I did go back. I call it the pursuit of knowledge. It's what educators do. I would say it was more like I caught Ms. Handler in a compromising position."

"What does that mean?" Nunn asked.

Golk answered. "We'll get to that. More importantly, after we'd told you to not leave the premises without telling us, it seems you also followed Ms. Handler from the Institute to her gym and made threatening remarks to her."

"Okay. Hold off a minute," I said. "I hope you can see through this. Ms. Handler stole money from the Institute and when I caught her and followed her, she had some physical specimens threaten me with bodily harm. She's trying to throw you off course by making me look guilty when she's the one at fault here."

"See, I told you," Jordana said. "He'd twist things. I've told you the whole story. He's the one who's broken the law and ought to be arrested."

"Hold on," Nunn said, raising his hands. "Please just answer the questions we ask you."

We both looked at Golk. Unfortunately, he looked at me. "Ms. Handler says you threatened her." Then he looked at her and continued. "Will you please tell Dr. Unger what you told us he said to you?"

"Gladly. He said, and I quote, 'I will beat the shit out of you if you don't give me the information.'"

"And what information was that?" Golk asked.

"He wanted to know about the ransom money. Fortunately, I was taking it to a more secure location. That's when he threatened me. I was afraid he'd do something violent so I left the Institute to get some friends at the health club to protect me and he followed me there. When I saw he'd stalked me, I asked the people at the reception desk to help me. They did so and evicted him. You can ask them. They'll confirm my story."

I was getting nervous. What if Golk believed this web of half-truths? Was there enough superficial evidence here for him to arrest me? They say the best defense is a strong offense. It was time to test the theory with my own half-truths.

"I object," I blurted out, thinking I was in court already.

Golk gave me a you'd-better-shut-your-mouth look and I kept the rest of my objection to myself.

"I told you he'd deny the whole thing," said Jordana.

It seemed like Golk wasn't totally buying her story. But, then, he wasn't buying mine either. He knew something stunk.

"What's the story, Dr. Unger? Is Ms. Handler right?"

It was time to dig deep into my therapy bag of tricks.

"Of course she's not right. Well, that's not entirely true. She has pieces of the truth here and there but she's putting a whole different picture in the frame. If you go to a museum, are you there to look at the pictures or snoop? If someone asks you why you're doing something, is that threatening? Now, we all know this has been a trying week for everyone, especially those closest to Dr. Goodst, so I don't want to say Ms. Handler's paranoia is deep-seated. But she has a way of viewing the world that might not exactly fit with reality."

Name-calling is a long-standing way of handling oneself in the middle of an argument and I'm sure we've all resorted to it at one time or another. Therapists have elevated name-calling to such a high level, they've produced a hefty volume called the *Diagnostic and Statistical Manual of Mental Disorders*. Nobody, including therapists, likes to be called names but that hasn't stopped the profession from labeling other people as neurotic, obsessive, borderline, narcissistic, or, in this case, paranoid.

Personally, I prefer to focus on behavior rather than on what to call it. But I didn't spend all that money on graduate school not to be able to employ the tricks of the trade. Just like the nasty thing your relative labeled you with could stick with you for life, so too can a therapist's name-calling dig its way into your unconscious. When I'd called Jordana paranoid, it was my low-handed attempt to discredit her story. I didn't know whether it had worked; Golk might have been a subscriber to the belief that paranoids are people who just know the truth.

"Cut the bullshit!" said Nunn. "Just tell us what happened."

Some techniques work better than others.

I related my side of the story, except, like Jordana, I left out a few facts. I'd followed Jordana because I hadn't believed she was taking the ransom money from the safe for the purest of reasons and when I'd confronted her, she'd had her cronies muscle me out.

Golk interrupted me. "Were you the one who made the anonymous tip?"

I didn't really want to own that but Golk had me fingered for the call. Nobody likes a stoolie, even the police. So I owned up to show him I was an honest one.

Golk seemed not to know what to do with us. He settled for another reminder not to leave the hotel without letting him know. It came with a threat of "measures" that concerned me enough to make me ask for permission to go to the send-off event at the Institute. Nunn was against it but Golk had a bit of a smile on his face when he agreed. I wasn't sure what that was about but was glad I'd gotten a hall pass.

# CHAPTER FORTY-SEVEN

# DISTURBING FACTS

**Saturday, early evening**

I OPTED TO spend time in my room. I was planning to leave the conference tomorrow and head home... not to jail. I'd come to the conference to learn about human sexuality, but at this point I had no idea how I'd put together a meaningful course. I'd spent more time chasing after the whodunit—and, I admit, skirts—than I had digesting the current best thinking in the field. I wasn't sure my efforts demonstrated my best thinking.

*Face the facts, David*, I told myself. *You came to absorb as much as you could so you could share that information in class. Instead of learning about vas deferens, you learned about Britt, Astrid, Trixie, Jordana, Gabriela, Layla, and Chet. People you'll probably never see again. Well, hopefully Britt. Maybe Layla, Gabriela in your fantasies, and Trixie in your dreams. But don't forget those other new people in your life—Lieutenant Golk and Sergeant Nunn. It isn't too late to go to the Surviving Abuse and Flourishing workshop. Better late than never.*

I splashed some water on my face, combed my hair, grabbed the complimentary pad and pen, and made my way downstairs. I found the presentation room, quietly opened the door, and took an empty seat in the back row. Not an unfamiliar place.

An earnest and enthused speaker dressed in a lot of purple seemed to be summing things up. I took my pad and pen and jotted down some notes: One out of four girls prior to becoming eighteen is sexually abused; one out of six boys. One out of five children is a victim of incest. Sixty percent of college women report some type of forced, unwanted sexual encounter. Eighty percent of rapists don't see themselves as rapists. Eighty-six percent of date-rapists believe rape is justified under some circumstances.

I don't know how those statistics sit with you but they shattered my bubble. Sure, I knew these horrible acts existed but I hadn't realized how prevalent they were.

I am not a victim of sexual abuse. Nor have I abused anyone. But, according to the statistics, just because I think so doesn't make it so. It was a disquieting thought.

My thoughts went back to the first workshop I'd attended where they'd talked about all sex being good sex as long as it was consensual.

The more I thought about consent, the more I thought it applied across the board in life.

My head was full of troubling thoughts as I saw Britt coming up the aisle. Our eyes met and she waved her hand toward the door, mouthing, "Come on." I scurried out of the row and caught up with her in the hallway.

"Have you seen Astrid?" she said.

"I saw her earlier. She said she was coming to this workshop. I thought you two were meeting here. What's up?"

"Let's go." She took off down the hall. "We have to find a private place to talk."

I followed her to the lobby and we found an empty sofa in the corner. "Something's wrong. I was supposed to meet Astrid at the workshop. She wouldn't have passed it up unless something had happened."

"I saw her about an hour ago and she was intent on coming. Maybe she took a nap and overslept."

"Don't be an idiot. Does Astrid strike you as a nap person? No. Something's wrong."

"Did you check the room? We could go up there now."

"I did that. When she didn't show up, I went and checked. Nothing. I asked at the front desk if she'd left a message. Nothing. So I came back and waited for her."

"Oh."

"She wouldn't just take off. And if she did, she'd leave me a note."

"Could she have met someone and decided to go off for a drink or something like that?"

"You really don't know what you're talking about. Why can't you just try and be helpful."

For someone who makes their living trying to be helpful, I didn't seem to be doing very well. "Sorry. I was just trying to work out what might have happened to her."

"Something has happened and I'm worried."

"Yeah. I can see that. I'm sorry."

"Knock off the patronizing therapist bullshit."

"I wasn't patronizing you."

"It's the same thing with all you shrinks. You don't know when you're being sincere and when you're just voicing phony concern."

Whatever I said wasn't going to go down well. She was worried and upset, and it was more invigorating to be mad at me than worried about Astrid. That said, her being upset with me irritated me.

"I don't get it," I said. "Why are you so upset with me? I haven't done anything but try to help. I don't like it, I don't appreciate it, and I wish you'd stop it."

"At least that sounded real. As I said, I'm worried. Sorry if I'm taking it out on you."

"Okay. That feels better."

And it did. I've learned expressing my anger is a positive thing for me. It's when I sit on it that it eats away at me.

"I'm just worried."

"Would you like me to make some phone calls? Try to locate her? I'm happy to help out. I know that might sound like therapist dribble and perhaps it is. I might not even know when I'm slipping into therapist mode, but I do really want to be helpful."

She stood. "Thanks, but I'll see you later."

Without waiting for me to respond, she headed toward the hotel entrance.

It didn't make sense. I was hurt, angry again, and confused. I'd spent a good part of the day—heck, week—helping her and in return I'd been shut out. Obviously, there were things she wasn't telling me and it didn't look like she'd be forthcoming any time soon. I just wished I wasn't so attracted to her. Then again, if she kept this up, I wouldn't be.

I decided to follow her and see what she was up to. I wasn't sure why I felt compelled to, but I'd come so far and I didn't have anything better to do—well, I did, but in for that penny, in for that pound.

I hurried out of the hotel and saw her get in a cab. I had an image of Lieutenant Golk and his warning about staying put. Was I going to play it safe and let the moment pass, or was I going to grab a taxi and say, "Follow that car"?

I got into the cab, said those immortal words, and felt a little jolt of detective adrenaline. We followed Britt into the recently cleaned-up tourist part of downtown San Diego. The bay was a few blocks away and restaurants and bars abounded. Unlike in LA, people were on the streets.

She got out in front of a brick building with a turquoise-neon palm tree with The Palms flashing in pink. I had the cab stop down the block and after a minute I followed her in. The evening was in full swing. There were enough people mingling that I could slip in without being noticed.

It didn't take long for me to realize I was the only man in the room. Too many eyes gave me the kind of stare that made me want to sing out like Cary Grant in *Gunga Din*. Some looks seemed to be kind—Okay, you made a mistake, now go back out. Others seemed more aggressive. I looked for Britt but couldn't see her. I hedged my way over to some of the more forgiving faces so I could lay low enough to spot Britt, who I imagined was seeking Astrid.

Helen Reddy was singing "You're My World" and couples were slow dancing. I'd never been to a place where I was the only man and all the women were dancing together. None were interested in me, which I was used to, but it was like a parallel universe. I was happy the place existed and yet I felt like I was intruding.

"What the hell are you doing here?" Britt's eyes hurled daggers as she strode past me and out.

I owed her an explanation so I followed her.

I caught up with her down the street. It didn't take any clinical skills to see how upset she was. "I'm sorry," I said. "I didn't mean to surprise you. I was concerned about you at the hotel and decided to follow you to make sure everything was all right."

"Just go away."

"I know you're mad with me, and you have good cause. I wouldn't want anyone following me. But something is obviously troubling you and we've been through a lot this week. And if I can, I want to help."

"You can't."

"Come on. Give me a chance. I've found out a lot of stuff since we last talked and I want to share it and see if we can figure out whodunit. But I can see there are other things superseding that so what can I do?"

"That's nice. But not now."

I kept up with her, stride for stride. I'd come this far and I wasn't giving up easily. We fast-paced it a couple of blocks till we were off the main tourist thoroughfare. We passed a dry cleaner's, a used-clothing store, a pet store with sleeping cats in the window, and a camera store with a cardboard brunette urging us to shop inside. She came to a halt. Turned and faced me. "It's Astrid. Something's definitely wrong. I was hoping she'd be at The Palms as that's become our local hangout, but she wasn't there and the couple of people I knew hadn't seen her. She told me she had to meet someone there earlier this afternoon. She wouldn't tell me what it was about. She was very secretive—that isn't unusual but it seemed off."

"She could have met them before I saw her at the hotel. Whoever she met, it must have occurred in the hour beforehand. Are you sure she isn't at the hotel? Want to go back and double-check or call in and see if there are any messages now?"

"What you don't seem to understand is I know Astrid. I know she'd have left me a message. She wouldn't just disappear. She probably went to The Palms, came back, saw you, and then what?"

"You could call the hotel and ask about messages."

"I did that right before I saw you in the lobby. I can do it again but I don't think it will help."

"But it won't hurt," I replied, scanning to see if there was a phone booth. We spotted one at the gas station down the block.

"I'm sorry," I said out of habit. "But I keep thinking if I knew more I could help more. And I know you want to keep things to yourself—which is certainly your prerogative—but I work in a profession that believes in talking things out."

"That, I've found out, depends on who you're talking to."

"Indeed," I replied, having had about enough of the piling on the therapist.

"Quit being a shrink," she said. She looked in her handbag, pulled out some change, and called.

"I'm trying to be a friend," I said.

"Well, right now I don't need a shrink or a friend. I just need..."

She asked Information for the hotel number and called, only to find out what she already knew. She put down the receiver and began to cry. And talk.

Britt and Astrid met a few months earlier at a press conference, hit it off, and began to spend time together. Britt had never been in a romantic relationship with a woman, while Astrid had only been with women. Gradually they'd become lovers. Britt's initial fear and uncertainty had given way to a newfound freedom that excited her and expanded her world view. Yet at the same time she was having doubts. She wasn't sure whether she was homosexual, bisexual, or just feeling sexual.

As she'd become more comfortable and embraced the process of discovery, she'd found herself attracted to me... enjoyed flirting with me. She wasn't sure what to do. Astrid had assured her their relationship was the real thing, that I was a distraction, just a manifestation of Britt's resistance to accepting her true self. Astrid had told her to not allow herself to be seduced by me or her fear.

Astrid had some pretty impressive knowledge and skills. She might not have liked shrinks but she sure thought like one.

Britt was torn and the more time she spent with me, the angrier Astrid became. They'd had a big blowout.

I had mixed feelings about that. Sad they'd had a blowout but glad because it meant maybe things were leaning my way.

I stopped paying attention to myself and listened as she told me she was making herself crazy over whether Astrid was seeing another woman. She'd taken a chance coming to The Palms but had wanted to confront the truth.

She hated being jealous and insecure, and uncertain about her own sexuality. Here she was, flirting with me but upset about the possibility Astrid might be doing the same thing or more. It was playing havoc with her and making it hard to think straight.

I told her I understood, I knew about jealousy and was

experiencing some at that moment. But that wasn't what she wanted to hear. She didn't really care about my feelings while hers were storming.

I related to her being more concerned with her own feelings than with mine. Since I was ultimately more interested in me, I was more focused on digesting the news than supporting her. As a therapist, I can usually put my feelings aside and attend to the other, but I was feeling disheartened about my prospects and not very available to her.

She continued to tell me about her jealousy and worry. Her pain was apparent. Mine was just starting to gnaw. It was hard to offer empathy when I wanted some for myself.

We ended up driving back to the hotel mostly in silence. She wanted to go to her room and be alone, and I didn't argue.

CHAPTER FORTY-EIGHT

# DÉJÀ VU ALL OVER AGAIN

**Saturday night—part 1**

THE BLINKING RED light called out across the room. I wanted to ignore it but I've never been that guy. To my relief, it wasn't Lieutenant Golk calling for my immediate surrender.

Trixie wanted me to meet her ASAP at the cabin. I couldn't figure out why other than it involving another round of my being tied up. I wasn't eager for that. While I might be able to temporarily soothe myself with some rebound sex, what she was offering wasn't really my thing.

That said, I was tidying up go to the Institute for the send-off soirée and could swing by the cabin to see what was up. While my romantic hopes had been with Britt—and some of my fantasies with Layla (and Gabriela)—Trixie was the one person I'd spent the most meaningful time with; being with her might be a good way to say goodbye to the conference.

I didn't know what to do about my playing detective. I hadn't gotten to tell Britt what Trixie had told me about Goodst and Johnny Trombone, or about Jordana and the ransom money. Whatever clues

I'd acquired were in my hands, and my hands wanted to wash themselves clean of the them all.

Britt was the reason I'd gotten involved in the whole mystery and now I'd lost the impetus. I'd enjoyed finding things out. It was akin to my therapy job, except sleuthing came with higher blood pressure and a different set of legal and ethical issues.

At first, I'd been helping out to get in good with Britt, but as events had unfolded, I'd realized I was enjoying trying to put my skills to work outside the classroom and office. They say those who can, do; and those who can't, teach. Maybe those who can are detectives and those who can't are therapists.

I ought to admit something. I have obsessive-compulsive tendencies. Well, so do we all in our own way. My way propels me to finish what I start. Once I find myself actively engaged in something, I need to finish it. I can't do some of the dishes. I can leave dirty ones in the sink, but once I've decided to wash them it's all of them. I know it doesn't make any difference whether I do or don't finish the dishes, but that knowledge only takes me so far.

Until I got in my car and started to drive home, I'd want to figure out whodunit. And, truthfully, I'd keep trying to figure it out…

Like I said, my need to complete things doesn't actually make much of a difference in real life, although I do get a lot accomplished. Of course, finishing the dishes, or the mystery, comes at the expense of not doing something else. How little of the conference I'd actually attended was a case in point.

Before heading for the Institute, I left a message with the hotel operator to deliver a message to Lieutenant Golk at 10:00 p.m. Chet and Layla had said something unforeseen would happen. If some of that unforeseen was coming my way I wanted Golk to know about the hidden cabin.

People were arriving at the Institute and the event had officially begun. I was enjoying the visual display, but my feet were taking me down the path to the cabin. The light was still shifting so I could easily make my way; when (and if) I left later, it would be more challenging. Of course, if I left in the morning, it would be easier to see but likely harder to walk.

I passed the *No Trespassing* sign and was cognizant once again I wasn't heeding the warnings I'd been given. Even though it was dusk, there was no light coming from the cabin. I wondered if Trixie had gotten tired of waiting and taken off.

I knocked. I waited.

Slowly the door opened and a dim shaft of light glowed before me.

"Are you alone?" Trixie asked.

"Yes, of course. Are you?"

She opened the door just enough to let me step in. Then she quickly closed the door behind me and locked it.

I could one light flickering and that she was dressed to play—a red-and-black leather biker outfit complete with over-the-knee black boots and a red whip at the ready.

Then I felt something hard pressing heavily into the back of my head. I became warm and gushy as unconsciousness enveloped me.

I awoke. I couldn't feel the sheets gently surrounding my body. I tried to open my eyes to see what was wrong but they wouldn't budge. The pain throbbing in my head was limiting my desire to do anything.

In my grogginess, I slowly realized there was a lot wrong, and not just the missing sheets and the grinding tectonic plates in my head. Any movement seemed out of the question.

I needed a visual aid.

I gradually opened my eyes. And quickly closed them.

The light was blinding; I'd changed lanes too fast.

I tried opening them again at little-old-lady-from-Pasadena speed.

I was back in the chair. Alone in the room. Tied up and ready for the adventures ahead.

I had no idea if it was still Saturday. That thought pleased me because it proved my brain was capable of having a thought. That was the only thought that pleased me.

I heard something else. Moaning. Was it me? Could be, but this sounded more distant. I twisted my head to see if I could find the source.

Big mistake.

I'd forgotten to remember not to move.

I got the reminder.

Being a healthcare provider, I've learned a thing or two about healthy living. I knew it was time to focus on some internal healing. I didn't have much at my disposal, just my breath. I inhaled deeply and held the air in my lungs. I remembered hearing there was nothing ten deep breaths wouldn't help.

I'm here to tell you that isn't true. I did a few more. The pain came down to a nine. It wasn't much but it was progress. I kept at it.

Then I heard another moan.

I wanted to find the source but knew I couldn't look. A masseuse once told me about the reparative qualities of sighing and how it enhances lung function. I figured it might be a good way to start. I sighed in slow motion, which may not have optimized the healing effect.

"I'm very upset with you," I heard Trixie say. "Why don't you tell me what I want to know. Then we can kiss and make up."

I was willing to tell her whatever she wanted for a couple of aspirin.

"And when we're done, I'll let you have the worm in there. You can do whatever you want with him."

Under the right circumstances, that might have sounded like a memorable way to start an evening. Right now, I felt myself shriveling.

"I'm not going to tell you shit."

*That's the right attitude*, I wanted to shout out.

Before I could get a fix on whose voice it was, I heard the familiar crack of the whip.

"If you don't tell me, I'm going to have to really hurt you. You don't want that, nor do I, but I need to know. If I have to hurt you I will. Don't worry, I'll find a way to like it."

I guess I wasn't the only one tied up here. Seemingly it wasn't enough for Trixie and Goodst to have one tricked-out chair; was there was another in a room I'd yet to visit?

"If you hurt me, you'd better kill me or I'll kill you."

After a pause Trixie stated the good news and bad: "I'm not a killer like you. I just like to have some fun. But you betrayed me and I want to know what happened."

"You'll never know. I'm not going to tell you anything except bringing that imbecile here will only make things worse."

I wondered if Lieutenant Golk would show up. Was it already ten? I had no idea if the cavalry would come save the day or even what day it was.

"I can handle him. I thought you'd like having him. I got him as a present for you."

"He's nothing."

"But he's yours if you tell me."

I wasn't sure who I was rooting for but the impasse seemed to work for me. I kept breathing and sighing.

"When are you going to give up? I'm not going to play this game anymore. Let me go, and we can play some other games. Then I'll take care of the shrink."

"I can't let you go now," Trixie said. "How do I know you won't hurt me?"

"Why would I hurt you?"

"Because I was able to trick you and tie you up. You'll want to punish me."

"Of course I'll do that. You want me to do that. But I won't go too far. You know that. And after, I'll take care of him."

*Well, that settles it. I'm on Trixie's side.*

We all seemed at an impasse.

Out of the corner of my eye I saw Trixie. My head slowly turned. She was framed in the doorway and moving my way. I tried to play unconscious. It wasn't that hard. The whip across my chest ended the pretense.

"Come on, dead meat. It's time for you to get up."

She leaned over me. I could see she was flushed and sweaty. Her eyes had a wired sparkle to them I didn't like. She seemed high on adrenaline, and some other substance. I tried to project some heartiness into the conversation. "Hi. It's good to see you again. I see we skipped the foreplay. How you doing?"

"I'm doing just fine. But you should be more concerned with how you're doing."

"Well, I'm aware I'm tied up again but I don't think we had visitors in the other room the last time. Is this part of the big event tonight?"

Trixie came close to me and whispered loudly, "It's going to be your big event, that's for sure."

"It looks like you're going to be a busy girl."

"A busy woman who's very upset," she said.

"Well, is there anything I can do?"

"You can eat shit," yelled the voice next door.

"As you can tell," Trixie pointed out, "Astrid is very upset too."

"Well, I guess we're all in this together. Hi, Astrid. How are things over there?"

I'd tried for cavalier but sounded more juvenile.

"Fuck you!"

"Okay, we might be doing that over here. You never know," I said to annoy her.

In a softer aside to Trixie I asked, "Why do you think she's so mad at me? What have I done?"

Trixie seemed to light up. She stood straight and said, "She wants to hurt you bad for messing with Britt."

"She sure is the jealous type," I whispered, in hopes of forming some sort of alliance. "I haven't had sex with her girlfriend. You and I have had some serious sex, good times, and meaningful conversations, and you and I aren't upset. Well, you, maybe a little. But Astrid wants to hurt me for flirting? I thought we lived in the free-love era. What's the big deal?"

I thought—hoped—Trixie was softening a little and decided to double down.

"I don't know if you've seen Britt but, frankly, she's not in your league. Astrid should be grateful you even talk with her. Come on, get real."

"Did you hear that, Astrid?" Trixie asked. "He thinks Britt isn't even in my league."

Astrid didn't answer right away. I guessed Trixie was the other woman Britt was worried about. Who knew how Trixie and Astrid's lives were intertwined? They certainly seemed to be more than new acquaintances. I could see Astrid and Trixie being attracted to each other. And Astrid being attracted to Britt. I felt the same way, more or less.

Astrid, not one for kissing up, told Trixie, "You're nothing compared to her. Or Jordana. Or Gabriela."

Ouch. That couldn't have felt good to hear.

Given the distorted way Trixie handled pleasure and pain, it was difficult to figure out how it affected her, though affect her it did.

*Okay*, I told myself. *You've spent years going to graduate school and practicing your trade. Now's the time to find out what you've learned.*

"You don't have to take that shit from her. You're much too smart and together to have to worry about her."

She liked that. Who doesn't like their ego massaged?

She took her own deep breath and her countenance shifted. Astrid must have felt the change. "Don't listen to that weasel. He's a wimp and a backstabber. You're a bigger fool than he is if you let him take you in with his shrink games."

Game on.

Trixie stared at me with a bad combination of distrust and displeasure.

I knew that to battle with Astrid I'd need to dig deep and fight in the trenches. Britt had told me the things Astrid had said to her. They were incisive, persuasive, and challenging.

It would come down to Astrid and me proving our trustworthiness. Who offered the road better traveled?

I knew I couldn't win by singing my praises and discrediting her. I needed to bring out another paradoxical intervention—discredit myself and agree there were good reasons not to trust me. It was a questionable plan, but I wasn't exactly in the best shape.

I began so only Trixie could hear. "Sure, I want to be nice to you so you don't hurt me or let her hurt me. But come on. We've been vulnerable with each other and had intimate moments together. Because we've trusted each other, I'm going to tell you something I don't want to tell you but think you need to know."

"Go on."

I wanted to think her tone was encouraging, but it could just as well have meant hurry up and get to the point. I get that sometimes.

"I'm really afraid. Being tied up by you was mostly fun and games. But this time I got knocked out, put in restraints, and I'm being yelled at and threatened. It scares me. I'm also afraid of what might happen to you. I want to protect us both but I'm worried you might think I'm not trustworthy enough to get us out of this mess. I get that. You have a longer, more involved relationship with

Astrid. That's a good thing. Or maybe it's been a good thing. But the question is, will it be a good thing going forward? Who's most apt to be able to help you? The person who got you into this mess or the person whose job it is to help people out?"

I hadn't said quite what I'd set out to, but I liked it. It was true enough.

She looked like she was listening to some of it at least. So I added, "Sure, I can banter and play with you. That's fun. But something else is going on here tonight. The good news is, you're in control. You can make things turn out the way you want. I want to help you make that happen."

I was warming up but she'd stopped listening.

Astrid wasn't listening either but that didn't stop her from replying, "I don't know what that asshole is saying but whatever it is, don't believe it. He's a con artist. Let me go and I'll deal with him so he won't bother us anymore."

Trixie didn't move. Then she said, more to herself than either one of us, "I've gotten myself into a lot of trouble and I don't know how to get out."

"Why not let me try?" I said.

"I can fix everything," Astrid offered.

"No one can help me," was Trixie's response.

To me she asked, "Will you tell the police we knocked you out and I tied you up?"

"I haven't told them anything up until now and I have no intention of changing that. I can keep this between us. No problem."

"Don't believe him," Astrid said. "He'll rat you out the first chance he gets."

Trixie remained still.

I kept pushing. "Okay, why not just keep me tied up and tell me what's going on? As long as I'm tied up there isn't much I can do. And maybe I can help you figure out how to get out of this mess."

It made sense to me.

She paused for a few moments, then went and found her answer. She downed a shot. Poured another, left it, and came over to me. Astrid must have been fuming but I was pretty happy. Small wins. An article I'd read in grad school had advocated for them. They build on each other.

Astrid wasn't a good loser. "You'd better keep your mouth shut, bitch. If you betray me, I'm going to kill you."

CHAPTER FORTY-NINE

# TOO MUCH INFORMATION

**Saturday night—part 2**

TRIXIE LOOKED BOTH spooked and excited if that were possible. I hadn't seen her face when earlier Astrid had said she'd kill her, but hearing it a second time didn't make it any less palatable. It was hard to know what was a game and what was real. Trixie was dressed up in her play clothes and I imagined Astrid was as well. But telling someone you're going to kill them is not exactly play-date material. Yet Trixie seemed to be drawn in and repelled at the same time.

I could barely hear her when she whispered, "Astrid told me she killed Goodst. She said she did it for me because she knew he had power over me and he'd ultimately destroy me."

I was stunned. While I wanted to celebrate discovering whodunit, I wasn't in much of a position to do anything about it. My only desire was for Astrid to remain tied up until we could get out of there and call the police. That is, if I could convince Trixie to call the police… otherwise I'd be betraying her trust and being that backstabber Astrid said I was.

Trixie must have seen my wheels turning because she filled in some of the gaps. "Astrid and I have used the cabin on and off for years. We planned to catch up this week. When it was announced Wilhelm was missing, she came to my house to see if I was okay. When I wasn't there, she came over here. Unfortunately, she caught me kissing Wilhelm goodbye in the doorway. When I started back to the Institute, she confronted me. I told her I loved Wilhelm and we'd planned the kidnapping so we could run away together. She got very upset. We had a big argument and she stormed off."

I wanted to say I thought you wanted to run off with Johnny but knew enough to shut up and listen.

"Astrid told me she'd come back to the cabin to 'talk' to Wilhelm. She really wanted to blackmail him. She's always had a thing about money and I'm sure she saw an opportunity to make some. Before she knocked on the door, she peeked in the window and saw Wilhelm in an animated discussion with Jordana. She didn't hear all the conversation, just enough to know Jordana had found out that Wilhelm and I were planning on running away and Jordana was also furious."

"I get that."

"Astrid stayed hidden until Jordana stormed out and they talked for a bit. Then she went in and confronted Wilhelm about running away with me and staging the kidnapping. She thought he was just using me. He got upset at her for interfering and their argument escalated. They both have trigger tempers and started to physically fight. She's much stronger. She said she beat him up pretty badly and was on her way out when he pulled a gun on her. Before he could shoot her, she jumped on him and…"

Trixie was shaken and on the verge of tears.

"What are you two doing in there?" Astrid yelled. "Are you fucking? It's awfully quiet. Can't he get it up?"

"We're talking, Astrid," said Trixie, as if to a child. "I have something I have to discuss with him and it'll help us all if you'd just be quiet and let us continue."

"Fuck you."

"When I came back to the cabin, Astrid was here and Wilhelm was dead. It was horrific." The tears came. "She convinced me if the police found him here, I'd be implicated. We just needed to keep our mouths shut and no one would suspect us. I was upset with Astrid for killing him and worried the police would blame me. It was terrible. I didn't know what to do."

"I get it. What did you do?"

Her story had changed some from her first telling. That time she'd discovered Goodst's body in the cabin and there'd been no Astrid and she was running off with Johnny. I wondered which version was closer to the truth. Or if there was yet another.

"Astrid was so sure of herself and I wasn't. I was terrified someone would find us with the body, but we managed to get him to his house and leave him there. The police would find out he wasn't killed there, but they don't know about this place and have no reason to suspect either one of us."

"Okay, I kinda get that. So why is she tied up next door?"

"I didn't know what to do," she said, yet again.

Too many times, I realized.

As a trained therapist it doesn't take long for me to hear what someone's really saying. Especially if they say it over and over. I'd been taught in graduate school I needn't worry if I missed something because if it was important, the client would repeat it until I heard it. It had taken me a while to clue in, but I was getting the picture that Trixie had difficulty knowing what to do.

"I didn't know what to do," she said. "When you and the police started to ask a lot of questions, I got nervous. When Johnny was killed, I got really scared."

"Okay."

"Then you told me Jordana stole the rest of the ransom money. Why? What was she doing? I was confused about everything so I called Astrid and asked her to meet me at a bar downtown where we used to go dancing."

"Got it."

"She tried to be reassuring but it didn't help. We had some drinks. That helped a little. When I told her about Jordana stealing the money, she was dismissive and said the bitch was just out to get something for herself. A gold-digger. When I told her I'd heard about Jordana from you, she said you could be lying and not to trust you."

"I seem to be getting that response more these days."

"Anyway, we talked and drank and agreed to meet back at the cabin in a couple of hours to blow off some steam. There was nothing more we could do to protect ourselves, so we might as well party until further notice, is what she said. I wasn't in any shape to argue so I went home, did some things, and came back to the cabin."

"All right. It's coming together. I must have talked with her after you two met but before she came back over here. She wasn't liking me but she didn't seem to be hating me. What happened when you both got here?"

"We got high and things got pretty charged. We were drinking a lot. She's a nasty drunk and things escalated. She asked about our night together and got very jealous. She started talking about hurting you and that you were a sexist, smug pig."

"Yeah, well I'm working on that."

"At first I thought she just wanted to yell at you but then she talked about hurting you for real. I told her that wasn't a good idea, that even though you were stuck on yourself, there was no reason to hurt you. She told me to shut up and then got the whip and told me it was time to really party. I know she likes to be dominant so we always start with her. But she really likes to be dominated, too, so sooner or later she'd want me take control. So that's what we did."

"And that's why she's tied up in the other room. She dominated and then you dominated. Okay, I get that too. But why knock me over the head and tie me up? I thought we were past that part of our relationship."

"Because I didn't know what to do. I wasn't sure about anything and things were getting out of control. I knew I'd feel better if I was in control."

For someone who didn't know a lot, she was pretty clear about that.

"I'm sorry. I had to knock you out because I didn't know how else to get you into the chair. You didn't seem to like it as much as I'd hoped you would."

"Well, there is that," I said. "How about I accept your apology, you let me go, and we figure out how to resolve this whole thing?"

She went and downed another shot.

She came over and released one of my hands. Just as I was flexing and feeling more hopeful, she took some handcuffs I hadn't seen and put them around my free wrist, pulled it over to my other hand and wed them. That done, she released my other hand, undid my legs, and told me to stand. My body wasn't excited about the prospect but she flexed her whip and I got up.

The good thing about pain is, usually, if you intensely feel it in one place, you don't feel it so much in others. Whatever tingling and discomfort I felt in my arms and legs couldn't hold a candle to the earthquake in my head. Even a lash across my chest didn't distract me.

Too quickly for me, and too slowly for her, she led me into the other room that was barely lit by the one light from the room we'd just left. Astrid was in a matching chair. She didn't look happy to see me. I wasn't sure how I felt about seeing her. The S&M regalia that adorned what there was of her outfit made me doubly glad she was constrained. I could tell she was seething; if she were let loose, I'd be in serious trouble.

Trixie pulled up a chair right in front of Astrid, sat me down, and tied me up.

"Okay, you two," Trixie said. "Make everything better."

"Fuck off," was Astrid's starting position.

"If you two can't figure things out, I'm going to have to leave you both here."

I wasn't keen on that. But if it was still Saturday night, maybe Golk would come and save the day.

"So, Astrid," I said. "Any chance you and I can figure something out so we all can get out of this in good shape?"

"Trixie and I will be fine," she said with a sneer. "It's you who's not going to be in good shape."

"I'm happy to hear you think you and Trixie can patch things up but I don't get why you wish me so much harm. So I flirted with Britt. What's the big deal? You're rooming with her, playing games with Trixie, and who knows what else. I thought you were a liberated woman."

"I am a completely liberated woman who can't abide sniveling losers. My life is of no concern to you and what I do is none of your business."

This wasn't going to get us anywhere but I didn't know how to proceed. I was feeling a bit Trixie-ish.

Then the front door crashed open and a voice yelled, "Hands up!"

The cavalry had arrived and I rejoiced.

# CHAPTER FIFTY

# THINGS AIN'T ALWAYS WHAT THEY SEEM

**Saturday night—part 3**

"HANDS UP" MAY be a tried-and-true command but it's not always adhered to. I was willing but Trixie was the only one in the room able.

I didn't recognize the man. He barged in waving a gun and repeated his request. He quickly assessed the situation. Astrid's and my restraints made him wonder just what kind of scene we had going on here. He went over to a wooden chest and pulled out some rope. I wondered whether he, too, had had some prior experience in the cabin. He grabbed the rope, pulled over a chair, and tied up Trixie next to Astrid and me.

Just a cozy little group.

"What's got into you, Rory?" Trixie said. "You just can't come forcing your way in here with a gun."

Too late for that observation, I thought, but at least Trixie was speaking up.

"Shut up, bitch," Rory said as he strode over to her and stuck the gun against her backside. "I know you're in this thing up to your neck. If you don't level with me, I'm going to give you a new asshole."

Trixie didn't say anything.

Too anxious to stand still, he left us and went into the other room. I heard him going through drawers as if searching for something. When he came back I took a closer look at him. He looked familiar but I couldn't place him. Had he been at the convention? He was definitely wired on something. Jittery and sweating, he paced about, searching for something.

"Okay. I know some shit is going on here. Where's the money?"

None of us said anything but I made the connection. He was one of the muscle-bound men from the health club. It didn't seem to be a hail-fellow-well-met moment.

"Shit shit shit," he said, appraising the situation. Not satisfied, he waved his gun at each of us. "If you don't tell me…"

Maybe I could use some of my communication skills.

"What makes you think we know anything about the money?"

As if noticing me for the first time—understandable given what Trixie and Astrid were wearing—he barked, "You set up Jordana, asshole. What did you do with the money?"

"What did I do with the money? I didn't do anything. I saw Jordana take it from the safe at the Institute and bring it to the health club. That's all I did."

"That's what you say, but Jordana says when she got to the club the money wasn't in the bag." He came closer to me. "She says you switched it out."

"What? That's impossible. I never touched the money. I never cared about the money. I was just trying to find out who'd killed Goodst."

"Jordana said you were a shrink. Of course you care about money. See? You're bullshitting me right now."

My communication skills weren't exactly paying off. But not one to give up, I plowed on. "The only reason I was following Jordana was because she was acting suspiciously at the Institute.

When I thought she'd stolen the money, I decided to see what she did with it. That makes sense, doesn't it?"

"Are you saying Jordana killed Goodst and stole the money?"

"Not anymore. Why don't you ask Trixie and Astrid?"

He looked at them. They looked at him. While diverting his attention had seemed like a good idea at the time, I now realized it might not have been the wisest choice.

"That sniveling shrink is the one who killed Goodst and stole the money," said Astrid gleefully.

"I knew it!" he said, as if glad to have his theory confirmed. "Jordana said not to trust you." He stood in front of me and pointed the gun right between my eyes. "Where is it?"

*Damn it, Astrid,* I wanted to say. But I'd given her the floor. Why had I thought she'd do right by me?

"Look, obviously I'm in no position to lie to you but I told you all I know about the money. Last I saw it, Jordana was stuffing it into her bag. And if you care about who killed Goodst, she did," I said, nodding in Astrid's direction. "She took the money too."

CHAPTER FIFTY-ONE

# HOUDINI, I AIN'T

**Saturday night—part 4**

THE MOMENT THE lights went out, I knew it wasn't the cavalry arriving. Just more trouble. It was Saturday night, after all, and if things were going to build to the ultimate climax, this was the time to do it.

Trixie, Astrid, and I were tied up in our cozy little circle and Rory had his gun pointed at my head. At least, that was the last place I'd seen it pointed.

"What the fuck?" yelled Rory.

No one answered him. An eerie silence took over the room. Then I heard a thud. And more silence.

My eyes had yet to adjust to the dark; I just saw paler shades of it. I heard some movement next to me but wasn't sure if it was one of us or one of them.

There was some indiscernible commotion and groaning.

Then I heard fast-moving footsteps headed in the direction of the door and it slammed shut. Then silence.

After a few moments, Trixie whispered, "Is everyone okay?"

"I'm okay," I said, reassuring us both. "But Rory might be napping."

"Astrid?" Trixie asked.

There was more moaning, then, "What the fuck?"

Ah, Rory was awake.

"Are you all right?" Trixie asked, knowing something herself about thunking people on the head.

"Yeah, I guess so," he said, to no relief on my part.

"See if you can find your way over to the table," said Trixie. "There are some matches and candles there."

Trixie asked again after Astrid.

Perhaps she was stonewalling.

Rory lit a match.

Or gone.

"Listen," I said. "Astrid is scampering out of here. Why don't you untie us and the three of us can go after her?"

He didn't have too much time to think, and maybe the bump wasn't helping his thought process, since it would have been quicker to take off alone. Or maybe the blackout had bonded us in some way. He cut Trixie loose and took off. Trixie undid my handcuffs, grabbed her purse, and we quickly headed toward the Institute.

The joint was jumping. I could see the party lights and hear the music blaring. People were engaged in all sorts of activities I wouldn't have minded joining. I wondered what Layla and Chet were doing and whether I'd have a chance to enjoy something that didn't involve bondage and threats. Perhaps Gabriela would be there and lower her standards for the night.

Rory was scanning the parking lot for any sign of Astrid and whoever had set her free. He must have spotted them because he ran toward his car, yelling over his shoulder, "They're getting away."

Trixie and I looked at each other and we each sprinted to our own cars. It was as close as I'd ever get to a Le Mans start. We made our way out of the lot and onto the highway headed back to town. Rory first, then Trixie, and me bringing up the rear.

I wasn't really all that interested in following Astrid or bumping into Rory again. I figured Astrid would head back to the hotel to connect with Britt, grab her stuff, and take off. When I got closer to town I took an exit. If Trixie wanted to find me, she'd go to the hotel. If Rory wanted to find me, well, I didn't want him to find me.

I checked my watch. It was nine thirty. I could get back to the hotel in time to tell the operator to cancel the ten o'clock call to Golk. And, what the hell, I might see about tidying up and driving back out to the Institute.

Or go to bed and call it a night.

When I entered the lobby, I went up to the front desk and told the unlucky soul on the night shift that I'd locked myself out of room 315. Could I have another key? He handed over their key and we wished each other a good night. I made a quick pit stop in my room to cancel my previous message to Golk and give him a new one. Then I headed over to 315.

I hesitated, then carefully placed my head against the door. No sound. Was there no one there? Was it just a quiet moment? Was the door mostly soundproof? It was a quality hotel.

Do I follow up with a knock or let myself in? Do I do the polite thing or barge in and catch whomever doing whatever?

A quote from Bertrand Russell popped into my head. "The fundamental cause of the trouble is that in the modern world the stupid are cocksure while the intelligent are full of doubt."

Perhaps my questioning was a sign of intelligence, I reassured myself. Then stupidly, I did a cocksure thing.

I slipped the key into the lock and pushed the door open. Astrid was changing out of her S&M outfit and Britt was packing. Neither seemed particularly surprised to see me. Mostly they were annoyed, but I'd gotten used to that.

"Good evening," I said, staring at Britt. "I'm sorry to barge in on you like this but, as Astrid knows, I've had a busy night. I just wanted to check in and make sure everything's all right. It looks like you've found Astrid as well."

"I'm fine," Britt said crisply. "We don't really have time to talk. We're about to leave."

"Okay. But, Astrid, how did you get back here? Who freed you?"

"Fuck off. It's none of your business."

"All right, we can pass on that for now. But, Britt, didn't you want to say goodbye, leave me a note or something?"

"No," Astrid said. "She didn't."

"That's not true," Britt replied. "It's just that I don't have time now. I'll be in touch later."

"Okay, that's good to know. But before you go, I deserve a few answers. Astrid has threatened to kill me, some hired muscle of Jordana's was going to shoot me, and I've spent the better part of this conference trying to help you get your tapes and keep your nose clean."

"What do you want to know?" she asked.

"Astrid killed Goodst. Do you really want to be running off with her?"

"She didn't kill him," she said with a matter-of-fact tone while continuing to pack.

Trixie told me Astrid said she'd killed Goodst. I thought she was telling the truth, but she was an adept liar.

"Okay, if she didn't kill him, do you know who did? And while you're at it, will you tell me whether all this running around really was about your tapes or is there something else involved here?"

"Don't tell him shit," said Astrid, supportive as ever. Having exchanged her cabin outfit for jeans and a flannel shirt, she'd lost none of her verve. "Let me just kick him in the nuts. Then we'll get out of here before Jordana's thug finds us."

"No, he deserves to know."

I was glad to see Britt stand up for herself—and me. Not an altogether easy task when Astrid was ready to pounce.

"I know I shouldn't tell you this. Astrid is just trying to protect me. But I want you to promise me you won't tell anyone."

"I know I asked you to promise not to tell about Trixie's part in the kidnapping and you agreed, but murder is an entirely different thing."

"Are you going to promise or not?"

"I know we've bent, well, broken some rules this week but I don't know about this. It's asking a lot and I could get in a lot of trouble if the police find out."

"Come on. Just promise or we're leaving now."

"Yeah, asshole. Do you want to hear what she has to say or not?"

"I do but I'm being put in a very difficult position. If the police ask me anything, and they've been talking to me, I can't promise I won't tell the truth."

"How about if I become your client?" Britt suggested. "That way you'd have to keep it secret."

"It would certainly be easier for me to keep your confidence. But I'd have to report your abuse."

"My other therapist already did that," Britt said.

"Right. I forgot."

"What if I told you I'd broken a law?"

"I don't have to report that unless you're planning on doing it again, in which case that might be considered harm to yourself or possibly others."

"Okay," she said, and went into her purse. She opened her wallet and handed me a twenty. "I want to be your client."

"Stop. Take it back. We were talking theoretically," I replied, not taking the money. "I don't want to be your therapist. I want to date you, take you to a baseball game, have a hot dog, peanuts, and a malt."

"That's very nice," she said, putting the twenty in my hand. "We can talk about it later."

"I don't know about this," I said, holding the money loosely. "If you're my client, I'm not supposed to have a hot dog, malt, or anything else with you for at least two years."

"That seals it!" Astrid said. "Now just take the money like a good shrink and listen to what she says so we can get out of here."

CHAPTER FIFTY-TWO

# IS THIS THE TRUTH?

**Saturday night—part 5**

"I'M LISTENING."

"You remember I told you Goodst raped me when I was his client?"

"Yes." I wasn't sure she'd used that term but my memory isn't that good. Either way, I knew he'd taken advantage of her and it was for the best she saw his abuse for what it was.

"Well, what I told you was the truth, as was my going back to the Institute, making a scene, and being kicked out. But what I didn't tell you was we'd slept together for several years, sometimes in the back cabin."

"The back cabin?"

"Yeah. I freed Astrid. I figured she might be there."

"Okay, I guess I'm glad you found her, but why free her if she's a killer?"

"She didn't kill him. When you couldn't find the tapes, I went up to the cabin to see if they were there. I found Goodst and demanded he hand them over. We got into a shouting match. He told me to go fuck myself. The tapes were his and I was never going to get them."

She took a breath.

"He said they were useless. He couldn't even get off on them anymore and he'd destroyed them because they were worthless to him. He said I was an egomaniac who just wanted to exploit him. I called him a crazy, evil man. He grabbed me and told me we should try again and see if time had improved my skills. We fought. I'm not that weak girl anymore."

She spoke fast, her voice cracking as she became increasingly upset.

"He could never take no for an answer. He tried to tie me up and put me in the chair but I knew all his tricks."

She stopped. Composed herself.

"He threw me down on the floor. We wrestled. He was talking dirty and telling me how he'd fuck my brains out and I'd love him more than ever. That infuriated me and I pushed him off me. He tripped, fell back, and hit his head on the fireplace."

She paused for a moment. "I thought he was playing games but when he didn't move, I came closer and realized he was dead."

She avoided looking at me as she continued.

"I didn't know what to do. I was terrified. I ran out and went back to the hotel as fast as I could. I told Astrid what happened. She convinced me he deserved it and nobody need know, but if I came forward they'd think I'd kidnapped him and planned his murder."

"That makes some sense."

"Astrid told me to stay here while she went back to the cabin and wiped off any fingerprints. She looked for the tapes too—searched everywhere—but couldn't find them. She cleaned up everything and left."

"That's all?" I asked.

"That's enough," said Astrid.

"But I thought the police said he'd been shot."

"They did," Astrid said. "But that was just to catch Britt off guard. Typical pig shit."

"But that still doesn't make sense." I turned and faced Astrid. "You told Trixie you'd killed him. Now Britt says she did. What gives?"

"You did that? I didn't know you knew Trixie." Britt said.

"I said that to protect you."

"Okay, I get that," I said. "But you convinced Trixie."

"Fuck off."

"Now I don't understand," said Britt. "I appreciate your protecting me. But why would you tell her? How do you know her? She could have told the police you'd done it."

"I would have told them she made it up. I don't really know her. They could never prove I did it. I wasn't worried about it."

"I don't know," I said. "The more I think about it, just like Britt believes you, so did Trixie."

"Shut up," she told me as she stuffed her clothes into a suitcase. "It's time for us to go. Britt told you what you wanted to know so we're leaving."

"I don't get it," Britt said, facing Astrid. "Why did you tell Trixie? What's this got to do with Trixie?"

"It's nothing."

"I don't believe you," I said. "You shot Goodst."

"You don't know what you're talking about. Britt just told you she killed him. I went over there and he was dead. I cleaned up, searched the place, and took him over to his house and dumped him. End of story."

"I don't think so. When you got there, he was either awake or unconscious."

Turning to Britt, I asked, "Did you check him closely before you left?"

"I did look at him but I didn't touch him or take his pulse or anything. There was blood behind his head and he wasn't moving so I assumed he was dead. But I can't say for certain."

"He was dead all right," Astrid said. "Now we have to go."

"I'm not so sure you didn't go back there and find him alive. You figured you could finish the job. After all, he'd betrayed your trust as well. Knowing you the way I do, you were jealous Goodst had fucked Britt in the cabin but never taken you back there. You weren't in her class even back then. So why not finish off what Britt had started? But you decided not to tell Britt. That way she'd be forever indebted to you for keeping her secret. It would give you some of the power and control you like so much."

"You're a jealous prick. Making up stories. Come on, Britt. Let's go."

Britt turned to Astrid and looked her directly in the eye. "Tell me, Astrid. Did you really kill him? Why would you not tell me? Tell me the truth."

"You want the truth?" Astrid said. "The truth is, he deserved what he got."

Someone knocked on the door.

It wasn't my place to open it but I did.

# CHAPTER FIFTY-THREE

# WHOSE TRUTH ARE YOU GOING TO BELIEVE?

**Saturday night—part 6**

THERE STOOD RORY and Jordana. He was armed with a gun, she with an unpleasant look on her face. He must have followed Astrid to the hotel, called Jordana, and they'd decided to come up and visit.

I invited them in.

"About to leave?" Jordana asked. "I hope you don't mind us holding you up for a while."

Astrid hissed. Britt turned, a questioning look on her face. And me? I worried.

"Okay," said Rory, also not one to linger on foreplay. "Where's the money?"

I admired his focus.

"Don't ask me," I said. "The last I saw of it, Jordana had it."

"That's not the money I want," said Rory. "I want the money that was stolen earlier."

"I don't know what you're talking about," replied Britt. "I've nothing to do with any money. I paid my ransom share. Why would I steal it?"

That made good sense but I could see some holes. Just because she'd paid up didn't mean she wouldn't want to withdraw later. And given her relationship with Goodst, I couldn't see why she'd even paid in the first place. Sure, she'd said she wanted him back so she could personally take him down, but that wasn't all that compelling.

Before I could focus on those disquieting thoughts, Astrid, never one to sit quietly for long, produced her standard reply, "Fuck off," then added, "I don't know where the money went or who Trombone is. I've never heard of him. You're barking up the wrong tree. Why don't you get out of here so we can go about our business?"

You had to hand it to Astrid. She plays a strong hand.

Of course, you don't spend years working with Goodst and not have some skills as well. Before Jordana could exhibit them, Rory wanted to show his.

"Don't fuck with us," he shouted, his eyes darting. "We know someone has the money, and if you don't tell us I'll fuck you over."

It didn't look like anyone would be confessing anytime soon and I didn't want to test Rory's abilities. I had one of those I-don't-know-what-to-do moments. Most likely something unpleasant was about to happen. I didn't have a lot of experience I could bring to the fore but that didn't stop me from doing something.

"Say, Rory, I have an idea. You tell us why you suspect us, we'll tell you who we suspect, and then collectively maybe we can figure out who took the money. There's no reason for us to be on opposite sides with this. We're happy to help you find it. We just don't have it. Or, at least, I don't."

Jordana stepped over to me. "You know, the more I see you the less I like you. You really grind on a person. We're not a team here. We're—"

Just as we were about to find out what we were, there was another knock on the door. Rory gestured for us to be quiet and crept over to the peephole. Then he flung the door open and pulled

Trixie in. The party was definitely picking up. Especially since she was still wearing her black-and-red leather biker outfit. Her entrance certainly garnered our attention.

We all stood there for a moment. While nobody had planned for this gathering, it seemed there were answers for the taking if only we could find a way to tease them out.

*Take responsibility*, I said to myself. *You know what Eldridge Cleaver said: "If you're not a part of the solution, you're a part of the problem."* I wasn't sure which part I belonged to, but that didn't stop me.

"So," I said, making quick eye contact with everyone, "the way I see it, we might be able to solve this mystery together. As far as I can tell, we have the person who confessed to Goodst's murder in the room. We also have the person most likely to have killed Johnny Trombone, And, the person who stole the money."

"What?" Trixie said. "Someone—one of us—confessed to killing Wilhelm?"

"Actually, two people confessed to killing him but I'm not sure either of them did it."

"What are you talking about?" said Britt.

"I'm happy to explain. If it's all right with you, Rory," I said, paying proper homage to the gun in his hand. "I'd like to ask a few questions and if you want to be helpful you could point the gun at the person I'm asking, just to encourage them to be honest."

He pointed the gun at me.

"Go ahead," he said.

"Jordana, I know you took that money from the safe, put it in your bag, and drove directly to the health club, where I assume you left it while you had me escorted out. Yes, we tussled at the Institute, but do you really think I had the time to switch out the money?"

"You could have," she said. "It all happened so quickly. You threw me down and could have made the switch then."

"Okay, we can debate whether I threw you down but let's be

real for a moment. There were a lot of bills in that bag. Do you think I could have switched them all out in seconds? I don't think so. No, you left the Institute with the money. You either took it into the club or left it in your trunk. If you took it in, it's still there or someone else took it."

I took a breath and looked at Rory. "If someone took it, I wonder who."

All eyes turned to Rory. He turned his my way.

"Don't listen to this asshole. He's just trying to make trouble to cover up his sorry ass," Rory said.

Before Rory got too upset, I said, "Moving on. I have a question for Trixie. Hi, Trixie. You're resplendent as ever."

All eyes turned her way.

"Trixie, I know you told me some things in confidence, and I don't want to betray your trust, but do you think you could share some information with us about Johnny? Not everyone here knows about you and Johnny. It might help us get a better grasp of the situation if you'd share what Johnny was up to this past week."

She, unfortunately, seemed reluctant to share.

"Tell us already," said Astrid. "Did you have something going on with him?"

Knowing Trixie as I did, I guessed she didn't know what to do. I've already told you how, as a therapist, I have a split mind about letting the client make the call and nudging them over the line. In this case I was clear.

"I really think it would help if you'd share what you know," I said. "And most importantly, it would benefit you to tell us about Johnny and his involvement in all this."

She slumped on the couch.

"Johnny was a great man," she managed. "When he cared, he cared. When he didn't, he didn't. He cared about me and I cared about him. Wilhelm was jealous of Johnny. Johnny had nothing to be jealous about. But, still, there was tension."

"Between them?"

"Wilhelm's jealousy was making Johnny crazy. He, who'd fucked more people more ways than anyone, was jealous about me fucking one guy. He kept interfering in my life and wouldn't leave us alone.

"So Johnny and I devised a scheme."

That got everyone's attention.

So far, she was telling the truth as I knew it. As if I really knew the truth—it kept changing each time someone spoke.

"I kissed up to Wilhelm and let him win me back. Once he felt there was hope for us, it was easy to get him to buy into running away with me. He always had money problems because of his lifestyle. The idea of staging his kidnapping appealed to him. He'd get to see how much his 'followers' loved him by their paying to have him released."

There was a snark to her tone as she said, "And he really liked the idea of getting those who'd sucked off of him to pay for it once again. All the while never knowing he'd fucked them. He liked that best."

The room took a moment.

Rory thankfully lowered the gun and said, "Stop. That's a nice story but it doesn't really help us find the money."

"Hold on," I said, raising my hand. "She's not done. Are you, Trixie?"

"No, there's more. Wilhelm and I set up the kidnapping and had an escape route. One of his former clients worked at the hotel and he blackmailed her into giving him the room numbers of the guests. I told Wilhelm I'd mail out and distribute the ransom notes at the conference, but Johnny had one of his men do that.

"It didn't take long before conference attendees called the Institute and Gabriela and Jordana quickly learned he was missing. They found their ransom notes, as did I. I went to them with my note and we quickly put together a plan for storing the money in the safe at the Institute. We each had the combination."

Jordana wasn't happy as she nodded her confirmation.

Trixie continued. "I was getting nervous about things falling apart and being exposed. A lot of money came in right away, so I told Johnny to steal it and to break into Wilhelm's house and get some videos we could use for insurance."

"So Johnny stole the ransom money from the safe?" Rory said.

"The first chunk," I said. "Remember, Jordana—and maybe you—stole the rest."

He eyed the gun and I shut up.

"Johnny stole the money and probably the tapes but he did it for us, or at least I thought he had. I'm not sure now."

She started to cry but managed to say, "The plan was for us to run away together. But then someone killed him."

"Wait!" said Rory. "The person who killed Johnny has the money?"

Not one to let a point go, I said, "That person probably has the first chunk. I keep telling you Jordana stole the second chunk and then you stole that from her. Well, maybe I haven't kept telling you that, but we're all thinking it. But, yes, the person who has the rest of the money is the one who killed Wilhelm and Johnny."

# CHAPTER FIFTY-FOUR

# IS THE MAGICAL EIGHT BALL REVEALING THE TRUTH OR DO WE NEED TO ASK AGAIN LATER?

**Saturday night—part 7**

I'D PUT MY cards, such as they were, on the table.

I didn't know if the person who'd killed Goodst and Trombone had the money that Trombone had stolen. But everyone else was lying. Why not me too?

Trombone probably gave Trixie $50,000 and kept the rest of the money. I didn't think his murderer would turn their back on stealing from him. Unless they didn't know he had it or he really had given it all to Trixie. If she did have it all, did that mean she'd double-crossed Wilhelm and Johnny and lied to me? Could be.

While I'd offered my theory with conviction, I might have over-played my hand. I was counting on two therapeutic theorems to help me out:

First, the more authoritative you are, the more people believe you. Even though I was guessing, if I sounded like I knew what I was talking about people would be more inclined to believe me. That theory hadn't worked that well so far but I'm a try/try-again guy.

Second, textbook group behavior was in play. If anyone left said, or did, the wrong thing the finger would point at them. I knew everyone would be watching each other closely and I hoped the extra scrutiny would pay off. As much as everyone might want to leave, the pressure was keeping us together.

I had a pretty good idea who'd done the killing but I needed to put one more piece into the puzzle. For that, I needed Britt to tell her truth.

"Britt," I said. "Can I ask you some questions?"

She glanced at Astrid, who was quietly fuming, then turned to me, her gaze intent. "Sure, if it can help us figure this out."

"Thanks. Can I ask you how long you've known Astrid and how you'd describe your relationship? Also, will you tell us about your relationships with the other people in the room?"

She hesitated.

"Astrid and I met a few months ago and started going out together. We're both journalists and got assignments to cover the convention. This was supposed to be a business and pleasure trip."

She looked at Astrid. "We also thought coming here would enhance and extend our relationship. It hasn't been the easiest partnership for either of us but I believe we're committed to each other."

I hadn't liked hearing that last part but she was my client now and I had to contain myself and help her as best I could. Out of the corner of my eye I saw Astrid giving me the finger.

"As for the other people in the room," she continued, "I know you. We met at the beginning of the conference. I've never seen Rory before or Trixie. Jordana I saw at the Institute earlier in the week and I vaguely know her from years ago. That's it."

"And what do you think Astrid's relationship is with each of these people?" I asked.

"I'm not sure. She knows you—she met you when I did. I just learned she knows Trixie, but I don't know how."

"Thanks," I said, acknowledging her and the group. "Now, some of you might know things to be somewhat different than what Britt thinks and it would be helpful for her to hear what you have to say. Astrid, you want to start?"

"No, I don't. Because I don't think you know what you're doing and I don't think we're any closer to resolving anything."

"That could well be," I replied. "But, come on, we're all sharing our stories. What's yours?"

"Yeah," Rory said with an enthusiasm that caught me off guard. "What's your story?"

"There's no story. I met Britt a few months ago like she said."

"That's very nice," I said. My condescension earned me a glare. "But what about you and Trixie? Want to share that story?"

"There's no story there. We've known each other for a few years. We run into one another now and then. That's it."

Britt looked surprised, Rory interested, Jordana inscrutable, and Trixie lost.

"Okay, and when was the last time you ran into each other?"

"I don't know. Maybe a year ago."

"A year ago?" I said with a certain mock surprise. "Not a few months ago?"

"No. It was over a year ago," she said, defiantly staring directly at me. "At a Take Back the Night rally."

She smiled. So much for my authoritative voice. I'd guessed wrong.

If at first...

"Trixie." I snapped her out of her reverie. "Does that sound about right to you?"

She gave her classic response. "I don't know. I think so." Then she added, "I can't think clearly right now."

I wasn't so sure I was thinking all that clearly either. I'd marked Astrid and Trixie as the originators of the kidnapping plot.

I didn't have a lot of lucid thinking but I knew a path when I saw one.

"One more thing," I asked Astrid. "How about you and Jordana? Want to share that story?"

"Once again, weenie," she said, sounding slightly giddy from having debunked my accusation, "there's no story."

"You and Jordana don't know each other?"

"That's right. I'm meeting her here for the first time."

"Wow. That really surprises me," I said. "From what I gather, you two know each other very well. You must have at least met her when you 'interviewed' Goodst."

That got some movement. Jordana stirred uncomfortably and Rory checked out Astrid a little closer.

"Wait. You told me you didn't know her. And barely knew Trixie. Why did you lie to me?" said Britt with some despair.

Astrid wasn't happy. I figured she'd continue to deny knowing Jordana but she didn't.

"Okay," she said, shifting her body to face Britt. "So I lied to you about being with other women. I never promised you exclusivity. I'm a free woman and I don't have to share everything with you."

"You're right," said Britt boldly, but I could tell she was distressed. "You don't. But you also don't need to lie to me."

Britt was upset but Astrid didn't get up to comfort her and neither did I. Sometimes I know to leave well enough alone. I also know how to plow on.

"So, Astrid, when was the last time you and Jordana got together?"

"Maybe four, five months ago. Our circles overlap."

"All right. Britt, I'm sorry that finding this out now is upsetting but it's important for us all to know how we're connected so we can come to the truth."

She gave me a small nod of understanding.

"How about it, Jordana? You up for sharing a bit of your story?"

"Why not?" she answered with the kind of cool-under-fire look that must have made her an invaluable asset to Goodst.

"Can you tell us what you and Astrid talked about the last time you were together?"

"The usual stuff. Work, friends, trips, this and that. Nothing unusual."

Trixie had told me Astrid and Jordana had spoken outside the cabin before Astrid went in, got in a fight and killed him. Maybe that wasn't unusual.

"Would that nothing unusual include some of your own history with Wilhelm?"

"Not that I can recall."

"When you talked about work, did you share your own frustrations with Wilhelm? Did you tell Astrid about your devotion and sacrifice and Wilhelm's abuse of you? Did she tell you she, too, had been abused by him, or did those conversations begin years ago? When did you start talking about revenge and wanting to hurt him like he'd hurt you? Was that during the last meeting or years earlier? When did the talk start to become real for you?"

Jordana wasn't looking at me; she and Astrid were focused on each other.

When Jordan broke eye contact with her, I didn't need to ask any more questions because I'd found the answer. Jordana's gaze moved up to the right. Now, it isn't the most reliable tell but it's got its believers—if you're trying to recall the facts of an event, you look up and left; when you want to construct something, your eyes drift up to the right.

That was good enough for me. Jordana was about to construct a lie because the truth would do her in.

CHAPTER FIFTY-FIVE

# THE FINAL PART?

**Saturday night—part 8**

It was starting to feel like that scene in the Marx Brothers' *Night at the Opera.* Too many people in one room with too many stories. But it wasn't going to last.

While I'd certainly been misdirected over the week and the people in the room were not as forthcoming as I might have wished, they were basically telling the same lies we all do when we meet. We leave things out. You might call it the sin of omission. We present our better selves and as relationships grow, truths emerge.

I thought I'd had that light-bulb moment when I'd caught Jordana's eyes moving up to the right—conjugating her story up there in the creative sphere of her brain. She needed to make up something to help cover her tracks. I thought I knew the rest but, as any decent therapist will tell you, it's better when you can get the client to say it.

"So, Jordana, you talked with Astrid about the usual stuff, but I'm not so sure Astrid fully knows what you've been doing to make your life richer. She might be surprised to hear what you've been up to. What do you think?"

"What's he talking about?" Astrid said.

"He isn't talking about anything. You know me. You know what I've been doing."

"I'm not so sure I do. I didn't know you'd stolen the ransom money. Why didn't you tell me that? What else haven't you told me?"

*Ah, Astrid. Coming to the rescue. Put that pressure on as only you know how.*

"You don't need to know everything. So I took the money. So what?" She stood up and, facing Rory, said, "You stole it from me. So fuck you." Turning to Astrid she added, "And fuck you too."

Rory didn't look happy. Whether it was because Jordana had turned on him, blamed him, thrown him under the bus, or made him the scapegoat, I didn't know. And, frankly, I didn't care. I did care what Jordana might do if she felt cornered. She was becoming very agitated.

"Anything else I ought to know?" Astrid asked forcibly.

This was why group therapists liked to have a co-leader. So much easier to ride tandem.

"That's it. I have to go now." Jordana stood up and headed toward the door.

Trixie cut her off at the pass. "Out with it," she demanded. "What else have you done? I know we talked about staging the kidnapping but what else did you do?"

Jordana reached into her purse and took out a gun. Pointing it at each of us, she said, "I'm going to leave now. Rory, don't give me a reason to use this. I don't want any of you to follow me. I did what I did for good reason and this will be the last you see of me."

And with that she was gone.

# CHAPTER FIFTY-SIX

# AND THEN THIS

**Saturday night—part 9**

EVERYONE BEGAN TALKING at once. Trixie wanted to call the police. Then she didn't. She didn't know. Rory was itching to follow Jordana but said he'd wait till she was out of the hallway. Britt seemed ready to take her packed bag and head home. Astrid was upset but having been involved with Jordana, Trixie, and Britt, she was the recipient of a lot of questions.

I opened the door.

Golk and Nunn stood in front of me, along with Jordana.

It was time for another group meeting and in they came. Jordana was now in handcuffs. Golk and Nunn were somewhat happier to see me. In my message for Golk, I'd told him I expected some activity in room 315 and if they hid themselves down the hallway, they just might catch themselves a murderer and thief.

I don't know what he'd thought of my message but in a world where trust was at a premium, he gave it enough credence to follow through. I felt good he'd had faith in what I'd said and thanked him. While he had his suspect in tow, I don't think he was happy about how he'd landed her. I'm usually not a believer in the end justifying the means but, in this case, I hoped he was.

Golk and Nunn didn't stay long. Before they left, they told us all to come down to the station to make our statements. It wasn't exactly the nightcap any of us wanted but it seemed like that was the end of it.

And it almost was.

At the station someone found Trixie an overcoat. Our group, minus Jordana, waited to make our individual statements. Fortunately, there was some overheated coffee to drink and catching up to do.

Rory was called in first, probably still trying to figure out where he could find the rest of the money. Trixie and Astrid huddled at one end of a bench and Britt and I made our way to a couple of chairs. She was distraught about not seeing Astrid for who she was and wanted to put the week behind her. She was glad she was my client so she needn't concern herself with what to do with me. She'd call me if she needed me; otherwise she'd reach out in a couple of years if she felt so inclined.

There really wasn't much more to say. I was disappointed she and I hadn't had a chance to explore a more fulfilling relationship. I held out some hope for the future but knew the moment had passed. When they called her in to take her statement, she gave me a perfunctory hug.

Astrid and Trixie finished up their conversation and I went over to speak with them. Trixie was deflated; she still didn't know who killed Wilhelm and Johnny or why.

The three of us tried to put the pieces together.

Astrid and Trixie both knew that Jordana wanted to be dominated because that was the form of abuse she'd endured at the hands of her father and, later, Goodst. She wanted it and hated it. Wanted it because it was familiar and made her feel loved, hated it because she knew it wasn't love.

Astrid and Jordana had met years earlier when Astrid first interviewed Goodst. They'd seen each other off and on over the years and shared their stories of abuse. They'd fantasized about ways to hurt him. But they'd never come up with anything they'd act on. Like some other victims of abuse, they felt a kinship in sharing their histories and ideas about revenge but Astrid believed it ended there.

Trixie had known Jordana since she first started dating Goodst and over the years they'd built a friendship. I guessed when Jordana found out about Trixie and Johnny, she saw a way to hurt Goodst. She likely fed Goodst stories about them, which Goodst in his jealous rages would then throw in Trixie's face. Trixie nodded with what little energy she had.

Jordana had known Trixie was becoming fed up with Goodst's pestering her so she suggested the kidnapping plan. Jordana had known Goodst would jump at the chance to reunite with Trixie and run away. She could help sell it by enflaming his money problems. Goodst would think he and Trixie were taking the money and running but, instead, Jordana and Trixie would split the funds and Trixie could run away with Johnny.

Goodst would be left with nothing and wouldn't be able to squeal on Trixie lest it be found out the kidnapping had been his idea. Plus Trixie had planned for Johnny to steal the videos so they could blackmail Goodst if he continued to give them trouble.

I asked Trixie if she'd taken a picture from the wall at Goodst's house. She admitted she'd taken one of Trombone, Goodst, and her taken at the cabin in happier times. She didn't want anyone to be able to link the three of them.

Trixie became increasingly nervous and asked Johnny to steal the money. Jordana exploded when she discovered the robbery and suspected Trixie had double-crossed her, or Goodst had stolen it himself, or the two of them were scheming behind her back.

So Jordana had gone up to the cabin to confront Goodst and found him and Trixie there. The three of them had argued. Trixie admitted she'd asked Johnny to steal the money. That had enraged Goodst and Jordana and the three of them fought. Trixie had taken out her gun, Jordana had wrestled it from her, and in the process Goodst had been shot.

I didn't know for sure but figured when Astrid had gone to the cabin she'd peeked through the window and seen the whole thing. She'd known she could use the information to manipulate Jordana, Trixie, and Britt. There was no way to prove that and Astrid certainly wasn't going to admit it.

Jordana left Trixie with the body and soon thereafter Astrid showed up and they removed it.

At least that's what I think happened.

Every time I heard this story it was different. First Trixie told me that Astrid said she'd killed Goodst. Then Britt said she'd killed Goodst. Later Trixie explained that Astrid had stood outside and seen Jordana and Goodst fighting and when Jordana left, she'd gone in and killed him. This time out Trixie, Jordana and Goodst were fighting and Jordana had killed him while Astrid watched from outside. All I knew was Golk was dead and some mixture of people were responsible.

I guessed when Jordana found out that Johnny had the tapes and money, she left the cabin and confronted him. The tapes would be good blackmail material or she could sell them. I doubted she'd been in a forgiving mood and when Johnny didn't come forward, she shot him.

I didn't know if she found the money Johnny had taken or if Rory had taken the money Jordana stole from the Institute. The money was somewhere. In the movie version a last scene of Britt driving off in a fancy car. Maybe with Rory. It was frustrating not knowing exactly what had happened but I consoled myself that I'd gotten the guiltiest party arrested.

Since I couldn't prove anything, I was hoping the police would be able to get Astrid and Trixie to testify against Jordana for Goodst's murder if Golk offered them immunity.

It all kinda fit together and yet, like a lot of things, it was disappointing in the end. I'd facilitated our group so the pressure built up sufficiently for Jordana to expose herself, but all I really had was some testimonials by Astrid and Trixie who couldn't be trusted and my own suppositions which were just that.

Astrid was called in to give her deposition. She hugged Trixie and ignored me. I'd grown fond of Trixie and knew she'd have some rough times ahead. I tried to comfort her but there is not a lot of comfort to be had at the police station. I was sad when her turn came and we shared a tender knowing moment.

When I got my chance, I told my story as best I could, and after being berated and grudgingly thanked, I got to return to the hotel. I didn't know whether the police would be able to make the case against Jordana but I thought I'd given them the pieces of the puzzle.

As I walked through the lobby, I saw Chet and Layla waiting for the elevator. They were wrapped up in each other's arms and it looked like whatever energies they'd spent at the big event hadn't diminished their ardor for each other.

I was glad someone was having a happy ending.

And maybe I was too.

Monday, I'd be in class and have a story to tell.

If you'd like a peek into what the future holds for David, take a look at what comes after the Acknowledgments and Apologies.

# ACKNOWLEDGEMENTS

I wrote this book in the 1980s when I was teaching at a college and was, indeed, asked to fill in at the last minute for the Human Sexuality teacher. I didn't have the benefit of going to a conference to learn more about the subject and fortunately only had to teach it once. Thanks go out to my dean, Sara Winter, who gave me the assignment and thankfully relieved me of it.

I decided to revisit this book some thirty years later when my friend Shaun Saunders asked about it, read it, and told me I ought to bring it back to life. I've tidied it up some and had my editors, Lulu Swainston, Cally Worden, Beth Hamer, and Ursula at owlproediting.com, clean it up. My audio narrator, Jake Robertson, brought it to life, and the artists at Damonza did the cover

I am also indebted to Kinky Friedman, whose mysteries have not only amused and engaged me, but provided me the model for my own series. In his books he is himself, a musician who happens to get involved in mysteries. If he could be a version of himself and do that, I figured I could too.

Ongoing thanks go out to my family and friends, who are the ones that teach and share life's lessons with me.

DAVID UNGER, PHD

# PROLOGUE

"The best I ever saw? Well, that's an easy one."

"Okay, what is it?"

"Well, I was at Woodstock."

"All right. End of discussion. You win. There's no way I can beat that."

"You can try."

"The best I got is I did see the Beatles at Shea Stadium. I thought that would have been the topper but you got me beat fair and square."

"You dudes left me in the dirt," another guy said. "I was gonna say I saw Janis at the Fillmore. I thought that was pretty cool."

"It is. I saw her with the Who and Jimi Hendrix at the Monterey Pop Festival."

"No way. I saw Hendrix with the Allman Brothers."

Standing in the will call line, listening to these guys one-up each other with their gig credentials, I was quickly put in my place. I hadn't attended any of those concerts. And though I thought my rock-and-roll chops were decent, I knew I was out of my league. That wasn't surprising given where I was, but it still made me feel like someone's younger brother.

"I saw the Allman Brothers in '70 or '71 at the Whisky a Go Go."

"Whoa. That's pretty heavy. The Whisky. I saw the Doors there years ago."

"Wow. The Doors. Very trippy. I saw them in Asbury Park. My good friend broke up with his girlfriend and I got to go with him. They blew my mind."

"I saw them at the Avalon Ballroom. I'd never seen anyone like Morrison before. I almost lost my girlfriend that night."

I could understand that. Jim Morrison had been a captivating performer.

I wanted to join the conversation but the closest dot I could connect was having seen Bruce Springsteen at the Santa Monica Civic Auditorium. Before I could get up the nerve to speak, they'd moved on to other acts and venues.

*I'll take music acts and venues for $20, Alex,* I thought about saying, but wasn't sure that was the best entry either. Truth was, I was a bit of an outsider here. While I was looking forward to the weekend of music, I wasn't really here to listen to it. I had another purpose. A client wanted me to help him out if he got into difficulties—a purpose that was both familiar and unfamiliar to me. I'm a shrink after all, and my job is to help people navigate the difficulties they encounter. I see clients in my office, their home, or pretty much wherever they want. When my client asked me if I'd come to the festival and help him out, it took me a couple of nanoseconds to say, *Sure.* If I could go to the festival and get paid, why not?

We never fully know what we're getting into until we get into it. But we usually have a pretty good sense of what to expect. I thought my client might find himself in conflict with some of the people around him and might want me to facilitate. He might need me to keep an eye on his substance intake. Or he might want to speak with me about life as he was living it.

Some of that happened.

# CHAPTER 1

# "What You See (Is What You Get)"
# Oingo Boingo

**Six Months Earlier**

I'M A THERAPIST. I'm also a teacher. A Los Angeleno. A thirty-five-year-old single guy who likes sports, music, time with friends and family, as well as an occasional joint and shot of Cuervo. A regular guy. Or so I mostly think. I've been told I'm annoying and my "cutesy pushiness" makes some people want to puke. My mother thinks I'll be a late bloomer. My dad is just glad I have a job. My friends think I have redeeming values. You'll have to make your own assessment.

I share a therapy office with Sarah. I met her in grad school and she's way more organized than I am. She found the office, decorated it, and sublets it to me two days a week. It's a good deal for me. I like Sarah. Every now and then I consider sleeping with her, but since it's hard for me to be in a room alone with her for over thirty minutes, that thought usually doesn't go anywhere. It's not so much she's intense. It's more she'll take whatever I say and lay it out for me in the most unflattering psychobabble ways that make me feel bad about myself.

When I was in grad school, I took a class where we learned how to give IQ and personality assessments. We had to take a battery of tests and analyze them. Turns out we all were crazy. Which you'd kind of expect with therapists. But we're not alone—you're damaged goods too. We all are one way or another. Aside from realizing all of us have issues, the thing I found most fascinating is if you gave everyone in the world these tests, no one would come back normal. There's no such thing. We're all a little off. I don't know if you'll find that comforting or not. But that's what I learned in class. Abnormal is the new normal.

I didn't meet Sarah in that class. I met her at a children's clinic where she and I were interning with a small group of grad students. She was a year ahead of me and we hit it off, mostly because we didn't get to spend too much time together. When she graduated she got the office, and a year later when I got out of school she asked me if I wanted to share the space.

It's one thing to ply your trade. It's another to find anyone who'll pay you for it. Over the years I've been able to build my practice because I started doing something that got me a bit of a local reputation.

Now, I'll apologize in advance for talking about my dissertation, but you'll find it has relevance, not just to how I built my practice but also to your life. Plus, it turns out what I learned helped me out a lot over the weekend when all the trouble happened.

My dissertation was about time. Pretty much every therapist sees clients for fifty minutes. I'd wondered why. My medical doctor sees me for as long as she needs to see me. Why didn't therapy work the same? I wanted to know what was so special about fifty minutes. Turns out nothing is special about it. Therapists go for fifty minutes because it's convenient for them. It has nothing to do with you.

Once I realized therapy could be fifty minutes long, or an hour and fifty, or ten hours and fifty, it freed me up to see people for varying amounts of time. Most people came to me expecting fifty minutes, but when I explained I was flexible, it wasn't long before I ended up spending afternoons or days with them. In and out of the office. My clients really liked it when I could join them in certain activities—a challenging discussion with their partner, a flight they were too scared to take alone. It really helped me to get an inside view of their life and help them where they needed it most—in their daily life. Therapists usually want you to take what happens in the office and apply it to your life, but I've been able to help clients apply the lessons of therapy on the job, with their partner, with their friends, pretty much anywhere they wanted.

I was a newly minted therapist so my rates were reasonable and I was less troubled about boundaries. Nowadays, I'm more expensive and I have to worry about things that weren't so problematic when I began.

A few months earlier I got a new client named Drew. I suppose this is as good a time as any to put in this disclaimer—Drew isn't his real name. I need to protect anonymity so I've had to change names and some facts in this book to protect people's privacy. But for the most part, this is a true story and one you might know a thing or two about.

Drew came to me ostensibly because his girlfriend told him if he didn't see a therapist, she would leave him. Not the best motivation for therapy, but I've seen worse. He really liked his girlfriend and didn't want to lose her. He didn't really want to have her either. Well, he wanted to have her, but he also wanted to have some of the other women he was involved with in other cities.

Drew was a musician in a band I'm going to call Magoo. They looked and sounded a bit like the Eagles, except they had a woman in the band and not so many hits. That said, if I mentioned their big hit, you'd hear it playing in the jukebox in your head. They'd been a headliner for some years, and though not in the same league as the bands I heard those guys in the will call line talking about, they were certainly living the dream and knock knock knocking on stardom's door.

I'm not going to get into the nitty-gritty of Drew's therapy, but since he's the reason I was at the music festival I need to fill you in a little. Drew had asked me to come to the four-day festival with him because the band had decided to spend the entire weekend at the event and there'd be a lot of time for him to get into a lot of trouble. By that he meant the basics—sex, drugs, and rock and roll, and the consequences thereof.

Drew didn't really need a babysitter. He'd logged in a lot of hours at music festivals and on the road, and mostly knew how to monitor himself. This festival would be different because his girlfriend, CeeCee, would be there. While that was a positive thing, he also knew some of his previous one-night stands from the area might be making their presence felt and he thought a steadying hand could be in order. He told me to mostly hang around the stage, food pavilion, and tech tent, and if he needed me he'd find me.

That's how I ended up outside sunny San Bernardino, California, on Labor Day weekend, 1982.

Made in the USA
Las Vegas, NV
13 July 2023

74665467R00173